THE BOOK OF GATES

This is a Kristian Becker book

brought to you by IndieMosh
a service of Mosher's Business Support Pty Ltd

PO BOX 147
Hazelbrook NSW 2779

www.indiemosh.com.au

Cataloguing-in-Publication entry is available from the National
Library of Australia: http://catalogue.nla.gov.au/

Title:	The Book of Gates
Author:	Becker, Kristian
ISBN:	978-0-9873798-1-8 (paperback)
	978-0-9873798-2-5 (ebook – epub)
	978-0-9873798-3-2 (ebook – mobi)

Cover image: DollarPhotoClub.com

Cover design and layout: Ally Mosher, MoshPit Publishing

THE BOOK OF GATES

OF GATES

KRISTIAN BECKER

Contents

CHAPTER I

"Come on, Phil, pick up," Dan Whalis muttered as he put files into his briefcase. With his free hand, he crammed the last bit of toast into his mouth while he cradled the phone under his chin.

"Arrgghh," as he put his dossier in his briefcase, he noticed that it was covered in stains. His friend and colleague Phil Grundsman had been working on it yesterday. Dan examined the stains. They looked like sauce and beetroot, and he instantly remembered Phil eating a massive hamburger with the works at his desk.

There was still no answer on the phone, so he hung up. If he didn't leave now, he would be stuck in morning traffic, and he hated that. There were days when he arrived at work already exhausted from sitting in the morning jam.

His wife Natasha was still in bed. She worked the night shift at Coles and would have his balls for breakfast if he woke her up.

The TV was playing an infomercial for a funeral home. That commercial was on at the same time every morning this week. He felt a little satisfaction in turning it off midway through the woman's spruiking.

For once, the trip to work was easy; everyone must have slept in this morning—including Phil, who was not at the office when Dan arrived.

"Tell Phil when he gets in to see me first, Rozz," he told the receptionist.

"You know, I think he was saying yesterday that he was going out after work," she replied.

"You're kidding? We've got a presentation this morning, not to mention the shit he's in for sending that dirty email to the wrong person. Sometimes I think he's dumb as dog shit, I really do."

"Well, he's your friend," she laughed and then answered a ringing phone.

Dan made his way to his desk. The papers that Phil had grimed up with burger juice would have to be reprinted. Then there was the email. Maybe he should just admit to it. *"Yeah, boss, I sent the email to Phil, but I didn't know he was going to send it to your mother."*

Just then, Phil came in. His hair was a mess, and his beer gut seemed more pronounced than ever before, especially with the tight shirt he was wearing.

When he saw Dan, Phil's face lit up. "Hey, big fella. Sorry I'm late. Got totally wasted last night and slept through the alarm."

Dan just shook his head. They were both in their early thirties and married without kids. But Phil still acted like he was in school.

Phil yawned, and Dan swore he could see right into his alcohol- and pizza-filled gut. Its fermenting odour seemed to seep out like vapours from an open sewer.

"Are you prepared for today?" Dan asked.

"Me? Everything's gunna be cool, man. It'll all work out," he smiled as he sat in his chair.

Dan wasn't so sure. He thought, *to hell with Phil*; he was going to look after himself. Dan's wife would kill him after cutting off his balls if he lost his job. Real estate was a bitching business, and opportunities were rare.

"Man, I wish I could retire," said Phil. "I reckon you shouldn't start work until you're forty. That way, you don't waste your youth working every day. Cause when you're old, you can't use your free time. I can't get pissed at night and get up the next day when I'm eighty."

"So, who's going to pay you until you get a job at forty?"

"Dunno. The government?" Phil scratched his groin. His eyes were unfocused in the bright light. Dan knew it was going to be a long day.

He was right. He got through the presentation, fixed Phil's burger mess and got a warning for the email business. Old Phil got canned, but he only smiled. He just didn't seem to care.

It must have been about 10.30pm when the phone rang. Dan was home alone watching the late news. Phil was dead. He had been killed on his way home from work.

After getting off the phone with Phil's wife, Dan sat there stumped for what seemed an eternity. Phil, the insatiable slacker, had met his end. Dan was shocked that it could happen to someone like his friend. People like Phil always seemed to land on their feet, no matter what they said or did. People like Dan were the ones to get caught speeding the only time they ever did it. Or they were the first to lose their jobs, or have their cars stolen. But today the universe had seemed to correct itself for once.

The night before the funeral, Dan and Natasha were making last preparations. She had ironed his suit and bought a new black dress. With that done, she went to bed and left him watching the footy on TV. His Rabbitohs were holding on to a six-point lead against Manly. That's when the phone rang.

"Hello."

There was no answer, and he was too tired to be playing games.

"Hello?" he said again.

"So, how's the game?"

"Um, okay. Who is this?"

"See ya tomorrow, big fella."

The call dropped, and Dan was left holding the phone. It took him a few seconds to register that it had been Phil's voice on the line. But that was impossible. Phil was dead.

He really didn't want to think about it. When he went to bed, it took some time for him to finally nod off.

Funerals weren't meant to be cheery, and it seemed that any thought or emotion besides grief was immediately deemed sacrilegious. But somewhere in the throng of weeping people were two people who were not following the funeral script. One hid away, choking on his laughter. The other sat on the cold, hard pew inside the church at Palmdale Crematorium, deep in thought. Dan had been asking people whether they had called him last night. When they said no and wanted to know why he asked, he just shrugged it off.

"Oh, someone rang but hung up before I could get it."

Most of the chapel was filled with Phil's family. Like Phil, they had loud voices, big bellies and hand-me-down clothes. One of Phil's cousins wore a flannelette shirt with jeans. Dan felt overdressed in his suit.

When the sermon was over, Dan went outside, watching the mourners mingle and talk about how good Phil was.

"Hey. Over here, man," came a voice from behind him.

He looked around and saw Phil by the corner of the chapel, hiding behind some scrub.

Dan was stunned and merely stared at his friend, who was dressed in the suit he was buried in.

"Don't come over here," instructed Phil. "Meet me later at your place," then he disappeared.

Dan couldn't believe his eyes; now he felt even more detached from the mourners who held each other for comfort only a few metres away.

The rest of the day was long. Dan had to endure the wake, where Phil's mum brought out baby pictures and cried over each one. Should he tell her that Phil wasn't dead? No, they would probably rip him to pieces for answers, and he didn't have answers. Besides, Phil should do it himself. Maybe he'd turn up soon and there would be more high emotion as mourning turned to joy.

With the coming of night, Dan and Natasha could finally leave gracefully. He knew Natasha hated every minute of the formalities. She had hated Phil, so naturally that extended to his yobbo family.

Natasha went to bed after a quick shower, leaving Dan alone in the kitchen. He grabbed a beer and some leftover tomato soup from the fridge.

He waited, but no ghost appeared. He decided then that he was going out of his mind. There was no way Phil was going to rock up at his place a few minutes before midnight and tell him the secrets of the universe after he had already been cremated.

"Do you think I know what they are?" said a familiar voice by the window.

Dan jumped and saw his friend's head at the window. It disappeared, then reappeared a moment later at the glass sliding door. Phil opened it and entered the house.

Immediately Dan was overcome by the smell of mortuary fluids and another scent he couldn't quite identify.

"Phil?" Dan exclaimed.

"Sssh," Phil put a finger to his blue lips and sat down opposite Dan. Phil's skin was snow white, and there were black bruises from the accident. His hair was neat, and his eyes had a misty grey colouring.

"What's going on? You're dead."

"I told you to shut up. Now listen, something good has happened to me. Look at me, I'm still alive after being crushed in my car! I'm immortal, man, free as a bird."

"But ... how? I mean, how?" Dan was having trouble thinking of anything to say.

"I don't know how or why, Dan. Just lucky, I guess," he shrugged. "Do you want it?" he added in a hushed tone.

"I'm not sure what it is."

"Come on, Dan. Think of it, not having to pay bills or work."

"What do you do all day?"

Phil sat back and cracked a horrible smile. "You're pretty calm for a guy talking to someone who's dead, Dan. Let me tell you you're not dreaming. Everything's cool, alright?"

"I can't do this."

"That's what I thought, and that's why I'm ahead of you. I know you think I'm stupid. That soup you're eating, it's got me in it."

"What?"

"My flesh is dissolving in your soup," he reached over and put his fingers in the bowl of red soup, pulling out a chunk of flesh. "See?"

Dan stood up suddenly, his eyes wide. "What have you done, you idiot?"

"Don't yell, man," Phil quietly ordered.

"Dan, what's the matter?" Natasha called from the bedroom.

"Ah, nothing. Just talking to myself," Dan looked back at Phil sitting there calmly, his bright smile now replaced by a slight crease across his face.

"It's done, Dan. You'll be dead in two days. Want to bring Tash with you? I got Susan on the way over. We can team up."

Dan couldn't speak. He had no words, and no strength to get them out if he did have them. His friend had killed his own wife and poisoned him, wanting him to do the same to Natasha.

"You better leave."

"I'm going, anyway," he stood up. "Don't forget now: two days, and there's nothing you can do to stop it."

With that, Phil was gone.

Dan immediately went to the toilet to try to throw up the contents of his stomach. It would be a long two days.

He died first, and then Natasha. He had never thrown out the soup; in the morning, she had heated it back up and finished it off. He was too ill to tell her, but seeing her fall sick, too, he knew.

Phil and Susan met them the day they died, but Natasha would not speak to any of them. She disappeared into the Red Hill Reserve, where there were kilometres of scrub and bush with no tracks. He never saw her again.

Phil looked like shit. His skin had gone grey, and patches of it were coming off. His eyes had gone black, and he stank like the hunk of rotting flesh that he was.

"Looks like we still rot," Phil said apologetically. "But we're free."

"Free from what?" Dan sneered. "You always were an idiot."

"So, where to now?" asked Susan.

"We drive, baby. Drive into the outback where there are no people and live the free life."

They packed up some items, furniture, and clothes and drove west, never to return and never to enjoy the freedom Phil had promised. For death could not be cheated—only delayed.

THE DEAD AND THE BURIED

He fumbled in his pocket for the rings. There was a small chain somewhere in there, too. Taking out his hand, he found the chain between his fingers. He let out a sigh of relief and then walked into the pawnshop.

The owner was paging through some paperwork and looked up as he approached the desk.

"Whatcha got there?"

"Oh, my mum just died, and she's got these rings and this chain. I don't have any sisters, and I can't wear them, so I thought I could sell them."

"Alright, let's have a look."

He handed over the items and looked about as the owner inspected them.

"These are nice; you got real diamonds in this one."

"Really? That would be worth more, right?" he said a little too energetically.

"Yeah, if they're in good nick. I'll give you five hundred for them."

"Is that all?"

The owner seemed annoyed. "This isn't Tiffany's, and these aren't the priciest rings in the world. I'd think parting with your mother's worldly goods would be a difficult thing to do."

"It is, but I could really do with some more money, for the funeral and all."

"Yeah, that's what a lotta people say. Five hundred, mate. I've got a cupboard full of them."

"Alright then."

Soon he was out of the shop with his cash. Five hundred dollars wasn't anything to baulk at, but he went through a lot to get those rings and that chain. He would just have to get more. He didn't really want to, but he needed his drugs, and he needed money to get them.

Later that night, he was flicking though the paper and stopped at the obituaries. There were two funerals scheduled for tomorrow, both at the same funeral home. He ripped out the page and folded it away. Then he got out his only black suit, making sure it was clean. There was a white shirt and black tie to go with it. While watching some dodgy movie late at night, he polished an old set of shoes to go with it. Then he went to bed and attempted to sleep.

As soon as he closed his eyes, he felt fingers poking at his body. Startled, he woke and caught a glimpse of ghostly faces.

"I'm sorry!" he cried, burying his face in his pillow. "This will be the last time, I promise! I promise!"

The fingers stopped. His small room was quiet but for the roof fan that twirled around on its broken axis.

He had made promises like that before, and they always went away—but then, they always came back, too.

In the morning, he cleaned himself up as best he could. He patted down his slick short hair while trying not to notice too much how ugly he really was. His nose had been flat since birth, the result of his face lying too hard on the surface of his mother's womb. Then there were his chipped gapped teeth and wide spaced eyes. No woman wanted him, so he found other ways to make himself happy. The five hundred he'd gotten yesterday was gone up his arm, and he felt better.

The train and then the bus got him to Palmdale Crematorium. The first funeral was at 10am, so he waited around and mingled with the mourners before moving inside with them.

He had to sit through the sermon, which was agony to him, as some relative droned on about the details of the corpse in the box. He didn't want to hear about it; he didn't want to know the body was a person. All he wanted to know was whether there was anything worth ratting the body for.

It seemed hours, but it was probably only one before the sermon was over and the family could say a final goodbye to the body.

He waited at the back while everyone formed a line and passed the coffin. Then he jumped in at the end of the line.

When it was his turn, he stopped at the coffin. There was an old man inside it. His sons were close by, so he had to be quick and flawless. There was a wedding ring but nothing else. He gritted his teeth in frustration. After an hour of sitting through crap, he had come up with nothing but a ring.

He pretended to pat the man's hands, but with a quick motion, he slipped the ring from the man's dead hand and put it in his pocket. He faked emotion by pretending to wipe nonexistent tears from his eyes as he walked out, then went back to his grumpy best when he was clear of the family.

He turned the ring over in his hands. It was solid gold with no stones. A name and date were engraved on the inner side, but he didn't bother reading it. He put the ring in his pocket. Now he had to wait for the funeral at midday.

While he waited, he wandered among the graves in the cemetery and found his way to the mausoleums. Each was a little house holding a few coffins; some mausoleums held a dozen corpses from one family. He had been here once before in the middle of the night, hoping that the mausoleums had been left unlocked. But none ever were.

Mostly Italians and Greeks had mausoleums here. He had learned from his Dad at a young age that they were buried with their jewellery. It tore him up that he could never get into them. In just one night, he could make his fortune, and he would never bother anyone again.

He made his way back to the chapel to once again play his charade.

The family were Italians or Greeks; he wasn't sure which. He only knew their kind as *wogs*. As he mingled, there were a few double takes directed at him. It took him some time to realise it was because he didn't look like a wog. Luckily, the beginning of the sermon saved him from closer scrutiny.

Taking his usual place at the back, he once again endured the weeping and long stories about a stranger. He just wanted to get to the end and get out of there with his stuff.

He found it hard to block out the mourners' cries. They were so loud that he winced every time there was a gut-wrenching howl. One particular woman was the loudest. He guessed she was the deceased woman's daughter. He wished she would shut the hell up; he was getting a headache.

The minutes wore on until, over an hour later, the sermon was finally finished. He sighed a breath of relief.

The usual line formed, and he took his place at the end.

When he reached the coffin, his heart raced. The old woman wore a large necklace, earrings, and a ring on every finger. He stood there for a few moments while he figured out how he could get all the jewellery off her. He reached in and handled the necklace. It was heavy and had plenty of red stones.

"Hello," came a voice next to him. He jumped, pulling his hand out in a flash.

"I was just admiring the necklace."

A middle-aged man who was balding and wearing heavy-set glasses stood behind him.

"Yes. It was Aunt Elle's favourite. It's a pity she wanted to be buried with it, as it's worth a far bit. But she was a stubborn old woman who hated giving her stuff away. I think she was afraid Sofia was going to sell it to buy herself some new tits."

He didn't know what else to say to the man.

"So, who are you?"

"Oh, just a long-lost relative," he managed to say, stepping away and setting a steady pace out of the chapel and away from the mourners.

This was almost perfect. He could pawn the jewellery, and the money would set him up for life. Maybe he could move to the Gold Coast, or buy a place in the outback. A little isolated sheep station would do him good, and he would never bother anyone again. But he had promised that before, too many times.

He paced the road outside the crematorium. How was he going to get the stuff from the old woman? Then he saw the pallbearers bring out the coffin and place it in a hearse, where it was driven to the cemetery. His chance to sneak back in to rat the corpse before its burial was gone. She was going into the ground. He knew what he had to do, though he didn't want to. He tried digging only once before, and he had never made it to the coffin. The dead always drove him back. He didn't mean to bother anyone, but he knew it bothered them. They told him in his dreams.

But this was the last one. The last dig, and he wouldn't bother anyone anymore. All he needed was one last haul.

He didn't go home that night, instead staying about in the bush close to the cemetery. He stole a shovel, a chisel and a hammer from the shed on the grounds and went looking for the grave.

It was not hard to find, as it was the only one with fresh flowers and loose soil. No gravestone had been erected, and he was glad people didn't spend money on making brick or concrete graves anymore. It made his job a little easier.

He started digging, keeping his mind on the prize. Dirt constantly got into his mouth, and he didn't have any water to spit it out. Dirt had run down his open shirt and was filling his shoes. But he kept going until he finally hit the wooden lid of the coffin.

He took the chisel and hammer out of his belt and was about to smash a hole through the coffin's lid when a cascade of leaves fell into the grave, blown in by the wind.

Startled, he looked up, but no one appeared at the top of the grave. All seemed still except for the wind. Returning his mind to his task, he steadied his arms with the chisel and struck hard. Too hard, it turned out. The chisel smashed right through the wood, breaking it completely into the woman's face. The sound of her skull cracking made him take a few moments to ease his stomach.

The leaves drifted down onto him again, and he could hear other noises. He knew.

"Shit," he muttered, closing his eyes. They had warned him many times. Their ghosts woke him up at night with their fingers poking into his body.

Hundreds of apologies rushed through his mind as he sank down and rested his knees on the coffin.

Under him, the ground seemed to move. At first he didn't notice it as he tried to think of words to get out of this mess. The wood creaked and groaned under him so much that it finally caught his attention. At first he thought his weight was going to push it in, but he very quickly realised something was forcing its way out.

Cracks appeared in the coffin's white-painted surface, splitting wider until it exploded and showered him with wooden flakes. He turned away to block the pieces. When he looked back, the dead woman was sitting upright in her coffin, his chisel still stuck in her brain.

His courage deserted him. Backing away, he stood up to leave. It was then that he saw the crowd that had gathered around the open grave. These were not ghosts; their foul, rotten stench drifted into his nose and polluted his lungs. He didn't know what they were; he only knew that they were after him.

"I'm sorry!" he cried, frightened tears welling in his eyes.

For a moment, they stared down at him in silence. The woman in the grave began tugging at his jacket. He tried to fight her off as the crowd moved closer and started throwing the freshly shovelled dirt on top of them. Its weight and taste unbalanced his efforts to save himself.

The hard bits of clay bruised his face, and the dirt blinded him as the grave filled up and retarded his movements. The dead woman's grip was tight, and he couldn't break her hold on him.

He screamed for mercy, but his attempts fell on closed ears. "Please! Please!"

Suddenly aware of his fate, he cried out in disbelief.

The soil built up around him as the old woman increased the strength of her grip. Finally, his strength was at an end. With a final scream before his mouth filled with soil, the woman pulled him down into her grave. The loose soil covered them both as the crowd filled the grave to the top, then returned into the night.

THE CAPTAIN

Detective Sergeant Barrel had known this would happen. Only three days ago, his major crime squad had captured a cult leader calling himself the Risen Christ. His real name was Paul Ball, and in the past five years, he had managed to gather about a dozen followers to help him cleanse the earth of evil people.

Ball's idea of ridding the world of evil had only extended to a young pregnant teenager who his group almost murdered. She wasn't pure enough for Paul Ball's utopia.

Paul and his cult had been given bail, and of course, the agreement between the accused, that he would hand in all his weapons and report to a police station twice a day, and the courts had not been honoured.

"Why did that idiot judge give these fucking idiots bail? It's beyond me, really." Barrel shook his head as he complained to his partner, Con Mathias, who sat in the driver's seat.

"Yeah, I hear ya." Con had been hearing it all morning.

"Now we've got to spend hours catching this bastard again. Unbelievable." Barrel had the shits big time. It had taken almost six months to build a case against the Risen Christ, and now some judge had let him walk. Now they had to do it all over again.

Luckily, this time they had a break. One of the members had become an informant and let Barrel know that Ball was headed south along the Hume Highway in a brand new black Mercedes van.

Somewhere along the Hume highway, Ball had a hideout, but the informant didn't know exactly where it was; it seemed Ball only ever took his most trusted lieutenants there. Barrel guessed that Paul Ball knew he had a turncoat.

"And another thing. I'm in my mid thirties, and I can't even get a date. But this guy gets six women to attempt to murder someone for him! How does that work, Con? Tell me!"

Con laughed. "I don't know." He was concentrating on driving, clocking almost 150km/h along the highway, dodging cars while he listened to Barrel bitch.

"*Crime 42*," came the voice over the radio.

"Yeah, Crime 42."

"Crime 42. Crime 50 has spotted the Mercedes on a track about fifty kilometres north of the Bowral exit. He's in position there and will wait."

"Copy. About thirty minutes."

Barrel was happy. Hopefully this day would end with the recapture of the Risen Christ, and hopefully Barrel himself could tell the magistrate to keep this bloke in jail.

~~~

Things went well as Barrel's team organised themselves down a dirt track a kilometre from the farmhouse. One of his team had surveyed the house. It looked deserted apart from the black Merc in the driveway. Barrel decided they would take up positions around the house to block anyone getting in or out. Then, if given a chance, they would move in. But as they began to take their positions, everything went wrong.

Machine gun fire peppered Barrel's sedan from over a hundred metres away, wounding Con in the leg. Barrel's other team had also been ambushed as they approached the farmhouse. Three men were wounded, and the rest had to pull back.

Only when Barrel got a good look at the house did he realise that the windows had been barricaded up and had peepholes. During their initial reconnaissance his team had reported the windows open and nothing suspicious to be seen. He guessed that they had cameras or binoculars and were watching and waiting for his unit to move in.

Barrel was mightily pissed off, but he was also puzzled by the fact that the cult had not tried to make a break for it. It would be the perfect time, and he fully expected it. The two sides sat opposite each other for about two hours.

More police turned up to recreate the ring around the house. It seemed the opportunity for Paul Ball to escape had passed.

Barrel waited at the forward command centre located in an old sheep pen about three hundred metres from the front of the farmhouse. He was constantly on the phone with top brass in Sydney who wanted to know what was going on.

Every few minutes, gunfire erupted from the windows. The rounds ricocheted off the dirt, trees, abandoned police vehicles and fences. It seemed the cult members were shooting just to keep the police on their toes.

As time ticked on, the sun began to fall from the sky. Darkness would come soon. It would be the perfect time to go in.

Over the phone, Barrel asked his duty officer, "Where's that tactical group?" It was the third time he'd enquired about it in the hour.

"Relax," came the voice on the other end. Barrel didn't recognise it. "I've got a special squad to deal with these types of situations."

"I thought the TRG could do this?"

The voice chuckled. "The Risen Christ will have to deal with the risen dead." Then the line went silent.

Barrel rang a few numbers to find out who or what this special squad was, but no one had heard about it.

So he had to wait, and anxiously wait he did.

At about midnight, a loud roar came up the road. A black bus bounced into view bearing no number plates and tinted windows. It stopped in the concealment of thick trees and shrubs close to Barrel's position, and he walked over to it. This must be the special squad he was meant to be waiting for—he hoped it was, anyway.

He waited for the door to open so he could brief the squad on the situation.

But the door didn't open. Instead, a man appeared at the rear of the bus. He was dressed in black overalls and a black cap. With his arms behind his back, he confidently walked towards the house. A column of black-dressed troopers followed.

At first, Barrel was annoyed that he had been ignored while the man scanned the farmhouse with a pair of binoculars. As the file of troopers passed by him, Barrel noticed a horrible smell. From experience, he knew it was rotting flesh. These troopers did not walk like normal men or act like the TRG. Their bodies were bent, and they dragged their feet as they moved. Only grunts and groans broke the night as they formed up. Helmets mostly hid their faces, but Barrel saw pale white skin and many unhealed wounds, some even bandaged.

With the troopers lined up, the man with the binoculars turned and walked down their line, tightening vests and checking equipment. When that was done, he looked over at Barrel.

By this time, a few other officers had joined Barrel for what they thought would be a briefing about entering the farmhouse.

"Detective Sergeant Barrel?" the man asked.

"Yeah, that's me."

"My squad is ready. I understand the objective is the house, the Risen Christ and his associates?"

"Yeah, that's right. There's him and about three others, as far as we can tell. They all have automatic weapons that they're not afraid of using."

"Excellent," the man said.

"Can I get your name? I'm Detective ... well you already know my name."

"I am the Captain, Detective. This will be over in moments. Your men can enjoy the show." With that, the Captain turned and went back to his troops.

"Weapons drawn!" he bellowed.

The special squad removed their batons.

"Advance forward!" the Captain called. The special squad began to advance in an open line right across the front lawn.

"Shit! He's just sending 'em straight in like cattle!" another officer remarked.

"Somehow, I don't think that's going to matter." Barrel's eyes were unable to focus on anything except the line of men running across the lawn. He waited for the machine gun fire to begin.

It was quiet at first; then there was movement in the windows of the farmhouse, and Barrel's fears were realised. Shots rang out and hit the marching troopers. They stumbled but did not fall as pieces of flesh and equipment flew off their bodies. Still the shots rang out and found their marks. Barrel's men took cover and returned the fire. Still, the troopers advanced.

Barrel and his remaining men stared with open mouths.

The troopers reached the farmhouse. They smashed their way in as mighty screams came out of the house. One member of the cult jumped—or was thrown—out of an upper-floor window, landing in a tangled mess on the ground.

The Captain's voice could be heard above the din, bellowing orders to his men. "Seal all rooms! Don't let them get away!"

More shots and screams came from inside the house before it all suddenly stopped.

Barrel watched the Captain exit the house, followed by his squad. They carried the bodies of the Risen Christ and two of his followers to Barrel and dumped them at his feet.

"You may enter the house, Detective."

Barrel had nothing to say at first. He watched the squad line up at their bus.

Barrel went to shake the Captain's hand, but it contained the severed arm of one of his troopers. He moved the appendage to his left hand, then shook Barrel's.

"Thanks, I guess," said Barrel.

The Captain smiled slightly, then went to the bus with the severed arm still in his hand.

"Back inside!" he called.

The Captain and his special squad disappeared into the bus before it drove off.

It took a few moments of staring at each other before Barrel's men finally shook off the strange sight.

"So, who were they?" an officer asked, staring at the Risen Christ who was tied up and visibly shaking with fright.

"I've been in this job long enough to know when you just don't ask."

THE HOUSE BEHIND ME

I'm lying awake in my bed in the middle of the night. The curtains are drawn and the window is closed, but still I can hear the couple in the house behind me screaming at each other.

I get up and part the curtains a fraction. I'm annoyed by the disturbance, but I'm also curious.

I hear a woman's scream, and the moan of a man too tormented to scream.

It's too cold to be peeping through my curtain at the neighbours. I get back into bed and fall asleep despite the woman's screams.

In the morning, there is only quiet from the house. I tend to my garden while looking occasionally at the house. Only stillness meets my gaze.

That night, the same woman's screams awaken me. It is exactly midnight. This time, I peer though my curtain longer and hear more than screaming. Furniture crashes, and glass breaks inside the house. I even see much of it being thrown out the rear window into the yard.

The situation does not look good for the woman. I don't want to get involved in other people's problems—but I'm not above snooping.

But it's late, and I am glad when it finally goes quiet so I can return to bed. My mind is twirling for some minutes, wondering what is going on in the house behind me.

I wander my yard again in the morning. Whilst tending the garden closest to the house behind me, I take the opportunity to peek over the fence into their property. But there is nothing there, no glass or furniture. I guess they cleaned it up.

Later that day, I am in my front yard when another neighbour, Mrs Hilton, stops to talk to me on her way home.

"Oh, have you heard the commotion going on in the house behind me, Mrs Hilton?"

"No, my dear. I sleep very soundly. There used to be trouble there, but that was long ago."

"Really? I must be a light sleeper then. What type of trouble?"

"Well, I hope they don't keep you awake again tonight, my dear. I will see you tomorrow." She said without answering my question.

"Yes, good day, Mrs Hilton." I wasn't sure if she had deliberately ignored me or was just deaf. I believe it was both.

On the third night, I set my alarm to awake a few minutes before midnight. At exactly midnight, the screams of the woman and the moans of a man start on cue. But I also hear another woman's voice.

"Leave me alone!" she cries.

The lights are on in the house behind me, and I see shapes dance across the drawn curtains. A woman comes out of the house and goes into her yard, beginning to dig with her hands. I open the window.

She digs franticly for a while before she gives up. She runs her hands over her head, and I can hear her crying. She runs back into the house.

Should I call the police? I wonder. But I still don't want to get involved in other people's problems.

Again, the house behind me has gone quiet. I go to my bed and try to sleep again, still wondering what was going on.

This time, I do not sleep but toss and turn for some time. More noise comes from the house behind me, and I immediately jump out of bed and take my place at the curtain.

The same woman who was digging in the yard steps outside. She is following another person who drags something heavy down the stairs and into the yard.

Is that a body? I really don't want to know, but I can't turn away from looking.

I hear the sound of digging. It goes on for some time before all is quiet again. Only the woman who was digging earlier returns to the house. Then all the lights go off, and all is quiet.

I manage to fall asleep, but awake tired. Having my sleep pattern disturbed is catching up with me.

I watch the house behind me with interest after opening the curtain wide. I even open the window to let the morning air in. There is no sign of the woman or any noise coming from the house.

But then the woman I have seen digging appears at the rear of her house. I hide behind the curtain and watch.

She is carrying a spade and, on her hands and knees, she begins digging where I saw her the other night. She digs quickly, and I can hear her loud breathing. I look around at the houses nearby but see no one else watching.

Then a wild shriek rises from the yard. The woman appears to have found something. She jumps up, her eyes showing horror.

I move the curtain away to see clearly. There is movement between the cracks of the paling fence. Something or someone rises up out of a hole in the ground. I see a bony hand, then a head and finally a body. Dry dirt falls from its mangled hair and torn clothes.

It—I cannot tell if it is female or male—looks over at the terrified woman who is now backing away. It climbs out further, and I can see it is a man as its head towers over the fence. I watch, fascinated, not realising I am leaning out of the open window to see better. Is it a ghost, or is it a real man?

The man bears down on the woman, towering over her. When he reaches out for her, she is too late to back away. Soon, he has her by her arm. I have never heard such screaming before. She howls for her life.

I feel sick. This thing is no ghost.

He is absolutely decayed. The long arms pull her closer to him. The stench and sight must be unbearable, for her face snatches away from his on contact. The dirty, bony hand caresses her neck, then cheek. Then, *snap*, he breaks her gentle neck. She falls to the ground and out of my sight.

I'm horrified, but there is no time for emotions. The man turns about. The sun blazes in his eyes as he stares at something. Then he grimaces and begins to walk towards the fence. The palings break easily in his fists as he steps into my yard, his face still a grimace.

"Oh no." He is staring straight at me.

Sometimes you should just let the dead lie. I know that now, but this morning, death was the last thing on my mind.

The soft body of Jess Howelston pressing against mine was all that I could think about. I didn't mind camping--it went back to my old scout days--but girls never seemed to warm to the idea of spending a few days with no water, no electricity, and no comfortable bed.

But Jess loved it.

"I like doing things in the outdoors," she said, with a wink in her eye.

I spent the rest of the day dusting off my old tent, swag, and managed to fill a cardboard box full of food, water, and alcohol to last us the weekend. Then we hit the road and I could not wait to get me a piece of Jess Howelston.

Now all things went well. I found an old camping site deep in the Watagans Forest that was thankfully deserted. I had barely unpacked when Jess whispered in my ear she wanted me to do her up against a tree. I knew then that this was going to be the best weekend of my life.

By nightfall, we had eaten and were now lying on a blanket drinking beer while watching the stars.

"How bout we go skinny dipping?" Jess asked, with a smile.

"Is there even water around here?"

"Yeah, I looked on the map while you were cooking. Down that way somewhere." She laughed while she pointed away from the camp.

"You've got no idea where it is."

"I do. It's down there, to the north."

"Alright, let's go."

We started walking north along an old path. It wound its way through the thickening bush for some distance, but there was no sign of water.

"So where's this magical water of yours?" I joked.

"It didn't look far on the map." She laughed.

"What about a centimetre? A centimetre is probably a few kilometres you know."

"Well I didn't know that; it didn't look far. You want to go back?"

"Ummm." It was probably best, but I really wanted to see her naked again.

"It really shouldn't be far, I promise." She sounded more serious.

So we marched on for almost another hour, before admitting defeat.

"I'm sorry, I really thought this was the way."

"Well, we've been walking for about two hours, in the dark, and in unknown territory."

"What are you saying? Are we lost?" She again laughed.

"Not yet," I said to myself. "Come on. Let's just go back the way we came."

It seemed just that simple, but as we retraced our steps along the path, something did not seem right. We had walked basically downwards on the way to the nonexistent water, but on our return journey we were not climbing, but continuing to go down.

The bush had become thicker and wilder. The paths were nonexistent and the night stars disappeared from the blackened sky.

We stupidly marched on; I didn't believe we could get lost and, as we saw a fire in the distance, we both breathed with relief.

But as we came closer, things didn't seem right. There was a strange odor that hung under the heavy canopy and infected the air. There was a group of people huddled around a fire but they didn't move.

"Hello," I said, but got no reply.

We should have backed out earlier. I should have said that we were sorry, that we didn't mean to intrude.

The people looked at us and there were suddenly dozens of them around us. These were not normal people. Their eyes were blackened holes, their skin was peeling from their very bones and the blood pored like saliva from their wretched mouths.

Jess stood there, too petrified to speak or move, but I managed to take a step back. That's when a crescendo of angst cries broke out from the crowd and they began to pounce.

I ran, while holding onto Jess' hand, but we didn't get far. They were fast and smart--too fast and smart for the dead. They circled around our flank and as soon as we were surrounded, they pounced.

31

I tried to help Jess, God's truth I did, but I panicked. They swamped us like flies; their rotting stench pushed away the fresh air. I fought, using my torch as a baton, but I couldn't get to her. I knew they had her. Her screams echoed out as I fled, dead skin still on my torch and hand as I smashed my way out.

Then I ran for my life. They chased me, panting and hurtling through the darkness. Branches slapped across my face and stung my skin. There were so many of the creatures I didn't believe I could get away. For every tree, there seemed to be one of them all converging on me, no doubt following my scent.

All I hoped for was to get back to my car and to get the hell out of there--but I knew that I really didn't know where I was or where I should go. So I kept running, the adrenaline and fear whipping at my heels.

Relief came over me when I came across a small hut in the corner of a clearing. There was no light coming from its windows, but the sight of the hut was like the rescue ship coming out of the fog to save a drowning man.

I ran to the door and found, to my surprise, that it was open. My relief turned to trepidation, immediately. The hut was a small fibro house and inside was a mess, with broken plates and furniture scattered about the rooms. There was no sanctuary here.

It was then that I noticed my torch still in my hand. Somehow I had turned it off. I turned it back on to reveal the rotting chunks over my hand and the lens. I looked about for a rag to clean it off, when I saw it. Startled for a moment I jumped back.

The light had caught the white bone of a human skull lying on the ruins of a table. The rest of the skeleton was scattered about.

Now I was overcome by a sense of foreboding and decided to get my arse out of there right now. But it was too late. I heard the first rush of footsteps and across the clearing.

I ran to the door and had just stepped out when a body appeared in front of me. Its stench immediately made my stomach turn and cost me my chance to escape. He grabbed me by the shoulders and leaned close and I saw the hunger in his rotten eyes. There was even a tight smirk across what remained of his mouth. A black chunk of flesh that had once been his tongue came out of his mouth and scraped across my cheek, putting me on the verge of throwing up.

In desperation, I kicked his groin. My foot smashed through the weak flesh and broke off his leg. His body crumpled to the floor. I thought I had made myself another chance, but there were now more of them surrounding me, all with the same hungry look on their grotesque faces.

They charged quickly and the force threw me back onto the house floor, where my death came painfully, but swiftly. They left only my bones scattered about the dusty floor.

POSSESSIONS

Collectors are the strangest of all people. They are a breed of their own. They can become so obsessed with the thrill of slowly collecting objects that their life becomes nothing but the acquisition of possessions.

A person with an obsessive passion of possession is a strong, narrow-minded individual. The search for more of the things they desire consumes every moment of their lives. If you were such a person, could you give up your life-long obsession? What if you died? What would happen to the collection you so painstakingly amassed? Could you really leave it all behind?

Long ago, a man named Samuel Brien lived on my street. He was a loner who spent all his time collecting books and artefacts from periods in history that fascinated him.

I remember seeing him at a garage sale. He spent some time going through Mrs Randle's boxes of magazines, figurines and odds and ends. Finally, he came across some medals. I knew them for what they were: antique campaign medals from the Crimean War. But poor old Mrs Randle had no idea. I wished I'd said something at the time, but I just watched as Samuel convinced the old lady that they were not really that valuable, and that twenty dollars for the two was a good bargain.

I even heard him chuckle as he walked past me. He was what some would call "deep pockets".

He never seemed to spend his money on himself. His clothes were always creased or worn. I don't ever remember seeing him in new clothes.

His house, though, was quite impressive. It had been built of sandstone and was one of the original buildings in our suburb. It was not large, but he kept it immaculate. Its garden was the finest in the area.

Every day, Samuel tended the garden or sat on the porch reading a book or looking over a new acquisition. His little piece of the world was his, and his alone.

Then the unthinkable happened. Time caught up with old Samuel. The neighbours became suspicious when no one saw him watering his garden for several mornings. For three days, he lay in his house, stiff as a board and perched in his favourite seat, where he could stare at the walls that held his best-loved paintings.

It soon became clear that Samuel was not prepared for death. There was no will, and his brother, Robert—who Samuel always hated—came up from Sydney to claim the estate.

Robert had always known his older brother was a bit weird. Samuel had been so disinterested in other people's lives that he became a recluse. But Robert had heard about Samuel's collection, and he knew it was worth quite a sum of money.

When Robert was going through Samuel's personal papers, he found strange drawings, notes and paintings. It seemed Samuel had thought about his own demise and had planned an Egyptian-style burial. Robert could only laugh. Samuel was not going to be buried with all his worldly goods like a minor pharaoh. He would be buried with little expense or fanfare in the local cemetery.

And so it was done. Behind Robert's façade of mourning, he kept going over the wonderful things he knew existed inside Samuel's house. He had even arranged for an employee from the Sydney Museum to come look at it, along with a real estate agent, to appraise just how much Samuel had left behind.

While Robert had made his decision, Samuel had also made his. That's when things became strange.

Robert arrived early after picking up the house keys from the police station. They had locked the house and kept them, as it took over a day for them to find Robert and inform him of his brother's death.

He opened the front door, but the overpowering odour that burst out made him think twice about going inside. He let the house air out while he waited for his guests to arrive.

Mr Walker, the museum employee, and Mrs Hayden, the real estate agent, arrived almost together. Robert was glad to get the show on the road, as he was keen to find out how much his brother's estate would be worth.

"Have you been inside?" asked Walker.

"Only once the other day, but what I saw was amazing. It's been years since I've been here and seen the stuff he was amassing."

As they arrived at the door, Robert saw that it was closed. He was sure he had left it open. It was locked again, and he opened it with the key.

"My, that is strong," Walker laughed, waving the air away from his face.

"You said he was found inside after three days?" Hayden asked suspiciously.

"Yes, but once it's cleaned up, there shouldn't be a problem," Robert assured her, stepping inside.

Dust covered everything. Books were piled up on tables and more books and antiques packed the shelves. Robert could just see the dollars stack up as he stepped farther into the house.

They wandered the hallway until they came to the rear of the house. "So, what do you think so far?" Robert prompted.

"It's impressive. Some items are very good," answered Walker. "But of course, we would need a good catalogue of what is actually in there."

Robert smiled. "Mrs Hayden?"

The young woman was looking up at the ceiling. "I like these double doors. Do they lead to a study?"

"I'm not sure. The police called it a sunroom."

Mrs Hayden opened the door while Robert looked back at Walker, who was picking through one of the shelves.

Then there was a scream, and the men swung around to see Hayden staring back at them with wide eyes. "There's someone in there?"

"What?" Robert exclaimed, stepping forward.

He saw shoes at the foot of a seat and a hand on the armrest.

"What are you doing here?" Robert demanded.

There was no response, and he stepped even closer. The sun shone into the room from a window, making the paintings in the room glow with new vigour and life.

Robert knew this was the room Samuel had died in and that this was the chair he had sat in for three days while his body began to ferment. He didn't really want to go any further, but he ignored his fear.

When he was closer, he almost lost his breath.

"Samuel?"

His brother did not respond.

"What are you doing here?" Robert now recognised the funeral clothes that his brother had been wearing when he was buried yesterday. "You're meant to be dead. We're here to collect all your stuff."

Only then did Samuel react. He gave a deep, dog-like growl, and his face became a sneer while his eyes bore into his brother's.

Robert stepped away as Samuel stood up. Walker and Hayden were already at the front door, with Robert not too far behind.

Robert called the police, and when they arrived, it got ugly. I remember a number of shots ringing out and much screaming. Eventually, the police dragged Samuel out of his home as he kicked and screamed. He had a wound to his head and three bullets to his chest, but he still managed to put up a fight.

Robert followed the ambulance to hospital, where he waited in stunned silence. Had he buried Samuel alive?

Surely not. But if he were alive, then Robert would not be getting anything.

"Mr Brien?" a doctor asked.

"Yes."

"Umm. I don't really know what to say, but your brother has no heartbeat. We pulled out three bullets from his chest and one from his head. We bandaged his jaw back in place. We believe there are two more rounds in his head, which we can't operate on."

"Why not?"

"Well, we can't anaesthetise him; even a local aesthetic isn't working. We thought it had, as he showed no sign of pain when the other wounds were treated. He should be unconscious or in great amounts of pain, but he just sits there."

"I ... I don't know what to say."

"According to our records, your brother died five days ago and was buried yesterday. Is that correct?"

"I thought it was."

"Well, we're keeping him here overnight for observation. I'll keep you posted; for now, you should go home."

"Yeah. Yeah, I might do that."

Robert went back to Sydney. He would not return to claim his brother when he was released from the hospital and taken to court on the charges of resisting and assaulting the police. When he did return he would never leave his brother again.

The magistrate did not know what to do with him. Here was a man who had died and been buried, then returned home to attack stunned police officers when they went to investigate the allegation of an intruder. Now, after having most of the rounds removed from his body without anaesthetic, he was sitting in the courtroom, a bandage around his head, looking through an auctioneer's catalogue.

"So, what is the defence argument?"

The defending legal aid representative was at a loss.

"Perhaps condition bail at this time, your Worship, for a court date to be set to allow both sides to ascertain what has happened in the case of Samuel Brien."

"I agree. Bail is set."

So Samuel went home, so obsessed with his collection that he had returned from the dead. That is the spirit of a collector who can't let go. His collection was his alone, and it always would be.

Samuel still lives in that house. He never goes outside, and his garden eventually died. Occasionally when you pass by, the face of a paranoid old man blazes out from behind a drawn curtain. His dead eyes watch you as you walk by. Watch out; don't try to make any offers for his wonderful house and collection. And whatever you do, do not knock on the front door, and never wander in the yard at night. You might end up as part of the collection he gazes at night and day. How else could I know all of this?

ANCESTORS

My nightmares have been coming for almost a week now. They began so abruptly that I cannot tell you what triggered them. Believe me, I wish I had the answers to the riddle of these visions that wreck me and leave me sleepless.

They are always the same, every night. That troubles me, too. The same bodies, strange colours, strange features. Bodies dragged from the earth, sleeping in metal boxes. I can tell that the dream takes place somewhere in the outback here in Australia. I recognise the rusty brown of the sand and the age-old craggy gorges and hills. There is a village of sorts, more of a camp, of Aborigines, who have stumbled onto these boxes exposed in a dried riverbed. There are five of the rectangle-shaped, smooth, silver boxes. The Aborigines pull each one from the ochre earth and inspect it with awe.

Of course, the boxes' appearance causes great excitement and talk among the people who have no idea what they are. Some say they are the gods, sleeping after creating the earth. None can decide for sure.

They try to wake them, shaking the boxes, yelling, tapping, banging and even dragging them around the makeshift camp. None stir. Not until the night. I see nothing of what happens at first. I see only the morning, when dead tribe members are found white as ghosts with small puncture wounds all over their bodies.

~~~

Another night ends with dawn and more death. The tribe learns quickly: five dead in two nights, five boxes. Suspicion and fear fall on the new discovery. Perhaps, they say amongst themselves, the gods should not have been removed from the ground. Then there is the elder, the chief. Tall and brave, he has the wisdom of his people peering from within his weathered eyes, framed by his white hair and beard. His orders are simple: put the boxes back into the earth from which they had been removed.

By the falling of the sun, it is done. The tribe goes into the night content that the wrong has been righted.

But the morning brings more death. Families have been slaughtered in their shelters as they slept. And for the first time, *they* had been seen.

A sleepless soul has witnesses the gods walk. Excitedly, he tells the elder that these beings did not look like other men, for they had red eyes and white skin, and they drank the red river straight from the body with their long fangs. The elder moves quickly to protect his people. He gathers his warriors together and sends the women, the elderly and the children away.

Once they are gone, the elder sits with his warriors and begins to speak to the mounds of earth. He speaks to the sky, appealing for the gods to show themselves so his people can plead their case and seek a way to appease the gods so they will leave his people in peace.

They wait for hours with no result. Then the sun begins to sink, and the first growls from the ground sound out. The dirt moves, and suddenly an arm strikes out from the ground, reaching to the night skies with a white stone claw.

The nervous warriors grab their spears, but the elder orders them to stand down with a sweep of his hand. Stunned, the men watch all the gods rise from the earth and stand before them. They are as white as solid cloud, and their red eyes blaze in the darkness.

There is silence for a moment; then, the elder begins to chant and sing. His men follow his lead, and the gods watch as the dust rises up in low clouds at the men's feet as they dance around the crackling fire.

The elder stops and beckons a man forward who is bearing a plate of fruit, meat and water. The man places it at the foot of the closest god. Again the elder speaks, wanting forgiveness for his people, hoping the gods will let them live.

One of these stone gods steps forward, then grabs the man still kneeling at his feet with the plate of food. The man shows no fear in the clutches of the white god. This being opens his mouth to reveal his sharp teeth. The man begins to panic as those teeth crunch down on his throat.

It becomes a signal for both sides to attack. Spears are thrown, and the men are horrified when the white men pull them out of their cold flesh and laugh, breaking the spears over their knees.

The strangers pounce on the terrified men. They fight back as best they can, but their stone knives and spears have no effect. Soon, the men's blood runs over the dirt, making sweet mud. The elder orders the men to flee. Terror deprives them of rational thought, and they run in all directions. They are almost as white as their attackers.

The elder reaches the camp of another nation and tells his tale. This chief is young and full of fight. He orders his warriors to prepare for war. For the remainder of the night and into the morning, they prepare by dancing and singing. They paint their bodies with white and red clay. By sunset, they are ready.

They march quickly, arriving at the abandoned camp soon after. They circle it, looking for danger. It is quiet. As they move in, they encounter the rotting bodies of the dead warriors. Even worse, they find bodies of woman and children who should have been safe far from here. The men don't know how the strangers found them, and they try not to think about it.

In the riverbed they see the large rectangular holes that hold the metal boxes. Around them are about half a dozen smaller ones, freshly dug. Moving into the edges of the encampment, the warriors find the body of a scout sent during the night. He hangs from a tree, his throat ripped out.

The warriors step over the corpses, moving closer to the mounds of dirt. All is still. Both elders order one of the smaller mounds uncovered.

They gather round the site. Their jaws drop. A face, then a body is exposed. It is one of the elder's warriors, killed the day before. His skin is pale and woundless.

The old chief covers the body with dirt again. He issues orders, and the remaining men begin to dig out the metal boxes of these dangerous strangers.

Both chiefs confer about what to do. They agree that they do not have the strength to fight these devils, and that the land they live in is too vital to their survival to abandon it.

The boxes must be taken away. First, the warriors wrap great barks of wood around them, winding them with long grass that has been twisted and treated to form a type of rope. The trek will take them through the night, and they will take no chances.

Four warriors carry each box, and the group walks for days without incident through the rough and hilly terrain. They finally arrive at a great lake that has almost dried up in the summer heat. Its banks still hold large tracks of bush and shrubs, and on one side there is a great crag of jagged rock that is the base of a plateau stretching into the horizon.

The group walks out onto the cracked, hardened mud and stops at the wall of rock. There, the men line up the boxes and begin excavating a small, natural cave at the base of the wall. All day they toil, and it is almost sunset when they push the boxes, one-by-one, into the muddy, damp hole.

Once they are all in, the cavern is filled with rock and dirt. Then a wall of more rock and mud is created over the entrance of the cave, entombing these savage strangers in their metal boxes.

Both elders say words to the wall and to the sky, prayers to keep these angry gods in peaceful sleep. When done, the elders and their warriors march back out of the drying lake, disappearing into history just as the first thunderclaps break out in the sky and the first of the winter rain begins to fall.

I dream no more of it, and I'm glad of it, too. I enjoy weeks of peace, sleeping quietly again. I even take up bush walking as I return to normality after my period of temporary insanity.

On such a walk, I come across a track that winds its way through the bush. Then I stumble upon a camp that is empty but for a number of police vehicles. I go on, then see a drying lakebed, almost a billabong, really, with plenty of green and grey shrubs and trees hanging on to the winter rains. And I see a crag of a wall, weathered over millions of years. I stop as I remember this scene. I know it from my nightmares. I begin to tremble when I see the dozen skeletons scattered over the wet mud, some still with flesh on them. In the corner of my eye, I see the wall of rock with a pile of rubble at its base. A chunk of the wall is missing, leading into a natural hollow. I swear I can hear the wind blow in its emptiness.

BENEATH THE
QUIET OF CUMBERLAND

William Hereford's carriage slid through the heavy rain, which had unexpectedly begun to fall, as it neared the estate of the Cranswell family in Croglin Grange. A stickler for time, he checked his pocket watch again. He was never late and tonight was no exception. Maybe it was a habit left over from his old military days. He took comfort that he was running on schedule and began to take in the green lush surroundings of Cumberland.

The soft gentle plains lay across the earth like an outspread blanket, here and there broken by the odd tree or small creek. He saw the sun, a misty fire cloaked by the thin veil of grey cloud. It seemed to fight to stay afire but the weight of the clouds pushed it deep into and beyond the horizon. Darkness was stirring, the sun was dozing in its cradle and the heavy rain washed all trace of the sun's warmth from the surrounding land.

The carriage turned into a long lane that ended at a gate. His mode of transport seemed tiny against the tall trees that made a thick wall from road to gate. The lights of the house blazed in the night signalling the only life for miles. He saw them through the grille of the gate and he could feel the warmth already as the gate swung open to let him pass.

Edward, the family's elderly butler, stood at the lower step to greet him as William stepped from the carriage. Edward seemed to be the stereotypical English butler of Victorian times. Tall, stiff upper lipped, and with short grey hair and polite but appearances can be deceiving. A smile broke across his Edward's face as William climbed the stairs. They greeted each as if there was no rain.

"Good evening, Mr Hereford."

"Good evening, Edward. I trust I am not late?"

"Oh no Sir, punctual as always. Mr Cranwell is waiting in the sitting room."

They made their way up the wet steps to an open wooden door. Here there was warmth as the house was brightly lit and with many an open fire.

"It's some shocking weather you have here, my man."

"Oh, it's always raining in Cumberland, Sir, keeps the grass green and air fresh. I'll see you into the sitting room first, Sir. John will take your luggage to your room."

"Thank you."

William entered a brightly lit room lined with paintings of ancestors and rare artefacts. Deep red seemed to be the favourite colour with the floors layered with rich blood-coloured carpet and the furniture padded the same. The family sat on lounges listening to their father Arthur retell an ancient tale of ghosts and treasure. The young children, George and Mary, took in every word as if it were true. The three elder children were old enough to remember being told the same tale a number of times and were content to let the little ones enjoy it. And older they had become, thought William.

Seeing his arrival, they stood. Arthur broke off his story and came to shake his hand.

"The floods didn't keep you away, I see."

"Absolutely not."

William could not believe the children had matured so quickly. Anne was a treasure to behold. Her hands were clasped in front of her and a teasing smile curved her sweet mouth. She knew he held her in awe.

"My word, Anne, you have become so beautiful."

She smiled bashfully at the compliment. "Thank you, Mr Hereford.

He turned to the two boys. "Richard and Daniel, now young men I see before me."

"Good evening, Mr Hereford," spoke Richard.

"Pleasant trip?" asked Daniel.

"Yes, thank you, it was. No leaks in the carriage, thank goodness."

Now he spied the two little ones again, still sitting on the floor. Both sets of eyes stared up at him, full of innocence and wonder.

"And Mary and George, you two have grown so much."

They didn't say anything in reply but smiled and clapped their little hands.

"Well then, William, we have much to talk about over dinner, old times to renew and new times to build. I want to hear all about your visit to Scotland. Come, dinner is served."

Arthur accompanied William, followed by the rest of the family, into the dining hall. Lit by electricity, its humble glow backed up by an abundance of candles made the room feel cosy and inviting. As Edward led him to his seat, he turned to look out the side windows that ran the length of the room. Already the sun had gone and there was the still of darkness across the land.

They were seated comfortably and dinner was served while they chatted over the family's recent history.

"Richard here is enlisting in Her Majesty's Army in the new year."

"Good show, man. Keeping the tradition flowing."

"Yes Sir."

"I'm sure you'll make as fine a soldier as your father and brother have."

"Yes Sir, I'm looking forward to it."

It was then that Daniel became distracted by something and took his stare from beyond the table and out the window.

"What is it, Daniel?" Asked William.

"There is something out there."

They all turned their heads as he stood up and took a candle from the table. He walked over to a window, opened it, and peered out. By the light of the candle, they made out a small tree but nothing else. He brought the candle back in and closed the window.

"Are you sure you saw something?" William asked again. Daniel moved to the next window and looked through the glass. Arthur had also stood up and left the room without saying a word.

"Yes, something passed the window."

"Perhaps it was a shadow of a servant?" reasoned Richard. Daniel had now given up and turned back to the room. "Perhaps it was," he replied.

He had moved away from the window when Anne suddenly screamed and threw her hands over her face. Daniel turned back to the window and his knees gave way at the sight. William saw it too.

A face was pressed up to the glass. It was a wrinkled face and its mouth was full of sharp damaged teeth all dripping with saliva. And there were its eyes, all red and blood shot but still clear even in the dark. They gleamed with evil fury and they were pinned on Anne but Anne had her face away from the beast.

William was struck with fear. Such an animal he had never seen before. In quick moments he had rebalanced his courage and thought only of the safety of the children. He called to Richard, struck dumb as he was, gazing at the face stuck on the glass.

"Richard, get the children out."

Richard woke from his disbelief and began to obey the order and ushered the little ones from the dining hall.

William now moved towards Anne who was still buried deep in her palms. He could hear her sob as he neared to embrace her. She jumped as he touched her but quickly realised that he was no beast.

"Anne, you should go to another room."

Her mouth was open in shock, her eyes fixed and her body trembling in fright.

There was no time to wait so he picked up her frightened frame and began to move her from the room when he looked over to the creature still in view. Its shark-like mouth spoke her name. He could just hear it spread from its lips and through the glass. He felt its temper change, rising higher and fiercer as he held Anne and ran from the room. He saw the face change into something more evil and terrible. It yelled her name now and began to pound on the glass as he took its prize away.

Pieces of glass began to fall to the floor but its sound became overlapped by Arthur's rifle as it echoed out and its shot pierced the glass and embedded itself in the monster's flesh.

It cried out as it was wounded, its rage feeding its strength. Still it hammered at the remaining glass. Again Arthur fired. Twice, thrice, and a fourth time with a revolver. Again and again the old man found his mark.

The monster, weak with the loss of blood, fell back out of sight below the ruined window. No sound rose from the unseen. Smoke wavered in the air blocking sight and infecting their lungs. Arthur stood triumphant and poised for another strike.

"What in God's name was that?" shouted William on his return from leaving Anne with her brother in an adjacent room.

"That is the local lunatic, William. Fresh from lady syphilis no doubt," said Arthur.

"This is a regular occurrence?"

"Of sorts."

"Well, I hope the asylum comes and claims it."

"We are miles from anywhere and no one has ever come to collect it. I actually think that no one will come, so I will have to put it out of its misery."

"Are you sure?" questioned William.

Arthur stared into William's eyes. He was as sure as the sun rising in the morning. He reloaded his revolver and like the old soldier he was he marched towards the front door.

Here Edward appeared, shaken from what he had heard.

"Sir, I heard gun shots."

"Yes, Edward. The lunatic is back. Now I am going outside to put a bullet through its wretched skull and giving us and it peace."

"Be careful, Arthur," William called as the old man stepped outside and into the night.

~ ~ ~

"It's been fifteen minutes, Mr. Hereford," stated Richard. His voice quivered with fear for the fate of his father. William, hands cupped over his face, looked up. He knew the end when he saw it.

"I know."

Daniel came in from the other room, full of his father's spirit.

"Perhaps we should get everyone upstairs?" he said.

William was pondering the suggestion when a girl's scream cried out from a back room. They rushed back into the sitting room where Anne and the children were resting.

On entering the room they saw the creature had opened a window and was perched on the sill, a grin on its vicious, blood-smeared mouth. Daniel raised his rifle he now carried and fired, hitting it between the eyes.

It lingered, unbalanced, blood trickling down the side of its nose. Richard ran up to it and used the butt of it to smash the monster's face. It cried out aloud and fell back out of sight.

Richard hung out the window with the rifle and fired a shot before pulling himself back in and locking the window.

"Everybody upstairs quickly!" ordered William. "Richard, gather up all the ammunition and weapons you can find and then join us."

"Yes Sir."

The terror-stricken family ran to relative safety on the second floor. William gathered up every living soul in the house. Cooks and butlers alike were all taken upstairs to Arthur's room. The small children were put under the large bed and Anne followed them. With the thick quilt that covered the ornate bed they were now invisible.

Richard gave over the family's weapons, four rifles, three revolvers, and enough ammunition to hold off a small army. Alfred, the elderly cook, looked dumbstruck at the weapon he had been given.

"I'm only used to the musket. I've never fired shot with a rifle in my life."

"Today is the day then," a nervous William replied. "Richard, show Alfred and John how to use them."

"What do we do next, Sir?" asked Daniel, who had already loaded his revolver. William was about to answer when the room went black. The children could be heard whimpering at the sudden darkness and all of them felt a shiver run down their spines.

"I don't believe it," a voice whispered in the dark.

They heard the monster smash its way into the house. The small group gripped their weapons and courage as the twinkling of broken glass died down. The monster screamed from the floor below them, tearing up furniture as it went.

"Aaaannneee," it cried. Under the bed, Anne shook with fright. The creaking of footsteps now followed.

"It's coming up the stairs!"

"Right then, Alfred, John come with me," ordered William, his voice fragile with nerves. His mind still did not comprehend the horror, did not comprehend that the beast stalking the family was no human being and would require more than an old man and boy to kill it.

They exited the room and went down the corridor, leaving the boys and Edward to guard Anne and the infants. Alfred, at his insistence, led the way. His lamp stripped away the dark from around him. The window at the end of the corridor let no light in; it seemed even the moon and stars had abandoned them tonight.

The footsteps on the staircase grew closer then stopped. Even though they could not see it they were overcome by its stench of decay. Slowly the three reached the top of the staircase.

"What do we do now, Sir?" A frightened John asked.

"Alfred, throw your lamp down the stairs, hopefully it will give us some light. At the same time we'll let it have it."

"Right, Sir."

"Now man, do it."

The three jumped from the corner, arms at the ready. Alfred threw his lamp down the stairs and it ignited upon the carpet revealing the creature in the firelight standing right in front of them. Instead of the flame falling before it, the lamp had overshot. It was too close and it pounced on the old man. There was barely time to get a clear shot and the bullets cemented themselves in the walls. No sound came from Alfred as his body hit the floor with the monster on top of him.

"Kill it!" screamed John, his hands shaking too much to pull the trigger.

William aimed again at the black mass upon the floor and fired. He heard the shot embed itself in the flesh but there was no scream of pain. Instead the monster moved and turned from the dead man and gazed up at the two living bodies.

"Run!" yelled William as he began to retreat back down the corridor, John at his heels.

But the creature got him, knocking John to the floor. He roared in terror as his leg was crushed by the angry beast that would not let go. William fell into the room and all the eyes that were there fixed on him were images of fright.

"Get out, right now!" He grabbed a nearby lamp and found to his surprise he still held his rifle. John's cries drifted into the panic-stricken room. He made up his mind to go back. There was no way out of the room, only a balcony with no stairs to the garden below. He would make a stand, there was no other choice. He peered from the doorway into the dark corridor, dark except the glowing of the fire on the staircase.

Alfred's body lay motionless with flames licking at his feet. There were black shapes in the corridor that he couldn't make out. He stepped out and moved forward slowly. The light from the lamp forced his eyes to squint and he fought to take in and respond to whatever fright lay up ahead in the gloom. He heard a noise and it grew stronger as he came closer to the shadows coiled on the floor. Slowly the lamp swayed away the blackness. He stopped.

There were bodies and blank empty faces. His heart jumped at the sight. The vampire lifted his head from John's throat as the light exposed it. Blood drops fell from its mouth as it grinned. The eyes glowed red in the lamplight and stared deeply at William, who stood frozen to the floor. The vampire leapt up to grab him and William stepped backwards letting off a final shot that didn't even slow its pace.

Richard and Daniel began escorting their sisters and brother into an adjoining bathroom. All of them were in tears and shock. They had heard the deaths of the others and now awaited their own. Edward had moved a desk across the door and stood back. All was quiet but for the crackling of the fire. Then a single voice began to call out and was mingled with the singing of the flames.

"Anne," it said. There was a scratching at the door. It repeated her name over and over as it hurled itself at the door. The lock gave way after two attempts. It jarred open a fraction and fingers could be seen pushing to widen it more.

Richard, Daniel, and Edward stood poised, arms at the ready and waiting for the vampire to reveal more of itself.

Slowly it did. The door creaked as it was forced to give way. The face, bloody and damaged peered through.

"Anne," it hissed again, the words lingering on its tongue.

Richard fired first, ploughing the shell into its forehead. It stood stunned. Daniel fired and there was disintegrating wood as it took one of its fingers away.

The vampire had finished destroying the door even with its injuries and stood there in all its menace and as the bringer of death. Its eyes and teeth glittered, the blood joining saliva as it ran down its chin. It stepped closer and all three fired again. The lead shot held him in check. Its blood now covered its ragged clothes and splattered over the furniture, walls, carpet, and men. Edward seized a lamp in his sweating hand. With all his strength he aimed it fair at the beast and hurled it.

It struck the vampire on the upper leg and the whale oil ignited on impact. Groaning in pain and fear for its end, the vampire ran defeated out of the room. Its arms flailed around in panic as it failed to extinguish its burning clothes. It ran and the boys followed.

They followed it down the corridor, passing their dead companions in the process.

"Mr Hereford!" cried Daniel on finding the man's white body, drained of all its blood.

The vampire kept on running and the fire became fiercer as if it had resolved to consume him. He had now mingled with the fire on the stairs, which had now began to fully take hold of Alfred's corpse and was licking at the corridor wall opposite.

It ran on to the window at the end of the corridor, smashing it as it dove right through it without hesitation. It was desperate for the cold rain falling in the night. The monster fell hard to the ground, and the shards of glass fell with the rain and landed all around it. The water was doing its work and the flames were begin to die already as the vampire lay exhausted and moaning on the wet grass.

Richard and Daniel made it to the broken window and looked out. On seeing them the vampire stood up and continued its flight, the bullets flying past him only driving him even faster.

"Damn!" yelled Richard.

"Watch where he goes, I'll check on the others," said Daniel.

He turned away and went back to the fire. The flames were spreading and the body of the old man sickened him, its stench unbearable. Edward appeared on the other side and threw him a box of ammunition and another lamp.

"Daniel, you must follow it. For that is surely a vampire and it must be destroyed. Follow it to its lair, find its sleeping place and set it ablaze. Burn it to ashes."

"Vampire?"

"Yes. Do as I say. I will do what I can here. Go now, destroy it or it will come again."

Daniel had no notion of what a vampire really was but he knew from tonight that he wished to know no more as he had seen its capabilities. He decided to do as the butler asked. He nodded and returned to Richard, still looking out of the window, watching the demon flee into the dark.

"We must follow it," he said to his brother, who nodded his agreement.

The boys exited the house by the servant's door and came out into the night. The light rain washed away the sweat from their faces and cooled the fear inside them. They followed the scent of burnt flesh that lay in the air.

Now and again they saw the monster's shadow appear in the distance. They quickened their steps after looking back on the fire that was getting out of hand in their home.

"We must hurry," said Daniel.

Quickly they trod across the flat smooth plains. Further they pushed into areas they had not visited since infancy. A building appeared, collapsed and ruined, overgrown and crumbling. Here the rain no longer fell and eased their vision. A shape appeared among the weeds. Richard aimed his rifle ready to shoot until stopped by Daniel.

"That will have no effect, we must set it alight."

Quietly as they could the two approached an overgrown graveyard. The odd statue and plaque rose above the grass. The boys had trouble finding a path; the grass had so thickly covered the graves it now looked like any wild field. Pressing on they penetrated further into the vampire's lair.

"Where do we begin?" asked Richard.

"Smell it?"

"Yes."

"Then follow your nose, brother."

The scent of burning was easy to pick up and they began to move away to a far corner of the hidden graveyard. A sudden scream of pain echoed out and rumbled off the stone. They crouched, believing they were about to be attacked but there was silence again.

Daniel sniffed the air.

"Over there." He indicated a cluster of graves in the far corner they were already heading toward. They moved closer, trying to make out what exactly was ahead of them with only a single torch and the moonlight as a guide.

Then they saw it. It was standing by a cracked and broken tomb, then to their shock and amazement it began to dissolve into a red mist that disappeared into the tomb.

"Did you see that?" exclaimed Daniel. Richard nodded, his mouth open.

They raced through the grass and graves until they came to the tomb. It was small and inconspicuous and was almost hidden under a tree. A fence of iron entwined with grass protected it and they noticed that the grass did not grow beyond this fence. The soil was dead and poisoned; nothing grew in it, only the hide of the thing that lay within its crumbling stone bed. They climbed the fence and were finally in the dead man's presence.

Daniel ran his torch over the outer surface, looking for cracks.

"Joseph Stadmann, 1581 to 1614. Died of the devil's curse."

"Let's get this over with."

With great effort they slowly slid the lid away and for the first time in over 250 years the inner hole of the tomb was open and its coffin with it. The lid landed heavily on the ground and cracked into pieces.

"Damn," Richard hissed.

"It doesn't matter. We will have to open it, to burn it better."

"Must we?"

Daniel just stared at his older brother before handing over the torch then reaching in to prise open the rotting lid of the coffin.

"Get ready to pour the oil in and light it."

Richard poured oil onto a rag, wound it around a branch, and lit it. The rest of the oil would go into the coffin. Daniel heaved on the old wood and the coffin gradually creaked open before suddenly cracking. The vampire was exposed, still blood splattered and damaged.

They watched it heal before their eyes.

"Now, Richard, pour it in."

Richard emptied the lamp oil all over the undead body.

Just as he finished, the vampire opened its eyes and hissed. It showed its fangs in an act of hatred and began to rise from its bed.

"Quickly, the flame!" shouted Daniel.

Richard hit the beast over the head with his flaming stick and it immediately exploded into flames. It screamed, clawed, and grabbed at empty air, desperate for survival. But its strength had already been weakened and the flames gradually began to consume it.

Daniel emptied his rifle into the creature's body with no effect. They stood back from the heat of the flames and watched the fire gnaw away the flesh. The vampire collapsed back into its grave, its undead life extinguished and the man dead for a second time.

Then it was quiet, quiet enough to hear a soul sigh as it was released from pain. They poked at the hot ash and smashed any large pieces they saw. Daniel reached in with his hand and scooped up the ashes. He spread them around the dead soil. The boys watched in awe as the first green sprouts immediately on contact with the ash sprang into life.

BEYOND THE FOREST

Rain and thunder rumbled through the blackened sky and lightning played in the distant sky. It danced, jumped and split the night with electric light. The massive huddle of tall trees of the forest rose high and it seemed their tips touched the clouds and attracted the lightning that banged and exploded in the distance.

Karlon sat uneasily in his seat, as he watched the rain clouds drain the remaining light from around them. The forest unnerved him and the lightshow in the sky added to his unease. He was a long way from the bright lights of Vienna.

The coach thundered its way along the peasant road. At each violent jolt, as the wheels sunk into the holes in the road, he was struck out of his seat and thrown in a collapsed heap into the lap of Lady Vannia.

"This is too much," he gasped.

Lady Vannia Carletta, a cousin of the King of Austria, blushed and smiled as he removed himself from her lap.

She nestled back into her trance of absorbing the countryside. The carriage was traveling too fast for her to take in close objects, so she decided to take in the horizon. There wasn't much to see. In between breaks in the wall of trees, she could make out dark snow-capped peaks and smooth grassy slopes that seemed to rise up into heaven itself. These dark woods seemed to stretch on forever and the trees came right to the road and wedged them in by their girth and number. They fascinated her.

Her party had been warned not to stop in these entombing walls of timber, especially at night. She noticed the people crossed themselves after any mention of the woods and ungodly souls. She remembered that they all wore crucifixes and hung garlic around their necks and even decorated their doors with it like pieces of jewelry.

"The night is for the dead," they'd say and cross themselves again.

To her, it was peculiar behavior. No such customs existed in her native Vienna, her home of cobbled stone roads, stone buildings and nights of brightness. Why had she ventured so far from home? She had just begun searching for that answer when something caught her eye.

A flickering light peeked out of the gloomy darkness. She turned her head quickly and very unladylike to spy, it but could see nothing.

"What is it my dear?" asked Dr Kinstein, her personal physician who had volunteered to escort her to her new appointment in Transylvania. His face conveyed the dearest and most truthful concern, but it also was like he needed proof that someone else had seen it too.

"I don't know. It was a light of some sort."

"Perhaps it was the flame from our carriage reflecting off some metal a peasant has left by the road?" offered Athol Galigata, in a matter of fact statement.

Lady Vannia didn't really like him--he was not upper class, but he was under the impression he was very much accepted. He thought his vanity could get him anywhere and the annoying thing was that it did; maybe it was little moustache of his.

Lady Vannia didn't know why he wanted to accompany her here, but her suspicion told her it was all a ploy for him to propose. She would just have to always be busy and not give him the chance.

Karlon nodded eventually. Obviously, the theory had some merit to the Diplomat and she greatly respected the man. He had always looked after her during state dinners with foreign dignitaries, as she could be very shy. In turn, she would help him in the finer details of etiquette, as he was a self made man without the upbringing of a Royal Court.

Athol, his ego undamaged and grateful for giving him an opportunity to show his brilliance, now stared out the window.

Dr Kinstein moved back into his seated corner with a face full of concern and confusion. Something was concerning him, she could tell, as his face did not lie. He ran a finger horizontally over his lips, deep in thought. He was far from home too; he had been educated in Budapest and knew this land better than any of them.

A crash--and for an instant the carriage was in slow motion, as the team of horses found the hole only a brief delay and hurtled the coach forward, knocking the occupants from their silence.

"This is damnable!" shrieked Karlon. He was half out of his mind with embarrassment. Another crash and the coach lurched to the left violently, tilting Vannia onto Karlon. A short cry escaped her mouth before she was muffled by a mouthful of fine velvet.

As quickly as it had begun, the coach righted itself and again they tumbled. Kinstein's head hit hard against the window and his body went limp, interfering with Athol's attempts to steady Vannia. He quickly turned his attention to the Doctor, holding him steady before he made contact with the floor.

Vannia stroked the hair from his face. There was no wound, no bruise. Karlon had ready a wet cloth and a cup of brandy. Vannia took the cloth and put it over his forehead.

"Will he be alright?" asked Athol.

"He'll be fine, just a bump. Look, he's coming to now."

Kinstein's eyes opened as slowly as the sun rises. "Oh my dear," he groaned.

"Can you get up?"

"Yes, yes," Kinstein answered.

Karlon gave him the brandy, which Kinstein drank quickly, then helped him to his feet. The Doctor was bashful with embarrassment and his cheeks glowed red.

Vannia smiled and took her seat. "Why don't you try to sleep?" she said.

"Not in this contraption and on this road, my dear!"

They all chuckled and went silent; their gazes returned to their own private thoughts. Vannia stared out the window; it was now too dark to see anything but the black trees that lined the road.

The carriage became silent and time seemed to move slowly on, despite its speed. Vannia tried to drift off to sleep, but it was impossible for her. Then came mumbles and words that started to seep into her mind. Finally, she took notice and began to listen. A soft mumbled voice seemed to come from nowhere. She listened more closely and it seemed to be rising in intensity, and then quietening, almost like a ship rolling on rough seas. She caught clearly only a few words. "Oh Father in heaven" and "Thy God protect me from thy devil."

"Do you hear that voice?" she asked of anyone.

They all strained to hear the voice.

"Yes, it's a prayer," confirmed Karlon.

Vannia was in the throes of asking a question when the Doctor answered it.

"It's the driver."

"Why?"

"Perhaps he is praying for us not to inform him of his dreadful driving?" Was that another biting piece of sarcasm from Athol Galigata of Linz?

"The Transylvanians are a very superstitious people, Mr Galigata," said Kinstein. "They believe they are permanently surrounded by evil and the root of all evil is in their tale of the fall from Grace. Do you know this story Mr Galigata?"

Before Athol could answer, the prayer grew suddenly in intensity and passion.

"Like the stream of clear purity, let me wash past the evil. God strike him down, God strike him down!"

They were all boiling with anxiety and fear, eyes glued to the windows.

"Perhaps we should say something?" suggested Karlon.

"No. He will not listen," answered the Doctor.

The prayers came on, rising and rising, and delivered in an ever-fearful tone. It was then that they saw the light emerging from the woods and coming towards them in great haste.

"It's another light!" cried Karlon. As the light came closer, the prayer from the driver grew louder, reaching its peak as they passed the glow at the side of the road.

"What was it?" asked Vannia.

"It's a grave cross," answered the Doctor.

"A grave cross!" Athol mocked Kinstein's theory.

"Yes!" The Doctor stung back at him with his word and stare. "Legends, as I was telling you before."

"Tell us, Doctor," Vannia requested.

"Vampires." Kinstein looked at them all. "The fall from Grace, the devil falling to Earth from Heaven. The people of Transylvania believe the devil fell here in these woods after his expulsion from Heaven. Here he became the Prince of Darkness."

Vannia stared at him then turned to look out at the night.

"I can understand why, but tell me, what was the light?"

"Because of the vampires, the blood suckers. It is believed that if a person commits suicide they, in turn, become a vampire, but it can be prevented by burying the corpse at the crossroads and lit with a light to show God where it rests and where to retrieve the soul."

"Vampires?" whispered Vannia. The Doctor nodded.

"That cross you possess will protect you, if you believe it will. Crosses, garlic, sunlight, holy water, waif and pure prayer can damage or even kill, but the only sure way is to drive a stake through its heart. That releases the soul.

Finally, cut off its head. Sometimes the body is burned and the ashes scattered."

She took out from her pocket a cross, given to her by the King himself. It lay in her hand and she looked deep into the sleeping Jesus' face and whispered out the words.

"The night is for the dead."

The coach still hurried on, the bad road still bruising its occupants. Karlon checked his map that he had picked up from the Romanian Consulate in Budapest.

"There should be a bridge soon, then it looks like smooth sailing as they say after that."

"Here it is," said the Doctor. Vannia looked out the window to see a tired, fragile looking bridge lying across the divide.

The driver cautiously drew the carriage up to the bridge. He eased it onto the weak boards and they creaked and groaned as the heavy weight rolled across them. A light lit each end, blazing away and revealing the length of the bridge. It flickered and blinded them temporarily as they looked into it. The group's attention then turned from the light to the depth of the ravine below the bridge. It was black and without any clue to how far it went down. It was up to their already overloaded imaginations to dream up what horrors lurked in the abyss.

Karlon pulled his head back into the carriage.

"I wouldn't want to drop anything down there ..." He broke off. Something had caught his eye. He looked at the road they had just passed. "Look, a dog."

They all strained to look back and to see Karlon's dog at the edge of the bridge.

"That's no dog. That is a wolf," corrected Kinstein.

"A wolf?" chuckled Athol.

"Yes a wolf, another creature of the night to fear. A vampire's companion, you see. They too can only be killed by chopping off their heads or with a silver weapon."

"What are you talking about old man?" Athol went on.

Kinstein ignored him, "Hopefully we will leave it behind but I doubt it very much. God only knows how long it has been trailing the scent of the horses."

Suddenly the wolf began howling and made everyone jump in fright. It howled loud and constantly, long and spine chillingly.

"It will scare the horses!" Karlon predicted.

The driver was unable to control them as they reared up and started to accelerate. The speed was too much for the old battered bridge, as it creaked and groaned under the weight. Eventually, the coach and occupants made it to the other side and rumbled on down the roughly hewn road.

The horses, still frightened and uncontrollable, finally slowed and stopped. They would not gallop any further to their destination. They seemed calm, but then suddenly reared up as their sensitive hearing and smell caught a presence ahead of them.

The driver began again his spells and prayers but this time mixed them with curses and foul words. He could not get the horses to move or calm down. So the carriage sat there immobilized.

"What is wrong with the horses?" an impatient and increasingly frightened Athol asked.

"They are obviously frightened by the wolves!" Karlon answered.

The howling of wolves started up again, this time closer and by their chorus there were many of them. Through the chaos of the wolves' howling and the horses' screams, a shot was heard, a yelp, and more growls. Karlon leaned out the window foolishly and saw a dead wolf lying by the side of the road.

"Put your head back inside man, or you'll get it ripped off!" the Doctor implored.

After having a look around, Karlon put his head back in. "One of them is dead, the other is coming across the bridge. They usually hunt in threes don't they Doctor?"

Kinstein was about to answer when the carriage suddenly began thundering off. "Yes, in threes. The driver must have calmed the horses down. Do you have any of that brandy left, Karlon?"

"I hope so." Karlon began rummaging through his carry case looking for the bottle he had earlier. When he found it he poured each of them enough to settle the nerves.

The carriage moved quickly, the horses eager to get to safety as much as the occupants. The forest grew darker as the carriage shot through the tall imposing ancient woods.

Unbeknown to these travelers, the coach was being watched. A figure waited, cloaked in the night, hidden in a tree. As the carriage got near, the figure jumped upon the driver's seat. With a swift kick, the driver almost had it tumbling over the side but its human hands held onto the seat while its body hung down the sides.

"What is that?!" screamed Athol.

None of them answered, all frozen in shock at the events unfolding in front of their eyes. The driver was fast in his actions. He leveled a pistol at the vampire's head and fired. Parts flew off and blood splattered across the window glass. Vannia shrieked in terror at the sight of it. The vampire still clung on and had managed to get a better grip. Even with half a face, it clawed its way up to the frantic driver.

His last chance was his only lamp by his side. He smashed it against its face and flames ignited the spilt blood, but still the vampire hung on. With one last reach, it grabbed the driver and dragged him from the seat. They both fell to the ground and were left behind.

"The driver!" cried Kinstein, as he watched the two bodies fall from the carriage. He opened the door on the still-moving coach, as it slowly came to a halt.

It was too late, the dying screams of the man faded out, as both bodies were consumed by fire.

"Now what do we do?" asked Vannia, from the blood smeared window. Kinstein said nothing as his mind searched for a solution.

"Karlon, you're the horse man. Can you drive this coach?"

"Yes I can." Determined, Karlon climbed out and took his position in the driver's seat. Kinstein climbed back in and they moved off again at a steady pace.

Karlon pushed the horses on, they ran fast, running to beat the devil. Karlon sat uneasy, the breeze watered his eyes and reduced his vision. He felt naked and exposed out in the open and moved his sight from side to side in nervous anticipation of being attacked.

In the carriage, things were quiet. The first death of a person Vannia and Athol had seen with their own eyes had shaken them. For the Doctor, it was nothing; he had seen countless deaths. He was more interested in what he believed was a vampire. Even in these dire straits, his curiosity begged him to return and recover the body for study. The old hunter in him knew that there were probably more lurking in the woods, eyeing the carriage as it carved through the darkness.

Athol held an empty stare on the rushing trees, oblivious to the other occupants. Vannia watched the troubled face of Kinstein.

"Was that a vampire, Doctor?" she finally asked.

Kinstein nodded. "Yes. There will be more of them and we still have an hour of travel ahead of us and four hours of darkness in which they prowl."

"What can we do?"

He leaned forward. "Drive."

"Doctor," Athol interrupted, "the wolves are running alongside us."

Vannia looked out her window. "This side too."

The horses too had felt the wolves and began to bolt even faster. Kinstein had decided he would warn Karlon, even though he was sure he knew. He leaned out of the window and shouted, "Karlon! Karlon!"

There was no response. It was dark and the shaking of the carriage side to side made hanging out of the window uncomfortable. Still, he could see an arm lying limp over the side of the driver's seat.

"Karlon!" he cried again. The only answer was a growl, its origin he could not make out, but it was close. Then the wolves all howled again and it seemed there were hundreds of them everywhere--rising in echo and song through the forest. He watched the wolves keeping pace with the bolting carriage, their mouths full of saliva and teeth, with eyes red burning coals. They watched him too. A wolf sang out again, loud and long. It was close and he guessed that it was on the driver's seat.

He saw Karlon's arm disappear and decided that retreat was safer than having his head hanging out of the window. He stared at the faces; they knew the answer but he confirmed it anyway.

"Karlon is dead."

Vannia burst into tears. She had remained strong but this was too much.

"What do we do now!?" a hysterical Athol shrieked.

The doctor said nothing, but thought about the situation. No driver, the carriage racing along uncontrollably and packs of hungry wolves waiting.

"We must remain in here; a driver is too vulnerable."

"Then what?"

"We remain in here until dawn, even if the horses stop. You understand we'll get no sleep tonight."

"God why did I come to this curses land!?" Athol's already low level of courage and spirit were dead and he huddled in his corner as the carriage thundered and jumped along the bad road.

It had been ten minutes of safety as the coach raced on. It was then that the bad signs reappeared. The horses had only slowed their pace slightly, but the constant battering that the carriage had taken was beginning to jolt the thing to pieces. Every pothole the axles and wheels hit strained the nuts and bolts that kept them together. Finally, they could take no more. A large hole took care of that and the forward axle and wheel snapped. The carriage smashed into the ground, grinding the horses to halt.

The occupants tumbled and collapsed in a heap. Athol bore the brunt of Kinstein's fall, but Vannia didn't fare well, smashing hard into the wooden door.

There was only the groaning of Athol. Kinstein moved about in the dark. It was silent, except for the frantic attempts by the horses to break away. They pulled hard on the leather straps and wooden poles that held them. Their strength still managed to drag the carriage slightly, until the straps broke and the horses ran, leaving the carriage a ruin and the whiff of wolves descending upon it.

"Is everyone alright?" Kinstein asked. "Lady Vannia? Speak, child." He patted her cheeks lightly until she came around.

"Athol, are you injured?"

"No."

The hungry wolves had resumed their howling, a signal to other wolves that the prey was down and ready for the kill. All around the carriage they moved into position.

"We're doomed," surrendered Athol.

"No, we can beat them off, or we die trying ... for other travelers' sakes."

"What!? You must be mad! How? With what!?"

"The driver kept muskets in his seat. Kept there for this very purpose. Now let's get out and put up a fight."

Athol didn't move and was either frozen in panic or stubborn as an old goat. He watched the old doctor climb out and begin his stand.

"Where is the Doctor?" asked Vannia, awakening fully from her sleep.

"Gone to kill us all."

"Pardon?"

"He is going to put up a fight. He means to kill as many wolves before they get us."

"And why aren't you out there?"

He merely looked away in shame. She left him and climbed out of the carriage and was met by Kinstein, who was loading two muskets. His eyes watched the blackness of the forest, looking for the unmistakable glow of red from the eyes of wolves.

"So, my Lady, ready to join the fight?"

"Yes, Doctor."

"I'm not sure if I can allow this--a lady of the court of King Matthias bearing arms."

"There is really no way out?" She voiced the question.

He looked down at his now loaded musket. "We could fight our way to the castle, if it isn't far, and I mean fight. These wolves will ..." He didn't finish but instead raised his musket and fired at the first wolf that showed its vicious blood thirsty face. "We must go now!" he cried.

Athol had, by this time, exited the broken carriage and began running down the road in a great show of cowardice.

"We must hurry and keep to the road, my Lady," the Doctor said. Vannia had rarely run in her life and now she found herself running for it. She saw Athol's white coat move in the distance and tried to keep up with it.

"Athol, wait!" Kinstein called out.

Up ahead, Athol stopped, but not because he had been ordered to. He stood there, his heart beating fast while the Doctor and the Lady caught up with him. All three now saw the sight that greeted them. Two wolves stood in their path, watching and waiting for the other wolves to move in on the flanks.

Kinstein wasted no time. He aimed his second musket and fired, killing one of them instantly. The other wolf rushed straight at Athol and threw him to the ground. Again, the Doctor was quick and produced a bayonet from his coat and plunged it deep into the animal's ribs. Again, it died instantly.

"Get up Athol. We have no time to waste."

Athol, already feeble, clutched his throat. Vannia saw the blood trickle from the wound and seep between his fingers.

"Strength, Athol. Find your courage and will," assured Kinstein.

They all began to run again.

"Why haven't they attacked us?" asked Vannia, between panting breaths.

"I do not know my dear but at least it buys us time."

They sprinted through the dark woods, the ancient tall and dense trees all around them. As they ran, they came to a clearing in the trees and were, for the first time, able to see out onto the world. There were lights in the distance.

"The castle!" cried Vannia.

Far from the dark woods, there was a black mass dotted with light. It lay atop a hill and only one tree stood at its walls. Reassured, the three pressed on; the wolves on their minds and on their trail.

Without warning, a grey wolf broke from the woods beside them and flattened Athol. No sound escaped from him and it seemed he died as soon as he hit the earth.

Another broke from the dark and aimed its attack at the Doctor. Kinstein dodged its attack and hit it fair over the head with the butt of a musket, knocking it out cold. He then turned his attention to the grey mass lying upon Athol. He leveled the butt of the musket and drove it into the wolf's head, smashing it and killing it.

Kinstein then checked Athol. His throat was ripped out and he didn't bother checking any further. The two human survivors breathed heavily, the first strains of shock beginning to seep into their bodies.

A sudden noise drew their attention; the sound of horses and wheels along the road. From around a corner there came a black mass with a swinging light. A carriage sped quickly towards them. Vannia began crying at the sight and Kinstein threw away his muskets. He put his arms around the girl, as the coach drew closer. He took one look around and was shocked to see a naked man sprawled over the body of Athol, where once moments before was a wolf.

"Werewolf," he whispered. How he would love to examine the body, but this wasn't the best time as his main concern was his distressed Lady.

Slowly, the carriage pulled up beside them. The driver, invisible in his black coat, called out to them.

"Lady Vannia of Austria?"

"Yes, she is here and I am Dr Wilhelm Kinstein of Budapest."

"Come aboard, quickly."

They needed no further encouragement and Kinstein opened the door for her to climb in. He looked up and as he did, he now could see the features of the driver. Young, clean almost feminine. The boy was staring at the corpses lying nearby. He turned back to look at his passengers and caught the Doctor's eye for a moment. There was no emotion in the boy's eyes before he turned away.

Settled in the cozy carriage, Kinstein and Vannia said nothing. Kinstein's mind was full of new discoveries and was beginning a plan to return and retrieve the bodies, all without the knowledge of Vannia, who should not be burdened with such revelations.

The castle loomed closer; only a few torches lit its outside walls. No doubt, most servants would have retired long ago. The castle gate was opened, the metal in desperate need of oiling, and the inner castle was revealed. It was dark and the only light came from a torch bearer, who stood near a number of people near the main door.

The carriage halted near this group. Kinstein and Vannia stepped unsteadily from the coach. They bowed and curtsied and were introduced to their host, Countess Bathory.

THE CHRISTABEL

The moon was high and its light lay upon the still lake. A stiff cold breeze stirred the sleeping trees and dispersed the smoke rising from the chimney of the house.

A man moved through the corridors, his candle the only light. It would be easier to turn on the light but he found the natural warmth of candlelight to be far more comforting. He climbed into bed and lay there looking up at the ceiling. The depression went deep, it hung heavy in his heart, an anvil around his life source that squeezed out any will to live. Once a week it hit him. He would be fine but with agitation just below the surface. Then he would fall into that black pit. And it was getting harder and harder to climb back into the light. Soon he would drift to sleep and in the morning he would be rejuvenated and ready to tackle the new day.

As he tossed and turned his mind wandered over dreams, wishes, and hopes. Would the future bring relief? Time after time he had failed as his ideas came and went. Names and people came and went. Faces of past loves and lost friends and he now hated for setting him adrift; left behind was more like it.

The man was a loner but not by choice. That's just how things worked out. The heart that beat in his chest was sore from too much solitude and his head hurt from frustration and stress over those failed dreams and hopes. No friends came to visit and he did not go to their houses. Some days he just sat looking out at the lake from his chair, the depression gnawing away at his motivation. It was becoming more and more difficult to return to the drawing board. Tired of picking himself up, he was being beaten by the anger of madness.

There was no wife, nor did he ever have any female company, though he yearned for it so. Desperately he wanted something to happen; stagnation was driving him crazy. Still he planned, worked, and waited.

The clock was ticking in the house as he lay in bed. This loneliness was quiet. Sometimes to his shame he would cry himself to sleep. His tears to God fell into the silence that swirled around his life.

But someone was listening and she hoped to bring happiness to his soul and youth to her old features. She came out of nowhere, it seemed. From the forest's dreams she materialised. Her old limbs were stiff but she didn't need them for walking, her mind moved the body. This body passed through the wooden wall, straight into the man's bedroom. She stood there watching him sleep uncomfortably. His tormented visions were music to her ancient soul.

For weeks she had been looking for such a man in so much misery. And misery loves company.

The ritual was second nature to her. For thousands of years she had come to the lonely, the boastful, and sick. The boastful she broke into submission, there was no love for them. An ego was an egg to be crushed. The sick she gave relief, comfort, and pleasure. Though none ever survived an encounter with her. Then there were the lonely. They were her favourites, giving out much more energy than any other. Every inch of them ached with the pain and for her services that energy was transferred to her own body where it filled every cell with new life and vigour.

The lonesome were in every city, town, and land. They were old and young. The best ones to harvest were the young who have been living a long lonely life. These were the diamonds in the sand and much sought after. She would play with them, lead them closer to the edge of the cliff. Let that frustration weave into energy. Let it build and build before the body collapsed into death.

Sometimes she left it too late and before she had consumed what she needed the soul had finished itself, usually in violence. This was true long ago but not now, she could judge the moment with precision. This one, this Adrian was such a diamond. He was near the cliff. She had heard his prayers from miles away, watched his dreams and felt his anger. She was lucky to have found him first.

With her crinkled hands she slowly removed her clothes while with her mind she penetrated deeper into his sleep and his dream. A dream she entered and manipulated. No longer was the vision of success but of women. It was now an orgy of exposed female flesh.

Gently she climbed into his bed and lay on top of him. Her game was not a quick one, not with this delicate flower. Tonight was just a taster, a teaser. She let him wake up and see her wrinkled face on top of him, moving slowly on his manhood. When his conscious mind told him he was awake she disappeared, leaving him in a warm sweat, which quickly cooled and left him unsure of what had just happened.

Her body was still there, invisible with the dust floating about the room. After a few moments she left, but he would be awake for some time thinking it over, leaving him in a confusion that she could enjoy somewhere else.

Adrian woke slowly. The morning was still chilly but would warm up in an hour or so as it always did. Last night suddenly became fresh. He sat upright while his memory delivered the events. There was no explanation, he could only put it down to one of those strange dreams that people sometimes have.

It was a new day with new plans. Yesterday he had decided to resume the painting of the lake that he had started months ago but had abandoned during one of his numerous bouts of self-pity. His attic was filling up with discarded or half-finished works. The whole room was an untidy mess. If he could only sell one he would be happy, and there would be a reason to continue.

He stepped out of bed and the chill of the morning hit him immediately. After dressing quickly he walked past the edge of the bed and noticed a lump of clothing on the floor. It didn't look like his. He picked it up and found to his surprise it was a dress.

The day was long and wasted. His brushes and palette were left packed and undisturbed and the picture he viewed and planned to bring to canvas remained in his mind.

A boat moved softly across the water, its size only slightly breaking the water. His seat creaked and groaned as he changed position. Today he didn't feel like doing anything. They were wasted days and he hated himself for letting them slip by without trying to seize them.

Today he had an excuse. Over and over he questioned his memory. How did this dress end up on his floor? Was the dream just that or the memory so blurry and his mind so tired that he took it to be imagination. All day he had moped about the house, the dress left on his bed. It was afternoon now when he regained some of his creativity. Always in the afternoon he had a last urge.

Out came his paints and he began to use their colours to create an image of his view. Boredom soon came so he replaced the canvas with a new one. Faces were not his speciality but now he would try again. The face of last night he could remember clearly and he began to bring it to life with paint.

The sun sank and the moon rose for another night. Beyond the lake, hidden in the dark, the frogs and crickets sang their tunes. Instantly they stopped en masse and the shoreline was quiet.

She moved across the still lake, riding the moonbeam that fell into the man's bedroom. The moon's light, magnified by her cells, burnt her shadow into the wall. It was another greeting card of hers to create the ultimate confusion and fear of the unknown in her subject.

She disrobed as last night. Then she climbed in with him, her mind connected as before. Her new brunette hair, the grey loved out, fell across his face. His arms wrapped around her, exploring her every curve of her body. Delicately she intertwined her own arms and legs around his sleeping form. Moving in time with his own desires.

Then she vanished, leaving only a snarling face in his mind.

He woke quickly in fright. Confusion and pleasure crashed and collided in his system. Another dream? That horrible twisted face in his mind wouldn't leave. He was sweating and his heart felt as if it would explode in panic. Then he saw the shadow burnt on his wall, illuminated by the moon's light. His stretched heart was forced to a stop. He looked out to the window and for a spilt second a faded face was visible before it disappeared.

For a few moments he remained upright in the bed. Every possible explanation ran through his mind from the reasonable to the strange. Was he dreaming? What on Earth had heard me?

Whenever he was out of the house it seemed like a huge weight had been lifted from somewhere inside him. Now as he walked the small distance into town, he felt uplifted, free from the house and whatever lurked about and within it.

The streets were busy with people out and about. It was rare for him to get out; his inner well being told him he should but he usually ignored it. He pondered over clothes and food in the stalls for some time. There wasn't much money to spend but he enjoyed being out and didn't want to go back home.

In one store he recognised Jane Astel. He went to school with her and had had a crush on her ever since. She was the usual popular girl and there would be no way she would recognise something special in him.

As she moved along the stalls he couldn't help but watch her. She had become even more beautiful as she had grown older. Her shoulder length brown hair kept getting in her eyes with every blow of the wind. He should say something to her. Would she even remember him? Suddenly she moved away. Go after her! He stood still as she disappeared in the throng. In his imagination he saw a great boot kick him square in the bum over and over. Gutless, there was no other explanation. There was the thin hope she was still somewhere in the crowd. He wasted more time weaving around the stalls on the lookout for Jane. Occasionally he would spot someone who looked like her and his inside would be awash with nervous venom, which made him freeze up.

Some products caught his eye, like golden statues and works of art. God he wished he were rich, he'd buy a castle and live in it like a King, churning out paintings while living in solitude with his only girl. He was dreaming away when Jane walked right in front of him. Her wonderful scent overcame him with gorgeous delight. She smiled.

"Adrian?"

"Jane."

"Wow. I can't believe we both still live here?"

He couldn't concentrate clearly. This was usually the moment when he would say something stupid or worse, nothing at all.

"I've never seen you around?" he finally managed.

"Well, I moved away but just came back. Mum's sick and ... you know."

He nodded not sure what to do next. Luckily she was a little more vocal than he.

"Maybe we should do something?"

"Sure."

And that was that. A time was set for a date and he felt the happiest he had been in a long time.

Twilight, the dying light, what dangers lurk beneath the stars so bright? Would she come again? Whatever she was. He was on a high all afternoon until the sunset. That dark well would not hold him tonight. He fought it by blocking out everything but Jane. He thought of how happy he was at that moment, the bliss and the teenage excitement. There was no sorrow, no depression. It had been left in the dust.

So the sun died as he sat on the bed. Sleep? He didn't want to but eventually the most human of comforts overtook him and he was in the most comforting sleep he had ever had when she came.

"Between the stars, it is I my dear who knows who you are. Your dreams aren't of me and my touch is not your source of happiness." Her anger seethed and its power was mighty. The scar on the wall was but a taste of what could be inflicted on every wall.

He met up with Jane again. They wandered the empty shores of his lake all day. The time spent shrank his nerves away though he was careful not to mention his visions of the woman that was stalking him.

"You seem preoccupied," she said.

"It's nothing. It seems strange but I was going to ask you the same thing."

She smiled and turned to watch the water stretch out to reach her feet with every gentle wave. Around her neck he noticed a red rash about the size of a hand on her delicate skin. He said nothing; if she wanted to talk about it she would.

Night again. The shadows formed. Tossing and turning, Jane tried to sleep comfortably. The tapping at the window broke the attempt.

"Adrian?"

"Come on out."

She climbed out of bed and began to get dressed hurriedly.

"Don't worry about that," he teased from the window. She now saw that he was completely naked. Playing along, she also stripped off her gown and followed him to the lake shore.

Here they hugged and kept each other close. Adrian took her hand and led her into the water.

The water wasn't too cold, anyway she had his body to keep her warm. When the cool water reached their shoulders they stopped and began kissing. His hands ran all over her body as he rocked her in the open space.

At the height of passion she felt something strange. His body quivered and shrank in the wrong places and expanded in the wrong. No longer did she feel him deep inside her but rubbing against her. His chest ballooned until they matched her own size. And his face changed from a man to woman. The very same woman who had tried to strangle her the night before.

"He's mine and you'll never have him. I won't let you bring him joy." Gathering her strength Jane hit this woman that held her tight but was still rubbing against her. She hit again and again without affecting her assailant. It only seemed to drain her own strength while letting the woman overpower her.

Slowly and surely Jane began to weaken. Eventually she wouldn't be able to hold out as her strength was drained away and her body lowered further into the water. There was no fight left. The woman grinned as she dragged Jane to the bottom and left her as a corpse.

~~~

He waited by the roadside alone. Where could she be? What could have happened? He waited an hour and a half after the set time they had agreed to meet before shuffling home alone. Every few metres he would turn to see if she was there, running up the road. But there was nothing.

"What have I done wrong?" He asked himself as he got home.

For the rest of the day he sat or moped about waiting for the knock on the door or phone call. Waiting, waiting, waiting. He was always waiting for other people.

He didn't bother eating but went to bed sulking as soon as the sun had set.

For some time he watched the burnt shadow on the wall. Even his dreams weren't sane!

"I'm insane," he told himself. "Everybody moves on but me. I'm stuck with the hard road." How could he sleep with his mind in complete overdrive? Too many questions about Jane and fear of the other one.

When he had finally fallen asleep she came. Came again with such strength. She was whole now and full of energy. He was broken, she could tell as she wiped the still wet tears from his cheek. He dreamt of the other one but she would soon stop that and throw any other desire but that for her out of his mind. As she began her tricks he woke up and saw the one who had been tormenting him.

"I'm the one who loves you, forget about any other. She was married and had no intention of screwing you every night."

Adrian said nothing but watched her with petrified eyes.

"Don't be scared. I want you and you can have me every night, all night."

She already had him in her and laughed as he came. Then laughed even louder when she did.

"Oh the nights are going to be sweet."

He wouldn't go out for days but remained shacked up in his little house, a prisoner of pleasure. To burn his time he painted with renewed vigour. He painted only Jane. Finding them punctured and torn the following morning only kept the fire of her memory and his spite alive.

The days went on and it became almost two weeks. She seemed to be getting stronger and hungrier with every night. He felt ashamed some nights for enjoying it. Other nights in complete exhaustion, he would just lay stupefied while she did her thing.

Then she stopped. No more visits, no more of her tongue and fingers upon him. No more the feeling of her hot and hungry mouths. It was absolute peace. Now he could rest and take in what exactly was happening to him. Did he really want all this sex and attention? Was this woman a nut or something more demonic? And did he want it to stop?

The respite was good and he regained some of his strength. He went out for the first time in so long. He wandered the same stalls he had met Jane in. Back in his mind he hoped history would repeat but he knew fate had a cruel hand. There were days when he mused that humankind had no say in their own lives and were a pawn in some egotistical God's fantasy.

As he simmered with his frustrations a man bumped into him. The jolt brought him back from his hate-filled fantasy realm.

"I'm sorry, I was chasing you to ask you a question," the stranger said.

"Oh?"

"Are you Adrian Donnell, the painter?"

"Yes." The man smiled widely, almost in relief.

"I've been searching for you for days, you're a hard man to catch."

"I've been a little busy lately."

He nodded and reached into his pocket and pulled out a card and handed it to Adrian.

"My name is Dennis Ritchie, I'm in the process of collecting unknown Australian artists' work. Are you interested?"

"Of course." He didn't need to think the answer through.

"Well, you've got my card and I hope to see some of your work soon."

With that Dennis walked away, leaving Adrian in a state of exhilaration. Finally something was happening, there was a light at the end of the tunnel.

As he began to walk home he tapped the card with his fingers. He wasn't going to put it away yet, he was going to enjoy every letter.

When he was on the edge of town it started to rain. Quickly he put the card in his pocket and began to run. But then a piece of paper on a telegraph pole caught his eye. On closer inspection he recognised the face. His heart jumped at the realisation. It was Jane's picture on a missing persons flyer.

The rain was coming down harder but he didn't want to leave. He was gaining with one hand and losing with the other. He ripped the flyer off the pole and stuffed in his jacket with the card and he continued running home, his tears camouflaged by the rain.

Deep down he knew who was responsible and it hardened his resolve not to give in to the demon.

~ ~ ~

"Yes you will," she whispered over his sleeping body. She slipped her hand under the sheets and woke him by grabbing his crotch. As he woke he found himself already in her mouth.

"Leave me alone," he was able to murmur. Ignoring his words she gently bit down harder, pressing her teeth into his hard flesh. He didn't moan but reacted by pushing her off to the floor. Even before he had begun to stand up on the bed she counterattacked, grabbing him by his shorts, and dragging him back down to the sheets. With one quick movement she ripped them in half, leaving him naked.

"I could rip this off if I wanted to."

Pressing her hands on his hips she pinned him down. He wiggled and moved but couldn't get her off him.

Sensing she had won she climbed on him and put his placid member inside her.

"Enjoy your rest my dear?" she gibed between moans.

He turned his face away and concentrated on staying soft. Her hand grasped around his head and turned it back to face her own. He had always been overwhelmed by her immense strength and now it had him again. There was no way to move his head or lower body. Her thrusting was more powerful than it had ever been.

With ease she brought him up to her breast and her arms tightly wound around his shoulders. Like steel they locked him in a cage and the moans in his ears drowned out his own thoughts.

Hours later it seemed, he was finally left alone. He thought of the future and its hazy movement. A decision was made.

All his paintings were placed in a box clearly marked for Mr. Ritchie and sent away.

Now he sat on the porch and waited, a hidden pistol in his lap. He would kill the bitch. There was nowhere to run, he didn't have a car and he knew she would find him anywhere that he tried to hide.

The steel was cold as he ran his fingers along the barrel. How did his life end up in ruins? Could they be rebuilt? His pondering was interrupted by the most ungodly scream, which came closer and closer. His railing smashed and the bits of timber flew about. And she was there. Transparent in the faint light but her killer snarl was still clear on her beautiful face.

"No you don't!" she screamed in a high-pitched voice.

His resolve wavered under the eerie sound but remained intact. He revealed his weapon and fired at her startled expression. The shot went through her and smacked into a post behind her. Panicking he fired again and again the same result. She stepped closer.

"You belong to me, Adrian. Don't you like being screwed every night?"

"Just leave me in peace," he managed to crackle out the words.

There was no way out now. He put the pistol to his head.

"No!" she screamed long and loud. He fired. Her eyes bled fury as his body went limp in the chair. The changes were immediate. Her hands wrinkled and her hair went grey in seconds. With her remaining strength she kicked his dead body hard. The chair was thrown back to the wall and Adrian's body slid to the veranda floor. She kicked it again before shuffling her old body back into the forest's dreams.

NOT ALONE ON THE OCEAN

Willy was the first to see the survivor bobbing helplessly on the wide rolling ocean. At first he thought it was driftwood or garbage dumped illegally from a passing ship. But as the trawler came closer the bright red blaze of a life jacket became ever clearer.

"Roy, Roy!" He called out to his skipper as he jumped up from his seat on the deck where he was enjoying the bright sunlight.

"Port bow! 100 metres!"

On the bridge Roy Miller put down his coffee, picked up his binoculars from a chart table next to him and scanned the green emptiness where Willy was pointing vigorously.

He saw it alright and didn't need to second guess what it was. Immediately he sprang into action by swinging his ship onto a direct course with the body. With one hand he kept the wheel steady while the other held his binoculars tight to his experienced eyes.

"Dull, get out here!" he called out.

The aboriginal boy put his head out of the radio room behind the bridge.

"What is it, Roy?"

"Call rescue services. We've got a body in the water. Then get some blankets and the first aid kit."

"Righto boss." He disappeared back into the radio room and began sending out the distress call.

Out on the deck Willy had tied himself to the side rail with rope. He climbed over the railing and waited, his hand raised in indication of speed and direction for Roy on the bridge.

Gently the trawler slid up to the body. Willy and Dull heaved the man from the water and onto the deck.

"Is he alive?" Dull asked as Willy checked the man's pulse.

"Yeah, barely. He's swallowed heaps of water."

After 20 minutes of warmth and strong brandy the man was conscious and talking. Roy watched him. There was something not quite right about this bloke in his late twenties with a scruffy seaman's beard. The way he twitched on nervous edge and how any subtle movement would make him recoil in fright.

"You must have some story to tell?" mused Willy as he poured the man another brandy.

"You bet," he said, his voice and hands still shaky. "Do you want to hear it?" he continued.

Dull smiled.

"Sure, we're all ..."

"Which way are we headed?!" the man pleaded, his grip on Dull's shirt, his voice quivering in fear.

"Back to Hawkesbury," Roy said bluntly, in revulsion at the man's antics. Roy had been at sea too long to put up with poofs and weaklings. There was no way this bloke would have stepped on the deck of Roy's boat if he had met him at another time or place.

Reassured, the man calmed down and gulped his liquor. He lay back on Willy's cot and closed his eyes.

"You don't want to go back out there. I'll never go to sea again, never."

"Are you going to tell us or what?" Dull pushed the subject.

"Alright but you won't believe me. We were about five hours out of Gosford heading back in from the fishing grounds when the motor cut out. Bloody thing just died on the spot. I was in the radio room when the boat stopped. Kenny, our skipper, was furious. He had a hot date that night and for the past week that's all we heard about. At his age getting a root was a hard thing and this chick was a bit younger than him. So anyway our boat just stops, I'm sure they meant it that way."

"They? Were you hijacked?" Willy questioned.

"You could say that."

"Fucking bastards," Willy steamed under his breath. He hated those scumbags who preyed on fisherman and stole money, cargo, even the whole boat sometimes.

"But it wasn't like that. We spent two hours trying to get her started. Mal, our mechanic and his son Eric, checked the fuel line, the battery, oil. Nothing. There was nothing wrong with it. She just wouldn't start. Kenny got me to call the coast but I couldn't get through because of bad reception, all I got was some fucking Asian radio program from god knows where. So we sat there, hoping that eventually we would be missed or spotted by a passing ship. We waited and waited but nothing showed up. Even the radar was on the fritz. Now we were stranded five hours and never moved from the same spot. No current moved us away, we just bobbed up and down on that same patch of evil sea. Kenny did his thing with the sexton and the sun, but he was as mystified as the rest of us. 'Never seen nothing like it,' he said. By late afternoon things were getting creepy. Kenny had us all in the engine room again checking over the motor. Mal was showing me how to pull apart the battery housing as I'm not too bright on mechanics and shit, when we heard a knocking on the outer hull.

"At first we didn't take too much notice, it's common for bits of driftwood to run into ships. But it kept going. It was random at first then as it caught my attention I listened more and I could make out a pattern. Tap, tap, bang, tap, tap, bang. It kept going on like this for a few minutes and the more I listened to it the more it freaked me out. I shook it off, convinced myself it was still driftwood and my mind was playing these tricks on me. We had too much on our hands anyway to worry about it but as the hours went on, so did this bloody noise. Sometimes I couldn't hear it, then when I tried to hear it, it started again. We were exhausted and as time went on the chances of us getting the engine started seemed more remote. Finally Mal spoke up. 'What the fuck is that banging?'

"I've been listening to it all afternoon," I said.

"We all pricked our ears and listened, then it … it was like it finally got our attention and started going crazy, showing off even. There was a rapid thump that we could clearly hear go from one side of the hull to the other virtually instantly. That was followed by a sort of drum roll that went from bow to stern, right along the keel. No person could do that, no shit, no way. Stupid as it sounds I thought there was a giant who had hold of the ship and was tapping on it to see if there was anyone home. We were shitting ourselves and sweating even more in the stinking hot engine room. Still the knocks came on all over the place. I kid you not, I felt a knock right under my feet, the vibrations made me almost hit the roof. The others looked at me with huge empty eyes. They were petrified, all except Kenny.

'I still say it's a debris field.' He said it strongly, but I saw him clutch the wrench tightly to stop his hands from shaking.

"Strange debris field don't you reckon?" I spat back. Kenny went to say something back to me but was interrupted by footsteps from the upper deck. We grabbed tools and anything that could do damage to a person's body and ran up from the engine room.

"All our nerves were frayed, we were tired, hungry, frustrated, and scared. So I was determined to vent some of that frustration on whoever was stuffing us around.

"Outside, we found no one. Mal and Eric ran up to the wheelhouse and bow, while Kenny and I went down to the stern. We looked in every box and room. There was nothing. It was just us bobbing on the ocean in the dark."

The man stopped and motioned for Willy to refill his empty mug with liquor. While Willy poured the brandy, the other three said nothing but watched him, even Roy seemed enthralled by the bizarre tale and was taking notes in a worn notebook.

"Get to the point, would you mate," Willy urged him on as he put the brandy bottle back down.

"Sure." The man laughed. "There was a scream, which turned into a cry of agony. It came from out on the ocean, then it begun to multiply. I could hear women, men, children all screaming, then a ship's horn blared out from the darkness. We all stopped and stared out, looking for this ship and people. We were ablaze with light and there was no fog, still we couldn't see the ship. We waited for something to happen but there was nothing.

"What's going on, skipper?" I implored Kenny for an answer.

"Kenny was still as stone, with a face like a white sheet and electric eyes that darted about in panic. He was just as confused as the rest of us.

"I don't know, Ed. Something's not right that's for sure."

"Skipper! Skipper!" Mal called from the bow.

"Kenny and I jumped, startled by the break in silence. We rushed along the ship to where Mal and Eric were hiding behind a crate. They were shitting themselves with panic and shaking uncontrollably.

"Look over there," Eric whispered, indicating the bow with his shaking hand.

"I peeked over the corner and almost jumped out of my skin. Standing by the fishing nets along the port bow was a man. He was transparent and I could see the white running board through his legs. I swear blind it was a ghost. When I was a kid all my friends would sit around out in the bush trying to scare each other with ghost stories, for a laugh, you know. But to see one was something else.

"Every part of me shook, partly with fright and amazement. I was too scared and fascinated at the same time to turn away. So I watched this shape of a man stare out to sea. I think it was Mal who said, 'What do we do?' No one answered. No one had could think clearly, I know I couldn't. We whispered amongst ourselves, with each of us throwing in a plan: run, chase it, run, you're all nuts, that type of quick panic thinking.

"Suddenly the ghost turned around to look at us. It glared at us with black eyes and a tight smirk across its weather-beaten face. We panicked in unison and fled, thinking it was after us. We ran like girls back down towards the engine room, screaming and fumbling our way down the corridor and steps. Shit, I even fell at the bottom but my panic was so great I jumped back up and almost knocked out Eric as he tried to help me up. We got into the room and the door slammed shut and was locked behind us.

"We all collapsed about on the greasy floor or up against the engine housing. Our hearts pumped like crazy as we tried to catch our breath in that horrible stale air. There were no words, only eye contact. I could see we were all petrified beyond imagination.

"What are we going to do Skipper?" Mal was almost in tears.

"Just stay calm, we'll think of something."

"Kenny looked over at me for reassurance but hell what was I going to do?

"Then there was a metal sound. I can still hear that scraping of metal on metal. All our heads shot around as one and our eyes were glued onto that turning wheel on the door. Slowly it turned until it locked up and couldn't turn any further then it turned back to where it rested.

"Mal broke ranks, picked up a wrench and stepped forward. At first I thought he was going to charge the door because he could see something I couldn't, that the ghost had somehow got in. With one mighty swing his wrench came tearing down and dented the engine covering with his first swing.

"'Come on, start you bitch!' he wailed in panic as he wound himself up for another blow.

"Nobody stopped him. I was hoping that it would work and it would magically restart, like in a movie. The only thing that started was muffled crying and splashing about in the ocean. It sounded like a choir of angst-ridden souls all thrashing about in boiling water. Like … I shouldn't say like, it was.

"The boat was rocking from side to side. The thumping of before had returned but this time it was everywhere on the hull. Hundreds of fists hammering at our wooden hull, all of them trying to smash it open. We were thrown from one side to the next as the moaning and confusion went on outside. We all covered our ears in a vain attempt to block out the horrible noise.

"I looked to Kenny who had frozen in place but his eyes darted about at every ear-piercing scream.

"Skipper! There are ghosts climbing onto our ship!" I yelled over at him.

"Bullshit!"

"Are you fucked up!? I can see their bloody legs through the porthole!" He said nothing in reply. Mal and Eric turned about in circles and tried to keep their balance as the ship rocked about. They had the same expression of fear as our Skipper.

"Then I heard wood crack and the gushing of water. More wood broke and still the hammering continued.

"They're dragging us under, we've got to get out!" I yelled to Kenny but he still stood there.

"I wasn't going to wait for an answer, I was abandoning ship and went straight for the door. Luckily my fear of what was coming through the hull was greater than whatever could be waiting for me on the other side. I turned the wheel, it unlocked and I swung it open.

"There was nothing there and I was able to make my way up the stairs and into the corridor. Mal and Eric were right behind me but there was no sign of Kenny and be damned if I was waiting around.

"On the top deck there was chaos. All the containers on deck had been ransacked, boxes were opened and the contents strewn over the place. Our lifejackets were out of the emergency box and were amongst the clutter.

"I can't jump, god knows what's in that water!" Eric cried out.

"It's sink or swim!" Mal cried back while putting on his lifejacket.

"Where's Kenny?" I finally asked.

"He was right behind us but I ain't going back down there, no fucking way!" Mal said.

"I managed to get hold of a lifejacket and got my first glimpse of the sea. It was alive with people all screaming and thrashing about. There were bloody and white hands hanging onto the side of the ship, and some reached out for me, their faces white, their eyes grey and their mouths open holes of blackness.

"Our boat was listing heavily now and we couldn't stand straight with the sloping deck. I had my jacket on, done up and was trying to grow some balls to either jump or go down with the ship, either way I knew that I would have all those wet clammy hands over me and that I would die. I cried out and made a jump for it.

"As soon as I landed in the water I felt the hands. I kicked and punched my way through and swam like the devil was after me. I swam until my arms ached and I was running on adrenalin only. Finally, exhausted, I stopped. I looked about and saw the mast of our trawler, its light still ablaze, go under the ocean. I called out for Mal and Eric and I heard them call back for me but I never saw them again.

"The sea was now calm and only pieces of wreckage floated on the surface. I started to swim again, the panic rising up again as I started believing I was seeing ghosts swimming under the water following me. I stopped when I was exhausted and just lay in the water thinking I was going to die. I must have fallen asleep as that's all I remember until you pulled me aboard."

The trawler's crew said nothing as the man finished. The story was incredible. Roy spoke first as he lit a cigarette. "So you're saying a bunch of ghosts sank your ship?"

"Yeah, that's right."

Roy rolled his eyes and walked away. "You probably were dropped overboard for drunkenness. I knew Kenny and he ran a tight ship, he wouldn't put up with shit like that. I hope nothing has happened to him, cause I'll come looking for you," he said as he disappeared down a corridor.

"I don't care if you don't believe me!" the man yelled out at him, "I saw it and everything I said was true, I don't make up bullshit like that. One day you'll fucking see it old man and you'll remember me!"

Hawkesbury River was only another hour away and once there Roy handed over his cargo to his brother Dave, the local copper.

"This guy's got a tall tale you wouldn't believe. More Captain Rats than a Mandala patient. Been at sea too long or for not long enough."

"Is he part of Kenny's new crew?"

Roy watched his brother for a moment; he had a horrible feeling coming on.

"Yeah," he said slowly.

"Kenny's boat's missing for three days now, but yesterday morning we found Kenny washed up on Pearl Beach. He had a lifebelt on, SS Stanton, 1909."

Roy didn't know it or make the connection.

"I can tell by that blank expression you've got no idea. The Stanton was a passenger ship lost in a storm. The Navy have confirmed it's an original. Do you know if Kenny kept any crap like that on board?"

Roy looked over at the man who was being helped off the boat by Dull. "Nah, I got no idea."

"I bet he's got some story to tell," Dave said while watching the man be loaded into an ambulance.

"Sure does, do you want to hear it?" Roy smiled.

His breathing and his footsteps on the gravel path were the only sounds that night. The moon and stars above were the only others present among the monuments to the dead.

Suddenly he stopped, looked and listened. Hearing nothing, he walked on past the plaques and the chiselled, fading names. He ignored them. He had work to do.

The mound of withering flowers lay upon the grave. Their brown corners hung heavy on their petals as they slowly decayed and were absorbed back into the earth. Kneeling down, he scattered them with a brush of his heavy hand.

He removed the remaining bunches one by one and placed them in piles beside the mound. The family and friends who'd laid them would never return or ever know that the grave had been disturbed. It was all memories now. There was work to be done.

One layer down, the pretty layer. How they disguise the dirt with flowers. Death is decay, dirt, stench and dull. Not colour.

"Work quickly."

The soil was still loose and cold to the touch.

"Dig, dig, dig!"

It was done. He brushed the loose soil and exposed the naked wood. A nice coffin, but its black paint repulsed him.

His chosen few were pure and should not be surrounded by darkness, and she was pure and beautiful.

He had watched her for months in the refuge, helping the homeless and going about her life. He saw her shopping, working and as she spent time with her family and friends. He was always watching. After some months, she died. He did not know why or how, as it was not of his making.

He felt the edges of the coffin.

"Time to have a peek."

He lifted the lid slowly, lest he wake her from her sleep. A slight squeak from the dry joints sang a little song in that grave hole. He was disappointed that neither sweet sound nor quivering shiver went down his spine as dry metal scratched against dry metal. It was the sound he liked best.

There she was. The only movement were his hands and decomposition. Her dress was still pearly white; her hands were now slightly shrunken and dry. Her pretty face was smooth no more; it, too, had begun to shrink and go dry. Her skin was tightly stretched across the bones, the nose on the verge of collapse and her once rosy lips had begun to dissolve to reveal her teeth, which were still white. He closed the lid. There was work to be done.

He arranged the four legs of his pulley over the grave, and the metal chain hung down into the hole like a noose. He hammered four large nails into each of the coffin's sides and placed a loop of rope over each nail. Next, he attached the four ropes to the hook at the end of the chain.

Everything was set. He clambered out of the grave and set to work bringing her back to the surface. It wasn't difficulty for him to hoist the coffin out and lay it onto a small flatbed trolley.

Now it was time to make his escape. He dismantled the pulley and placed beside the coffin, along with his trusty shovel.

"Wait!"

The grave was still open. Curse his impatience. With great speed, he shovelled the dirt back into the grave ad replace the flowers on the mound. With the coffin removed, the grave was lower now, but he didn't care or have the time to worry about it.

"Quickly!" he said to himself. "Mustn't be caught, must not be caught."

He began his homeward charge, running, panting and pacing with nervous excitement. He took his familiar path.

His house backed up to the cemetery. He ran until he reached the fence that divided his property and the cemetery.

Long ago, he had constructed a swinging door in the fence that would allow him to push the trolley and its cargo through without fuss. It was hidden behind a tree, smothered in darkness, and looked like an oversized doggy door. He was proud of his ingenuity.

Once his prize was safely onto his property, he walked down a path that bordered the side of his house and into his yard.

In only a few minutes' time he had moved the trolley from the doggy door to the back of his garage, which held an old truck and shelves packed with tools.

He closed the garage door with a sigh of relief. He was safe now. He moved to another door in the garage. Behind it was a concrete slope that disappeared into the darkness of a room underneath the house.

His hands were trembling with anticipation; his breath turned into fog in the cold air. Gently, he manoeuvred his charge down the slope and into the basement.

He placed the trolley in the centre of the room and went to turn on the light. The explosion of light exposed the misconception that the room was a mere workingman's storage area.

No matter how many times a person had been down in his dungeon, the unexpected sight of the dead bodies still in their coffins but encased in glass like a display piece could turn the blood cold.

There were five of them, each standing upright with tight grimacing faces. The coffins were filled with flowers and the outsides were decorated with flags and streams of colour.

He moved to his new gift, debating what to do with her.

"Why did you act so quickly?" he told himself. Patience next time, his little crypt was nearing capacity. "But she would have gone if I left her longer in the ground."

He relaxed his mind and body as he looked around to plan where to put her. As he did, he inspected his little family for the hundredth time. Approaching the first glass-covered tomb, he remembered.

Mary Watts. Entered salvation June 10, 2004. She was the newest member of his collection, bar his guest tonight. They stared at each other, one in true death, the other only suffering mental decay. She had served as a nurse in the Korean War and continued her work with Legacy and the Salvation Army.

He stiffened in his boots with pride, breathed deeply and moved to the next troop in the parade of the dead.

Joseph Black. Entered salvation March 27, 2004. He bent down to wipe the dust from the brass plate that bore the inscription, and then looked into Joseph's cloudy eyes. He had died in a car accident; his left was arm crushed and his were ribs broken. He had survived many days before losing his fight for life. He was a fighter in real life and someone who had to be in his collection, he deserved it. Here was a man who gave his life helping the poor and made sure they got what they needed. Thank you, Joseph.

Alasia Downer. Entered salvation September 11, 2003. She was the jewel in his crown, his first. It all came back to him now: the hot nights, the chase, the sex. She turned him into an animal and he loved it. The smell of her flesh and the sound of her whimpering drove him wild.

Death came to her by her own hand, drugs. She was messed up and from a broken home, always depressed, never seeing the light. But he had held the light; he'd made sure she would bathe in it. She was the only one who had loved him.

Once, all deaths saddened him. He didn't know why we were born or why we died. There were so many souls, but he couldn't save them all. That was the only thing that saddened him now.

As he looked at her closed eyes, he thought more of life beyond death and the end times that were coming soon. God would be pleased, he knew, and it was no coincidence that these people had each died suddenly. It was all part of the plan.

He missed Alasia, though. He wanted to hold her tight, to pat her hair as she cried in his arms. "*The world sucks, I just wanna die!*" she'd say, and she did.

Soon they would be reunited. She went away but she'll come back, they all will, he told himself. He'll keep their bodies waiting for their return at Judgement Day. More patience was all he needed. Then he will be rewarded and they could all be together in their own little world. They would be so happy to be some of the few to have their bodies waiting for their souls. Alasia would embrace him and scream his name in delight.

Her coffin held pride of place and always had, with flowers on it. Always.

Jennifer White. Entered salvation November 7, 2003. Now she was a pearl. She was a nun with a soul of light, caring for children and just about anyone in need. Her touch was soft as a feather, her smile like warm sunshine. He would never forget her tender voice. She was his angel and had taken him in when he was at his lowest, when his love and job had gone. *Curse his big fat pig of a boss - such a pity he died a short time later, such a pity, tut, tut.*

He had found her obituary in the paper and was glad he had worked quickly to save her from the fires of cremation. No one had ever known that the ashes were just old wood. She didn't deserve to die from cancer, but she would remain forever in his care.

Robertson Bull. Entered salvation December 16, 2003. His own father. He had learned much from him, and now the debt would be repaid. His mother had left years and years ago. He didn't know where she was and didn't care.

"*Well done, Boris,*" he would say.

He looked at his watch. It was almost midnight. His excitement had masked his tiredness. It was time for bed. His new bride would have to wait until morning.

He made sure the room was secured, and then turned off the light. Next he checked the doors in the garage, which were all heavily padlocked.

The house itself was dark. There was a heavy, horrible smell in the air, but he was almost used to it, though anyone else coming in would not be able to stomach it.

He went down a hallway and into the front room. The smell was even stronger here, so much so that he coughed and his nose twitched as his lungs refused to accept the foul air.

Only the nuisance streetlights and the occasional, intrusive passing car's headlights that made strange shapes on the walls lighted the room.

A car passed by as he stood there and its light bled through the closed curtains. The room was illuminated for only a moment. Plumped here and there in the corners, sitting on couches and nailed on the walls were more stinking corpses.

The highlights revealed their silent, screaming mouths and their mushy, empty eyes.

It was quiet but for the passing car. He ignored it and ignored his trophies for a moment. He felt miles away; a bit of drool came extended from his bottom lip and his eyes were red from lack of sleep.

When the car had passed he awoke from his stupor.

"Hello, friends. Are you well? I see your scent is much stronger tonight. I fear the time will come soon when I must take you away from here. The neighbours will begin to ask questions."

As he moved to the foot of the staircase, he spoke to them. "Don't worry or cry. Be grateful that I remember who you are while your families have forgotten you. I was there to see you in your new face. But yes, the time has come to part, 'cause you'll give me away. That can't happen, they can't take away my family. But remember, I love you all."

~ ~ ~

James stood by the window looking through the light rain at the only house he had ever taken notice of. It was old and boarded up. The house seemed dead to him, odd, out of place and diseased.

The curtains were drawn, as always, a faded pink with another layer behind them in a darker colour. The house was two storeys tall and painted orange; all the others in the street were either white or grey. The paint was beginning to wear and patches of white could be seen on the walls, between the moss and cracks. There was a small yard of dying grass in the front, bound by a rusting fence. James hadn't seen the back of the house, but knew the cemetery was there. That was probably what scared him the most.

He had heard at school that the old man who lived there ate little kids. He believed it. He hated the house and wanted it gone from his street.

Today the house haunted him even more. He had been dared by his friends to look into one of its windows tonight. If he didn't, they said, it meant he was a chicken and girl. Some days he just hated school. James watched the house like a bull watching a matador. His heart jumped when he saw the curtains move and a head peered out of the window for a split second.

He ran from his room and downstairs to the kitchen where his mother was making breakfast.

"Mum, mum!"

He felt safe when reached her and could see her pouring cereal.

"What is it?" Came a tired response.

"Nothing." He could tell she was in a cranky mood and had learned the hard way to not bother her when she was like that.

"Well, you better be off to school then."

He went out into the morning. The overnight rain had stopped, but its fragrance lingered and the streets were wet.

With his hands deep in his pockets, he moved as fast as his twelve-year-old legs could carry him to the bus stop, but first he had to pass the house. The corner came up quicker than he liked, and he stepped into the main street.

115

He didn't want to look at it as he went by. It was only a stone's throw across the street. Up ahead stood the bus stop where his friend Jason was waiting. James couldn't help but look at the house.

His heart beat faster. He felt naked and alone, as the house stared him down. It seemed bigger and fiercer today than even before. Water poured off its roof, flooding the dirt patch in the front yard. No faces looked out, but he was waiting for them. He got felt a cold shiver down his spine. *"That's just someone walking on your grave,"* his mum would say, laughingly. He thought this was a horrible idea and would watch people's feet, imagining himself buried one day.

He was past the house now and came to the bus stop. "Ready for the dare tonight?" Jason asked while eating a donut.

James swallowed hard. No, he wasn't.

~~~

Morning. He sat on his bed and listened to the howl of the woman next door as she grilled her small daughter about spilt milk.

He could hear the little girl crying and the sound of the strike from a hand on her body. The woman was a bitch. Every day he had to listen to her yelling. Her constant high-pitched screeching was beginning to make his quiet existence intolerable. She had to go, and he had a plan.

He had dead bodies, sure, but the idea of actually watching the transition from a living person to a corpse had been his fascination for the past few weeks. He was anxious to watch death's invisible hand take hold and watch over time as the rot set in. Now, he had found his subject.

She would not be missed. In fact, he believed he was doing a service to the community by getting rid of her. Her daughter would surely agree; he had even heard her say she hated her mother. All would fall into place. What luck a creature lived next door. Luck indeed. Everything was ready.

Soon, the little girl left for school and the woman was on her own. Now was the time to strike. He jumped from his chair and went to a drawer. He removed an old Luger pistol that his father gave him when he was a boy. He loaded it and hid it beneath his jacket.

He was happy and he danced about the front room, surrounded by the stinking bodies as the morning light showed the contents of the room in all their gore.

On a couch was a blackened female corpse that he had picked up. Seizing her from her sleep, he danced with her, around and around the front room.

He stopped and put a hand over her to face to steady it. It didn't matter pieces fell off, it just didn't. He could smell her perfume and he feel her fragile body as he looked into her empty, blackened holes that were once were her eyes.

"You're so beautiful."

He stole a kiss, then another and another. A normal person would have been revolted, but not Boris.

"But now it's time to go. I have things to do."

He dropped her to the floor and stepped away. Now she was just another twisted heap of bones. Her skull lay undignified, face down, and her hair spread like wings beside it.

He left the house through the back door; he never went through the front, there were too many people out there. He went through the side gate and pathway. There was no one there, though usually there was a string of runners and walkers who came through the cemetery. Maybe it was to motivate themselves?

He jumped the fence and landed straight into her backyard. The grass was long. An old rug hung on the washing line, and old, moss-covered furniture was strewn about the yard. He could hear the sound of dishes being moved about in a sink accompanied by the faint sound of a radio coming from inside the house.

He felt the coldness of his pistol, now fitted with a silencer, the pounding of his heart and his deep breath making faint clouds in the morning air.

He made it to the backdoor and reached for the handle but stopped suddenly. Should he knock or just enter? He knocked.

She was only a few feet away, in a back room, and came quickly to the door.

"Hello?" she said in surprise.

"Hello."

She looked annoyed.

He hated the pleasantries of conversation and was always impatient to get to the point. That's why he had trouble waiting for The Day.

"I've been watching you," he said as he stared at her ample bosom. "And I want your body."

"What the hell are you talking about? Are you the weirdo who lives next door?"

He stepped into the house and she stepped back. "*She's afraid. Good.*"

"I want your body, to watch it."

She continued to step back and he could see she was nearing the phone.

"Get out of my house," she snarled.

He pulled out his Luger to make it clear who was in control of the situation. For some reason, she didn't scream but stared at the barrel of the pistol that was pointed in her direction.

"You know I've got Hep C, so you'll get it too," she whimpered.

"What's Hep C?"

"A disease, you prick! You rape me, and you'll die too."

He was shocked, and then let out a small chuckle. It wasn't like that at all. It was like this.

He fired a shot that hit her in the right leg, knocking her to ground instantly. She still didn't scream, but her mouth opened and closed in shock, her eyes wide at the sight of the blood coming from the wound.

Her agony and fear fascinated him. He watched intently at every whimper and tear. He fired again, this time into her abdomen. Stomach wounds were always a slow, painful death.

His whole body was trembling with excitement at her whimpering, crying and pleading. Blood was spilling out of her even more now. She knew she was going to die.

"Please," she whimpered.

"Shh." He put his finger to his lips, "You're spoiling it."

He sat on the floor and waited for her to die. He ignored her pleading and soon reached the point where he just wanted her to hurry up and die. It took half an hour but, finally, her eyes closed and she did not move again.

Now he could watch the body begin to break down. For hours he sat in the kitchen, watching. The blood had flowed out until the supply had ended and there was now a red pool that almost reached his feet. His mind was empty of thought and emotion, but he simmered in his excitement at the scene. Everything had gone according to plan.

Time ticked on. Soon, the little one would be home from school. He wrapped the body in a blanket and put it in the backyard. He would move it once it was dark.

He returned home and waited impatiently. He used the time to prepare his newest family member, the body from the night before, for her new destiny. He poured the coffin with flowers and found a place for it. His little room was now full. This worried him.

The hours passed and he was annoyed that he had missed the early stages of decomposition, but what else could he do?

He moved his trolley out of the doggy door and then jumped the fence. He moved it to the neighbour's back fence and jumped into her yard before he brought her body back on the trolley. He didn't look twice at the house or care if the little girl was all right. Soon, he was back in his own yard, the body went through the doggy door, and he went into his garage, where he could relax.

He took her body into the front room where he had cleared a table. He unrolled her from the blanket and was pleased. Her limbs had gone stiff and her skin different was shades of purple where the remaining blood had pooled.

Now he could watch nature take its course right through the 'melting' phase, as he called it, to when she would be a skeleton.

~ ~ ~

James had been dreading this all day. Now it was almost 8.30 pm on Friday night. His friends, Michael and Tyson, all met at Jason's house, ready for their dare. They wore coats and caps, as it was cold. Tyson brought a torch; James had a bottle of Coke and block of chocolate. Jason supplied a bag of mixed lollies, while Michael brought only a dirty magazine of his brother's.

As they neared the house their chatter stopped. Now it was the real thing. All four stood outside the ugly orange house watching for movement and having second thoughts about this little expedition.

"Do you still want to do this?" James checked with the group.

Michael shrugged his shoulders while the other two smiled and nodded.

"Okay, torch."

Tyson handed the torch to James while Jason continued to eat from the lolly bag. They all took a handful and put them straight into their mouths so they could hardly breathe as they chewed the mass of confectionary.

"Come on," James mumbled.

James tried to open the gate, but it wouldn't move, so they jumped over it. Each held his breath, waiting for a light to go on in the house, but nothing happened.

They crossed the dirt yard in single file, went around the side and stopped at a window.

The glass was low enough that they could all look through. There were curtains at the side of the pane and through a gap they had a clear view into the house.

James turned on the torch and shone it through the window while his friends looked on, their faces close to the glass trying to look in, too.

"It's too dark," moaned Michael.

"Hang on," James said as he cupped the torch with his hands on the glass. Immediately, hey could see shapes sitting on lounge chairs. The boys instinctively jumped back from the window and crouched down.

"Did they see us?" Tyson asked. He had already taken a few steps back, ready to run.

James slowly stood back up and looked through the window again. This time he caught a glimpse of the rotting face of an old man sitting in a chair. His mouth was gaping and stiff, his eyes green masses of goo that ran down his rotten, bloated cheeks.

James shot back in shock, and the torch dropped to the ground. Jason had been standing next to him and saw the old man, too. The others had taken this as a sign they had been sprung and had started running.

James and Jason followed. They were expecting the old man to come out of the door and start chasing them. Panic-stricken, the four ran all the way back to Jason's, where they regrouped.

"Did he see us?" Tyson pressed James for an answer. "Was he coming for us?"

James and Jason exchanged worried glimpses.

"What did you see?" Michael was sceptical about the whole thing. "You're probably bullshitting."

"It was a dead guy sitting on a lounge," James whispered.

He couldn't get that face out of his mind, the blackness of the open mouth and those rotten eyes. He was beginning to shake, and his fears multiplied as he thought more about it.

He and Jason weren't interested in doing anything else that night, so they parted ways. James just wanted to go home. It was a long walk back, and he deliberately went a different way so he didn't have to go past the house. With every new shadow and noise he thought the dead man was coming after him, so he ran most of the way back, all the time wishing he had never gone to that house.

~~~

The body was cold and rigor mortis was beginning to set in. The lower parts of the body, its bottom and back, were even more purplish now.

He was eating hot chips he had fried himself for breakfast as he watched, still fascinated by the stages of decomposition, but he couldn't sit there all day. The rain from the day before had come through the roof and he knew he had to have a look at the downpipes and roof.

He went around to the side of the house. The sun was up, and there were no clouds in the sky for a change. He didn't have heat in the house, only an open fire. Heaters made the bodies smell worse; even he couldn't stand it during the summer. Only his bedroom was heated, and now, with water coming in, that made him uncomfortable.

He spotted the torch straight away and immediately his heart sank. Under the front window were heaps of footprints and a bag of lollies that had been spilled everywhere. He looked through the window and saw the curtain had moved, making Henry visible to all.

His heart beat faster as it dawned on him that someone had seen into his world. Someone knew! His time was up.

Quickly he went back inside to think, back to the lounge room where his newest body lay rotting away on a table. Decisions had to be made, and made quickly. Why couldn't they just leave him alone?

~~~

James woke up early the next morning, sweating and grumpy. He hadn't slept at all, as the nightmares came every time he closed his eyes.

His mother entered the room and began to pick up clothes to be washed.

"Are you alright?"

"Why?"

"I heard you tossing and turning all night. I thought you'd stay at Jason's?"

He didn't say anything. Would this nightmare haunt him forever? What about tonight and the next night?

"You didn't get drunk did you? That Michael is too old for his little twelve-year-old boots." She had stopped picking up clothes and stared down at him, her hand on her hip and half expecting him to say yes.

"No."

"Good." She left with a bundle of clothes. He just lay there wondering what he was going to do.

~~~

He watched the report on the television. The disappearance of the woman, Debbie was her name, had been discovered. Police conducted door knocks in the neighbourhood. Anyone with any information was asked to contact them.

Police cars drove up and down the street, and they were all over her house. They even knocked on his door, but he didn't answer. They left a card. They'd be back; he knew it.

He looked down at his fingernails. Usually they were filled with dirt, but this time he had chewed most of them off. It was time to leave this place. Tonight.

~~~

James and Jason stood outside Debbie's house, which now had a barrier tape around it and a patrol car parked at the kerb.

"Do you think she's in that house?"

James shrugged his shoulders. "Don't know."

They both knew her daughter, Janelle. She was a year younger than them. Michael thought she was good looking and had her on his possible girlfriend list.

They kept on walking and past the cold, orange house. Their pace quickened and they said nothing as they passed.

~ ~ ~

Inside the house there were busy preparations underway. Boris had been lifting and storing his family into the back of the truck in the garage. He was their protector and he mustn't let them be discovered, never.

He had already found a new house far from this town and any large population. This time he didn't want any people around, so the countryside seemed a perfect choice. There was even a bigger room for his little family, and room for more. He would plan it all better so he didn't have to move again and waste all the time and effort needed for his modifications.

He came downstairs with the last of his clothes in a suitcase and went into the lounge room where the corpses sat unmoving. The sun had fallen and it was now time to go.

"I'm sorry, my friends, I can't take you with me. It's time you went back into the graves from which I took you. But remember, I was the only one who cared about you; you'd all be bones now with no one visiting your graves. Remember that."

He clapped his hands and was only slightly disappointed that he had to leave Debbie there on the table, but he knew there would be others. He'd be more careful next time.

He picked up the lady he'd dropped on the floor from yesterday. Her features were even more horrid now than before, and danced his way about the room.

"No more nights in my bed, my sweet, no more, I'm sorry. I must move onto other lovers. Shall we kiss one last time?"

He kissed the shrunken bits that were once lips and then dropped her to the floor where she landed, once again, on her face to hide her broken heart.

"Goodbye!" He called out as he left the room.

~~~

Jason and James wandered back along the street. It was late, the sun had gone down and they didn't want to be out at night anymore. Besides, they would probably get an earful when they got home.

The two had met Michael and Tyson at the local shops where they played the pinballs and the in-store Play Station. They also talked about the other night. Michael didn't believe them, but Tyson did.

"Go to the cops?" he asked.

"We should," Jason replied strongly.

James thought the same - they'd have to tell someone. He couldn't put up with the nightmares any longer.

They went past the house and kept going. Up ahead, the patrol car was still outside Janelle's mum's house. They would have to tell.

When they got to the house there was a man talking to the police officer, s the boys stood by waiting.

"I'm a relative and need to know what's happening," the man pleaded, obviously distressed.

"Janelle's fine. You'll need to go to the station because I don't have any information here on where she is staying or what's happening. I'm only guarding the place."

"Okay, thank you," the man as he left and went to his car.

The policeman noticed them now. "What can I do for you boys?"

Jason nudged James in the ribs.

"Um. You know that house down there, the orange one?" James pointed next door.

"Yeah, sort of."

"Well ..."

~ ~ ~

The door wouldn't give way after four powerful kicks from the policeman. He was getting annoyed with it, but on the fifth kick, he brought his boot crashing against the door harder. The door cracked and he and three other policemen were immediately overcome by the foul odour of death that rushed forth from the hole in the door. They all recognised it for what it was. The stench filled their noses and lungs. It was impossible to get any fresh air and they were still outside the house.

They had thought the kids' story was just boys' wild imaginations, but seeing that the detectives had been trying to get in touch with the man living in the house, they had gone there anyway and looked through the same window the boys had looked in.

One by one they went in and stood, stunned, in the lounge room.

"Holy shit," one of them exclaimed. None of them could stay in the house; the stench was unbearable, even for the older policemen who had seen plenty of dead bodies. They all raced out in one group.

Inside the house the bodies sat unmoved, stolen from their eternal sleep, slowly rotting away in the quiet. On one of the lounge room walls was a message written in red paint.

Judgement Day is coming.

THE DEAD OF NIGHT

Central Europe.

Through the sounds of squealing pigs, the bell of a church and the laughter of merry children, mingled the sound of the boots of the man. He trod quickly through the muddy streets of the town, hell-bent on reaching the forest, until a child stopped his step.

"Now isn't the time to play with snow, get along little one; it's far past sundown."

The little boy said nothing, but sped away from the man and disappeared. The man moved on; a smile smacked across his face, pleased that he had frightened the boy.

The forest loomed closer; its darkness inviting and teasing with the possibilities that it offered to the thief that he was. His eyes focused on the trail that led into its abyss; a tunnel that was his to enter--a doorway into which he was master of the room.

He could feel the change, the coldness, as he entered the gate--just as when the sun is blocked by the clouds and the Earth becomes cold for a few moments. He stopped; no birds sang, neither light nor star showed itself in the canopy. Quiet prevailed, except for the light footsteps in the far black distance. A single echo sounded in his ear.

The inviting and teasing beckoned again. He followed. His mask was off. He was now the hunter.

In the darkness, he couldn't see his prey; he could only hear the breaking of twigs and heavy breathing. Shortly, the distance would be closed, as he dodged and weaved through the undergrowth.

Soon he saw the small figure moving away from him. He closed the gap to a few feet, without detection. He could hear the man's breathing, the money jiggling in his pocket, the pulsing of the heart and blood. Only a small man; a small man carries less blood, but no matter. The enjoyment would still live and so it all climaxed inside him.

He was so close now. He opened his mouth to let the fangs show. He loved to take this slowly. Easily, he slipped his arm around the little man's waist. In fright the man turned quickly and sharply in response to his presence. *"Too late, my friend."*

He bit down hard, sinking his teeth deeper into the soft throat.

"Scream, yes scream, man! Let them hear your terror and pain. Let them hear your death! Scream as your neck relinquishes the stream of blood. Let it wash down my face and into my mouth."

He drained his victim, as the terror faded from the man's voice and the night was quiet once more. The empty corpse was thrown into the bushes. *"Let the worms have it."*

Moments later he was sitting upon a log, contemplating his desires. His desires told him he was not satisfied. Tonight he might visit another. The night had only just begun.

On the edge of the town closest to the forest, they heard the scream. The mothers took their children to bed and the fathers bolted the doors. Garlic was hung, crucifixes set, and prayers said. Tonight, the vampire was out.

~~~

Celestine sat astride the male. The silver dagger, now lodged in his chest, the blood spilling and seeping from the wound. She cut down, dragging the weapon towards where they had been joined in pleasure. In the space around her, whispers danced between the gentle glow of soft candles. Chants of dark poetry spoke in time. Breath, deep and heavy from the heat they had been witness to...

She slipped the dagger from his abdomen and the blood fell from its tip, falling to the thick river running from the steaming wound. She stopped and lost concentration, the dagger fell to her side.

"*He has killed again.*" She could feel it.

The words didn't need to be spoken, most knew. Most silenced their mouths, while others continued with the ritual, not feeling what the others sensed--still not understanding, they too fell silent.

"The Nosferatu runs tonight," said Celestine.

"Every night is the night; he takes every night. You should know this Celestine," a deep voice answered her from the dark.

"Yes I know, but nor do I understand why; why do we feel?"

"We are the lovers of the night, the devil's brides. We feel the passing of death. The sounds of death sing for all to hear. We hear the soul leave the body, hear the music of the soul ascending to heaven, and the screams of the souls dragged to hell."

Celestine felt a touch on her shoulder and a kiss on her cheek. "But what exactly is it?"

The woman behind Celestine brought her head up. The light withered away the darkness and showed her fine features. Her lips full and red, long black hair, sunken white smooth cheeks and narrow green eyes that stabbed those who gaze upon her. Emmarah was her name.

"Celestine. Get dressed, take Lucian, and fling this monster in the pit to rot, then return here."

The two rose, Celestine put on her black cloak and the two began to drag the corpse away. When they had left, Emmarah sat upon the bed. Only a few spots of red blood stained the whiteness of the sheets. She sat there, quietly waiting for the girls to return. When they did, she began to speak.

"Now, my children, listen to me. The Nosferatu has reigned long over the night. He drinks the blood of the living to exist and sleeps the stinging days. He is strong; stronger than ten men. We sense his presence, we sense the death he takes. Why? I do not know. You know the legends; some know the truth and woe be to those who do not or those who ignore it. He is as real as the rivers and wind. He has not made contact with us over the years, but I sense the time is drawing near when our black eyes finally meet. What better partner for the devil's son than the blood of witches?" Emmarah rose to her full height and gazed into all eyes. "He will come and be our mate and we will be immortal. We'll lure the lovers, the innocent, and the wicked. We'll feed on them all and sip the blood of our enemies. Forever immortal, forever in darkness." She bent close to a burning candle and with a soft blow extinguished the light. "Forever as the vampire."

~ ~ ~

It was a deep sleep. Then images not his own flowed into his mind. Women teased him with their nakedness, moaning louder, beckoning to him. He tossed his head, desperate to shake them out. He tried until he was worn out. Slowly, he was becoming entranced by their beautiful faces; all of them wanting and calling to him. *"Come to us, immortal. Fill us with your blood."*

Screams. He struggled again and fought to wake and escape. It felt as if the women were holding him back from waking; but he knew he could not wake, as his body was aware that the sun still shone above. He couldn't wake; he must endure the torment for further still. "Witches! How is it you play with a god?"

"Make us immortal."

He laughed so evilly. "So that is your play, witches. Rape me with your tricks and steal my sleep. Let me lay and I will come."

Peace and tranquility came as the witches left his mind. He could hear his heart thump in the confined box, banging like a clock. Like a child, he snuggled in a comfortable bed and fell back into peace.

To him, it felt merely a moment, but it was hours later when, like lightning exploding in his mind, they returned. Their beautiful faces and beautiful breasts flashed in his mind. There was thunder that shook the earth, as he roared in pain and anger at the thieves of his sleep. *"Time to come to us, immortal."*

His eyes burst open to the new night and the witches only lingered in his memory. With a lion's strength, he smashed his way into the new, cool night--rising like Christ from the tomb.

The rain he barely noticed as it hit and washed away the dust from his face and clothes. He pushed through the dense forest, stomping and crushing small trees and fallen ancients alike.

The lights of the town hung in the distance and it seemed they hung from the very trees. His agitation was almost forcing itself from his insides as he carved his way from trees, between houses, and down the streets. Like a maddened wolf, he sniffed his prey and found it.

There was no sound as he stood beneath the witches' window. The windows were locked to halt the few flakes of snow that had been falling over the past few days in dribs and drabs. It was the end of winter. He smelled the air, a drifting mist of burning candles, the witches' scent. He could hear their whispers behind the walls.

Effortlessly he sprang, head on, intent on smashing his way through the window.

"Emmarah, he is below us."

"So he has come." Emmarah spoke to all, as she stared into the candle's flame. She moved closer to kill the coldness in her skin.

They heard the roar; they heard the dark warrior's scream and then saw the figure of a man smash the glass as he came through. The glass showered over the women nearest the window. He landed on his feet and in the distance, dogs woke to call out at the intruder of the night.

The women screamed as they fled the cold air and the red eyes that pierced them all.

"Who dares to enter my life?" The cuts from the glass bled the red fluid from his face and it glistened in the candlelight.

"I do, immortal." Emmarah rose to meet his imposing height. She was the tallest of them all, but was still dwarfed by the beast.

"We wish to be as you."

"Wench! Curse your imagination. You rape my peace and I shall not speak to you."

Emmarah stepped closer to the vampire and near to Celestine, who rose as she neared.

"We are your wives; drink from us. We have all you want. We too are the devil's children and it's only natural that we become one."

The vampire turned in rage, upturning the bed and smashing it on the wall. His voice ranged far above any noise created by man or God. The women pushed their hands into their ears as his deafening bellow became more than they could stand.

"I serve no devil! And if he is the one that has cursed me with his blood, then I shall never serve, as hell I am already in. And you wish to join me?"

Now Emmarah joined the war of words and raised her pitch, in an attempt to match his.

"You are the devil's creation! And so are we. Drink us, bleed us, and let us become one!"

The vampire fell silent, his fangs shone in the light. The evil sneer, the wolf's eyes, and his ugly face peered through the dark as he moved upon the fire. His stare dug deep into Emmarah's. In a slippery whisper that carried all that was venom, he said, "Then bleed you I shall."

The witch nearest to him screamed as the vampire grabbed her neck and ripped her clothes, exposing her nakedness. He bit down as he squeezed her young flesh.

"Lucian!" Celestine cried out in fear.

Emmarah held her close, not sure what was happening herself.

The blood spilled down her face and neck as he sucked. There was no sound from Lucian's mouth as it hung open, her eyes fixed to the roof. The vampire kept his clamp jaw fixed on her soft neck, but bit down deeper. The blood no longer flowed from the wound, but he continued with his hunger. Now it was her flesh. He tore as he tightened his grip on the back of her head. He pulled and tore. The neck bone cracked as it broke and he pulled the head free.

The witches shrieked in terror as they witnessed Lucian's mutilation and the rising of the vampire from the floor with a blood covered face and a head in his hand. He laughed at their fear and the mockery of their failed plan.

"You are nothing compared to me."

A flame lit the darkness as it swam through the air. It burst into fire as it struck his chest, igniting his clothes. He cried out in pain as his hand tried to smother and brush off the flames.

Emmarah's voice carried a spell from her mouth. It was dim in sound under the wailing of the vampire. Still it needed nothing else, just the words.

Lucian's blood that was smeared all over his face bubbled and steamed. Like acid, it began to eat away at his skin. Again, he cried out in pain and fear. He cried so loud and long that the glass in the windows shattered, sending the piercing cry across the town.

Now off balance, the vampire stumbled back and jumped from the window. He didn't bother to land on his feet, but fell in a smoking heap. He rolled in the melting snow that lay on the ground and which killed the fire. Fingers of steam now rose from his chest as he lay on his back, exhausted, but still with Lucian's head in his hand. He groaned and roared as he lifted himself up and ran for home, with the spell of acid blood still eating away at his flesh--running down the streets and away back towards his beloved dark forest. Finally, he became conscious of the head in his grasp and let it drop to the street.

The blood he had stolen from the witch and that lay in his stomach had boiled and ripped his insides. It was the worst pain he had ever imagined and could not be wiped away like a blood-smeared face. He cried out once more like a wounded dog as the acid dug deeper. He needed clean blood.

He chose a house at random, crushing the door as he broke in. With his vision and smell he found the family easily; buried deep in bed, mother and father. He crushed and bled them more violently and quickly than he had done to anyone in years. He usually took his time to enjoy the event. Not tonight. The clean blood soothed the burn slightly, but he needed more.

Their children's blood he took and he felt calmer. Now he could flee home as the pain had been muffled, although it still lingered. He still wailed as he fled down the streets and into his forest sanctuary to recover.

Streets away, the witches heard his cries, heard the door smashed, and the family killed. They heard the screams from the forest, until they finally stopped.

~~~

Emmarah tried to comfort her flock by wrapping them in her arms one by one. Lucian's headless body still lay where the bed had been. Crying and muffled sobs revealed the shock in the room. She saw Celestine in a corner, face down and shaking. This was not right; it was not meant to be this way.

"What have I done?" she whispered. This was all a mistake and now she had let loose a wild animal upon them. Bricks and mortar will not hold him; she would have to channel the secret world to protect her family.

She would use a dark spell, a secret spell; one not used by her ever, but often in the past by other witches. Their mark she recognised in the Bible and in history. It was, she was told once, used to create the vampire itself.

139

She moved to the open hole where the window had been and read from her spell book that she always carried. She spoke in a language foreign to the girls.

"Dark Lord! Dark Lord, hear me! I have a soul to wager for vengeance against my enemy!"

There was silence, but then a voice loud and deep, but that only Emmarah could hear, broke the night.

"I have your soul already."

"Your name has been insulted; I have been wounded and I am suffering! What will I wager for your service?"

"All of them," replied the voice.

Emmarah immediately knew that the prince of all the fallen wanted her coven. "So be it," she replied.

"What is your will?"

"There is one marked with fire, curse him by binding him to the light and let him suffer with the heat and damn. You will see his suffering," Emmarah said.

There was a cold laugh. "For my sport, it is done."

Now the wind blew as she finished and the rain came down harder and heavier, as if wishing to smash the town away--smash it until the floor of hell was exposed. The curse was out tonight.

In the houses of the people now caught in the middle of a war, the men and women held their crying children who been awakened by the breaking glass and howls of the beast passing by all the while, the people pushed down their own fears, as they looked for protection to the garlic rotting on their doors. The crucifix hung on the walls smoldered with heat. The people listened to the dogs howling and the women's screams and prayed it all would pass them by.

~ ~ ~

"There will be no hunting tonight," he lamented. The venom still swam in his veins. The new blood that he had taken had smothered the witch's curse slightly; more was needed but he was too tired to hunt the rest of the night.

He made his way along the well-trodden path through the woods and back to his grave, still smashed from his violent exit at sunset. He was too tired to care and repair it tonight. He would sleep; let the pain be dormant until the following night, when he would kill again and regain his mighty strength. Those witches would pay.

He lay back on the wet soil. The rain fell through the protective umbrella of the trees and blurred his vision. The stars he could still see and the rain fell from no cloud, it seemed.

Suddenly, he began throwing up blood as his body began rejecting the cursed slime in his stomach. It splattered and ran all over his already-stained and torn shirt. He felt better, nonetheless, and for a slight moment, there was no pain. Sleep was the only thing to which he could look forward; revenge was far off, but stirring in the dungeons of his subconscious mind. Finally relaxed, he was able to concentrate.

"Let me slip between the open mouth of the soil," he commanded.

The dirt parted and his body slowly slipped beneath its surface and closed up again. In utero, he slept with the thick, rich earth barring the sun from burning his flesh to ashes in seconds.

~~~

The witches remained stunned. Some had collapsed and cried where they fell. He was not one of them, that was for sure. None thought capable of speaking words and none tried. Their room was in ruins and the townsfolk would surely be highly suspicious, but they would do little. *"Perhaps a death in the family would finally push them into action? No, they are weak and terrified."* Celestine reassured herself as she sat in debris and cried.

Emmarah remained at the broken window, her mind turning over the deal she had made. Her heart was heavy with uncertainty. She knew the devil loved to see people suffer. He would not strike the vampire down, as she had wished, but would merely disable him and watch as he sorted out his own revenge in a demonic game for the devil's pleasure. They would be played against each other until one died.

The room was shattered and there was blood everywhere; too much blood. Lucian's headless body was crumpled on the floor. The wound was seething red but there was little blood flow. The backbone stuck out, broken and twisted unnaturally, its white outshining the crimson pulp it reached out from.

The witches couldn't bear to look at the sight. Some were seeing death for the first time. Emmarah surveyed the damage. Appalled at the sight of the corpse, she ordered a girl to go out and retrieve the head and to do it quickly and quietly.

"The people will be alert. Better to not make any more noise."

"Pearlise, Doleen, prepare Lucian's body for burial. We farewell one of our own." They nodded and exited the room to collect and assemble the necessary candles and potions needed for the burial of a witch.

Celestine got up off the floor and approached Emmarah. Tears still lay in the pools of her eyes.

"Emmarah why has this come to us?"

"I was wrong; very, very wrong."

"All of this?" Celestine was confused by Emmarah's words.

"I will explain it later. Right now we have to protect ourselves," Emmarah stated.

"He'll be back?"

Emmarah nodded. "Only the sun can kill the Nosferatu, but we can prevent him from ever setting foot in our home again."

With that, Emmarah walked from the room and they would not see her again for the rest of the night. She knew the devil himself would come to her bed and there ravage her for hours. It had been like that for years and she had been proud of it. But tonight, she was beginning to see what exactly making deals with the devil would cost.

~~~

Something gnawed at his mind and dragged him from his slumber.

"No!" He cried out. His mind was active but he could not wake, his body was not strong enough to rise. "I'm too weak, leave me alone, witches. You have done your deed."

Slowly he could feel a strange sensation. His flesh was disintegrating without pain. Not burning or decomposing, but falling apart, cell by cell. Just like when a body is a fetus and the cells come together, now they were coming apart.

There still was no pain as it went on, just fear. As he faded from the earth, the soil fell into the empty space where his body had slept moments before. He could see himself disappearing in his dream; he did not realise his eyes were still nailed shut. Then his mind began to break apart. He screamed an empty bellow as the dirt finally filled the void where he had lain.

"Witches! Damn you, witches!"

He imagined it as a tunnel and he traveled through it. But this was no dream. From the light, he sped through the darkness until another light beckoned in the distance. It came closer and grew. He felt his body breathe and his mind forgot the terrain passed.

Slowly the pieces materialized and came together. He was no longer in the soil; instead, he was in the open and the town lay around him. The morning sun crept up from behind the far wooded hills. It had already begun to singe his tender flesh. *"My God, it's the end."*

Though initially naturally terrified, it was a vampire's worst nightmare, to be cornered by the sun. Soon a strange sense of relief came over him. Finally, it was to end and he braved the sun's coming rays. It had been many years since he had ever seen the dawn; it would be a welcome end.

The fire burned his skin and, to his surprise, he did not burst into flames like the countless others he had seen.

The pain was so great that he could not even scream or thrash about in wild animal furor. Panic began to rush around, frenzy-like, in his mind as his rushed plans of escape vanished one after the other. There seemed no way to get into shade; his body wouldn't respond to his commands.

"Witches! What have you done?"

He finally managed a long silent moan as he realised his true predicament. He had been paralyzed and left to die in the sun.

~~~

None of the coven got any sleep. All of them were too frightened and there was too much to do. For the first time in many years, they welcomed the rising sun. Its heat was now a protective field against those who loathed it. All through the twilight hours, they had toiled to rid their home of the spilled blood and broken glass. The women had ventured outside to clear the debris from the slosh of melting ice. They had even flirted with the notion of clearing the bodies of the dead family from their house, but Celestine terminated any thought of venturing too far and so close to dawn. The coven would remain where they were.

By the time the sun had awakened and pulled itself out from beyond the horizon, the witches had removed all traces of last night's battle as best they could. With that done, they had retreated to a lower room, where Lucian's body lay on a table. Her head had been retrieved and a black blanket had been draped over the corpse to hide her indignity.

Emmarah had reappeared in the morning, to great relief and many questions. She bade them patience and to put aside their questions until after the mourning period. She led the prayers and ceremonies that would continue all day. Celestine watched her and she seemed distracted, disorientated and miles away. Celestine knew that her mother and she were connected telepathically, although her gift was basic compared to Emmarah's.

As the sun rose, she had wanted to speak to Emmarah about the vampire and the future of their coven. She had even felt a strange feeling about the vampire. Something was not right with him. But the chance to speak did not seem to come and Emmarah's state had made her put it far behind her. "*If she had felt something,*" she thought to herself, "*then Emmarah must have felt it on a greater scale?*" Celestine tried hard to break into her mother's thoughts. Emmarah suddenly looked at her; she had been caught.

"Yes my child. I have felt it greater."

"*What is it? The Nosferatu?*" Her mental voice broke in fear.

"Yes. The curse has taken effect but we are still not out of danger."

"What curse? I thought he had fled!?"

"No. We must prepare ourselves for his revenge."

Celestine became overwhelmingly agitated at the sudden waste of time mourning Lucian. She had been a close friend, but the coven was at risk.

"In time my dear."

For so long, it seemed they mourned and prayed for Lucian, until Emmarah finally ushered the women upstairs.

To Celestine's relief, they would at last begin the defense.

Emmarah sat them down and quickly began, the dread in her voice constant, "I have failed in my first duty--to protect us all from those who wish to harm us. I should have destroyed him, but I merely disabled the brute. That monster that we dared to know, I now admit, stupidly unleashed, will come again."

The women's faces only slightly showed their fear; the strength in their mother held it off from growing any stronger.

"I would understand if you wanted to leave, but I believe we can win and we will win. We are many and he is just one. Just before sunset, we will circle our home three times, then bar all windows and doors. Our spells will enchant and strengthen our foundations, so he will never set foot in our coven again.

"Mother?" Doleen interrupted. "And Lucian?"

"I know it was our intention to put her in the earth tonight; instead, she will be sent on her journey after victory."

The words filled them with resolve.

"Yes after victory, we will put her in the earth."

Emmarah stood up. "Now, we have just a few hours before sunset. Collect all candles you can muster and each in her own mind find the courage and strength. I will take Celestine into the town and will return soon. When you see us return, you will leave the house and commence our battle."

They all understood and began to go about their work, while the two women stepped outside.

They walked quickly, desperately trying to reach their destination unseen. Their black skirts stuck out amongst the coloured clothes of the occasional passersby. It was in vain; most of the journey they were gawked at every turn of the road. Mothers held onto their children; men grimaced, ready to strike. A quick glance and stare from the witches in their direction was enough to stop them cold. Who would dare bother with a witch?

Obviously, the discovery of the dead family had spread quickly. Aggression was common now; the witches could read it in their minds. Never had this aggression come to anything physical. Today was a turning point. Today revenge was plastered all over the townsfolk's faces and minds.

"I have never felt such anger," Emmarah whispered.

"Will they attack?" questioned Celestine, without fear.

"No, they are still frightened and weak, but their courage is building. It will only take a few more houses of dead children for them to slit our throats."

That was not what Celestine wanted to hear. Bad memories began to stir long and forgotten times and places.

"We will soon be there. I want to show you something."

It had been so long since Celestine had walked the streets here. She had not been born here; some place in Bavaria, a town long forgotten. There had been a girl, her own age, who dressed as she does now. A little girl witch, Skylance was her name and her birth mother was Emmarah. Celestine had watched them. They talked to her without moving their lips. She would sneak over to their house in the middle of the night to watch the other women move things without using their hands. On certain nights, they would all sit in a circle holding hands and bring the dead back to life. Her blood went cold when her own grandmother appeared to her.

But it had all ended. The villagers had grown strong and attacked the coven, after a child had been found near the house, drowned in the creek. Two girls were killed on the spot without mercy, another two were captured and hung in the town square. Skylance was one of them. Celestine could hear Emmarah scream from the woods, as her little girl's life was terminated.

So Celestine ran away to the woods and joined the remaining women. She changed her name from Maria to Celestine. The words sounded so comforting when Emmarah had said them as they walked across the land. After days of wandering came the night when they silently slipped into Aideon and made their new home.

"Here we are." Emmarah announced.

Celestine turned to see her face. There were tears in her eyes. She had been watching Celestine's memories along with her.

Looking away across the town square there was nothing and no one. Then Celestine stopped and shuddered, a heartbeat pulsed in anger. She looked further, only a statue of an ancient boy Prince who had given all his possessions away to the poor. She gazed at this golden statue then realised ... it was alive!

"Yes it's him," her mother said with a slight hint of dread. "Cursed to stand as gold by day and by night he is free."

Celestine was too dumb for words. The violence and vulgarity that spewed from the statue's unmoving lips was far greater that she had ever heard. Such words and curses she could barely understand. The vampire's pain could be felt in her own body and soul as the sun burned the exposed flesh, as if there was no gold protecting it. She felt no pity.

"Let's leave now, Celestine."

They turned their backs on him and left the vampire to singe in the sun for a short while longer.

"We will not go home just yet. We will circle the town to prevent those who also wish to harm us from entering.

"Other vampires?" Celestine asked.

"Possibly. He may have allies. We cannot be sure, only prepared."

The two headed out of the dirty, cramped streets. They walked on the edges, passed the outer houses and through the woods.

Celestine knew this was the time to ask Emmarah.

"I told you I was wrong." Emmarah said.

"What did you mean?"

"After Skylance's death, I totally rejected god and naturally I believed that Lucifer would be help me. He came to me you know, or what I believed was him. He told me they would kill her, but I didn't believe it. So I made a pact, Celestine. He would give me the secrets of the universe in exchange for my service. But I never could kill the innocent and that is why we have preyed on the vagabonds and thieves of the world."

"But Lucifer wanted innocents?"

"I believe so. Lucifer told me about the vampire and I believed we could become immortal and our little family could live forever. But I was naïve and stupid--I should have known that a soul cannot pick and choose what it wants from both sides. It must pick a side and stay on it. So now, because of my stupidity, I have put us all in danger."

Celestine said nothing at first. She too had long lost her faith and naturally believed she was a child of the devil. But only now had the full reality of what that meant dawned on her.

"But can we protect ourselves from the vampire?"

"We can, but not from Lucifer."

"Then we're damned?"

Emmarah did not reply.

"Our ideals were misplaced, but I still truly believe there is power out there that does not belong to god or the devil. I thought that I had found it, but it is power that has been usurped."

Celestine's step had fallen behind Emmarah's. Her mouth was open in shock.

"You can repent, but I don't know whether that will do any good."

"What about the others?"

"Don't tell them."

"Why?"

"Because they will kill us."

151

"It seems we're going to die anyway."

"I need time to think, Celestine. We can drive away the vampire and then we can take on the devil. I believe we can do it. We must find that power. Will you help me?"

"Of course."

"Then let's finish this and get back."

Out in the woods, they encountered no man or beast. It was as if nature had fled the town in fear of the coming storm.

They timed their return perfectly with sunset and the women exited the house, ready to plant the final ring around the house. Together, they recited words and sayings from the Grand Grimwar, the black bible of witches. The coven circled the house three times and assembled in front of the door to hear Emmarah speak the seal.

"Three times thy rope has been turned, Oh Lord. And now I stamp the lock and key. To seal in those who serve only you and let those who do not, fall into oblivion. As the Earth breaks away and the two sides revealed. So it has been done and it shall be delivered."

The invisible steel wall now built, the women, in pairs, entered their bunker to wait the final sunset and the first assaults. The windows and doors were barred with furniture and candles were lit in every room.

The coven gathered in a circle. Dark prayers were recited from their lips. There was nothing else they could do tonight, until the vampire arrived to begin his bloody task.

As the sun melted away and the chilly empty night swarmed in to take its place, the people ran for shelter, as was their custom after months of terror. They now knew that to walk the nights was to meet your end. It had been taught hard. The night was for the dead.

~~~

Over in the town square, something welcomed the new cool night. The vampire transformed; the gold disappeared and his red sore skin was revealed. He stepped from the mount; the pain stung like a thousand knives and he moaned out in agony. Blood ran from his wounds and the skin fell away from the bones. His eyes were flooded with crimson wine and ached with blindness. The stench of burnt hair and flesh hung around him like a vulture over a disabled animal. Blood and revenge were on his mind as he stepped from the square and disappeared into the dark shadowy streets with a long pain riddled moan.

The coven shuddered as they felt him wake. The townsfolk buried themselves deeper in their beds as he walked. He felt himself come alive as revenge spun in his mind. This town now belonged to him.

He was no fool; he knew the witches would protect themselves with their prayers and whatnot. Another way must be found, but not yet. The pain of his wounds was too great and kept interfering with his train of thought. Running warm blood he must find and have.

After his body did its best to carry him through the town, he came to a halt in the middle of a cobbled street. The cold breeze kissed his open sores, soothing the ache, easing his mind so that he could think. The house nearest to him was the random target. The door smashed easily, his strength, though undernourished, was still greater than any man's. A scream escaped in a dark corner, mixed in with the sound of breaking wood. He followed it through the dark until he came to another door. He tore it apart with his hands; the scent of blood behind it fuelled his aggression.

As he stepped into the room, something hard struck his face, which split his already weak skin. The impact stopped him for a moment. His assailant attacked again, taking advantage of the confusion. Now the vampire had regained his composure and counter attacked. The attacker went for another blow, but was held by the beast and the beast wouldn't let go. Screams of a woman and children echoed in the tiny room; a companion to the sounds of his thirst as he took his pleasure on the man.

The body was drained and dumped on the floor. His attention now focused on the next victim. His raw hands seized the children by the legs as they cried out. He normally never bothered with children, but tonight he was desperate. The mother screamed and held onto their bodies, but her strength was not enough and she had to endure the torment of having to watch her babies bled before her eyes.

"You devil's monster, go back to hell!"

He grinned. The blood was good and he could feel his skin heal itself as the fresh blood swam and filled up his empty veins.

"You're next, my love."

"No!" She cried and lunged at the vampire in vain. The monster wrapped her tight in his arms and ripped the bedclothes from her voluptuous body. He forced her back on the bed gently and slowly, as a lover would. She whimpered and sniffed the hot breath from his decaying mouth, which made her stomach turn. She closed her eyes and waited for what was to come.

The vampire was gentle as he could be. It had been years since he was this close to a woman in this situation. But what she thought, was not his caper. He put his burnt lips all over her face and breasts, slowly working his way to her throat. He lingered a little before plunging his sharp teeth into her tender skin.

It was done. The occupants were dead. He stood pondering by the door. The blood had cleared the pain and his cruel mind could now wreak its havoc. He went back into the room and collected the bodies and blankets. The two adults were thrown over each of his shoulders, along with three blankets off the beds. The two children were put on top of their parents. Their combined weight was not too much, but it was enough to make him cringe with pain. He was determined to manage the short distance to the witch's coven.

The women hovered in the dark, behind the candles. They stopped their words, as each felt the presence of the vampire outside the wall they had planted before sunset.

"What do we do mother?" Celestine asked calmly.

"Nothing," stated Emmarah, almost brushing away the question as irrelevant. Then she had a change of thought.

"Spirit, go to the window and observe."

The girl did as told and got up and went to the boarded window. With all her strength, she removed a piece of the plank and glanced out at the pitch black night.

"I see him. He looks bigger." There was uncertainty in her voice at the sight of the shadow.

"Was he now stronger or is it a trick of the night?" Emmarah asked herself.

"He knows of our protection," she finally said.

"Will it change anything?" Spirit asked, turning back to the group.

"I don't think so."

Spirit turned back to the vampire out in the openness of the plain that led to the forest.

"He is moving over to the trees."

"And?"

"He is trying to climb one."

This was not right. All the women expected a fury of assaults aimed at smashing the house to pieces and their blood drained while in his arms. This suspense only tormented them.

Emmarah picked herself up and went to the window to see for herself. It was pitch black and she could only see a faint movement in the edges of the wood. She even doubted her sensing of the beast but no, it was him. He was just playing tricks.

He lingered by the trees for some time. A crow digested its meat among its branches. Then he climbed down and walked away back into the town. The witches could hear his silent mental laughter in their minds. The vampire walked fast and eventually disappeared amongst the houses and buildings. Emmarah turned back to the tree and saw what resembled bodies hanging from the branches.

It was almost dawn when the witches ventured out. All night, they had worried over the bodies in the tree. To their frustration, they would have to wait until the curse's effect took hold again and the vampire was once more caged in his gold armor. Still, none would dare go out at night to do the deed.

They ran quickly over the white ground. Snow had fallen during the night and made the speed difficult. It was very cold and the women could not stay out long with the freezing conditions numbing their fingers. As they neared closer to the edge of the woods, the strange shapes dangling off the branches revealed themselves without doubt. Bodies. Four of them. The mother and father were hung separately with their two sons attached to their backs. All still wore their night attire, except the mother, who was completely naked. Even the torn apart bodies they had witnessed over the years didn't seem to compare to the sadness of the sight of the little bodies covered with snow and their sleeping faces.

"Cut them down," ordered Emmarah, her mouth barely moving in the cold. The witches cut the family down, one by one, and as each was liberated from the blanket that gripped tight around their throats, they were carried back to the house. Two women to an adult and one to a child. As the last, the father, was cut down a loud moan lifted up out of the sleeping town.

"We are safe now," the witches' adopted mother reassured them, as she looked over the man's neck, hoping to find his probable cause of death. She found it quickly enough and it was what she had thought. Two red marks lay exposed on the side of his neck. As the body was taken away, she scanned the surrounding area, hoping on fate that no one had seen them.

A lone farmer gazed out of his smudged window at the sight and crime. He watched the women retreat back from the woods, across the snow and into what he knew was a witches' coven.

The town was in much fury by midmorning. Three houses of dead had been found, all brutally drained of blood. The more outspoken demanded the priests rid Aideon of all this evil.

"In time," they answered. They themselves were still reeling from the shock of the unchallenged existence of evil. Slowly, the smoke was rising from the embers of a bitter people. They had been suppressed and frightened for so long. Now there was a stir in the dark deep coldness of the lion's den.

~ ~ ~

The sun fell from another day and released the vampire from its burning grasp. He stepped from the mount, his skin again raw and bloody. This was far worse than he could ever imagine. It was living in damnation; it was pure hell. Every inch of him seethed and cooked.

"An eternity of this?" he cried to the dark sky.

His body simply couldn't take much more and he believed even god couldn't take this pain.

All through the day, he had listened to the people express their anger and repulsion over his actions during the night. Retribution, justice, and violence stirred in their veins. But he was not their target. The witches bore the brunt of the people's damning curses. All that was needed was another push, to finally throw them over the cliff and into open revolt. That pleasure was all his tonight.

There was no time to waste. First, his wounds needed to be healed. Only after draining twelve bodies did his skin look normal--a fact he had discovered last night when his thirst devoured three families. If this hell were to continue, then the entire population of this miserable town would cease to exist in a matter of weeks. That's if he could hold out that long.

Violating houses was slow and the blood was not enough; he needed a lot of sweets in one jar. He turned his body in a circle, thinking as he did.

"Where? Where would I find enough blood?" He stopped.

"*The orphanage.*" Almost every town had one, he was sure this one would also. But where? "*The church!*" The pieces fell together in his mind, giving a sense of joy when everything just clicks. For a moment, he adjusted his bearings. His memory desperately tried to find the church's whereabouts. He remembered; he knew where it was and set off down the dark empty streets.

He found it easily enough. At this moment, as he stood at its gates, it occurred to him that he may not be able to enter this house of God. So he waited and collected his thoughts, while the stinging of his burns ate away at his patience.

He circled the grounds, looking for another way in. Here, by the back, he found the building that was his target. He lifted himself up so he could peer over the tall wall. The hard stone gnawed at his tender hands, making him cry out as the pain became too much. Without command from his brain, they gave way on their own and he crashed to the slush on the ground. The wall was too high for his damaged body; if he was at full strength there would be no problem, but tonight ... But it would be worth it.

There was a stone building not too far from the wall. He just needed a way in. Nearby was a large tree; its branches hung over the wall and disappeared over the churchyard side. That was his way in.

The climbing was agony. Every grip was burning red metal and he left bloody hand prints all over the wood. Branches slapped his face, leaving ugly welts on the skin, even the soft leaves would sting his open blisters. Determined, he pressed on until finally he was clear of the wall and he let himself drop to the wet grass.

Here his forgotten question of the powers of God was answered. Steam rose from the grass where he lay exhausted. He screamed among his tears of torture as the heat further damaged his body. With his remaining strength, his mind pushed his body to save itself. Moved by desperation and anger, he got up and raced to a stoned pathway and collapsed in its safety.

He lay there, panting and breathing heavily, wondering if this was all worth it. The melted snow on the cold surface was good and he soaked it up, not wanting to leave its chill. Then something caught his ear, a heartbeat. He became alert and ready. With his night vision, he scanned about him. The vampire turned in a circle and saw a man staring back at him; a candle lit his petrified face.

"Who goes there?" the man asked, his words riddled with fear. The vampire stepped forward and closed the gap.

"By the law of God, answer!" The courage was building in the priest's voice, but it was too late now. He had only a moment to gaze into evil's own eyes, as the vampire appeared in his candlelight.

Quickly he was drained and the body thrown through the church's stained glass window, smashing it into a thousand pieces and shredding the priest's corpse before it landed broken on the cold altar floor. The tinkling of falling glass sang out into the night until its song dimmed down to silence.

"*No time to waste now*," he thought to himself, as he bolted to the building window. Voices and footsteps were muddled in the dark end of the yard, but that's the direction he didn't need to go.

He shattered the glass as he flew through it and landed in a rough heap on the floor. All of the children awoke without a sound, as the man crashed in. Some were already awake because of the event a moment before and ran from the window as the glass sprayed over them.

First, he went to the door and threw a child from his bed and tilted it up against the door to create a barricade. Now he could turn his attention to the frightened children, shivering in their beds.

One by one, he bled them, only being interrupted when a lone brave priest showed his face at the broken window. The vampire blooded this face with a bed, thrust through the hole where glass had once been.

The children cried in terror, too frightened to escape. Slowly, as he moved around the room and did his dirty work, the cries became silent. Only in the far end of the large room were there any signs of movement and sound. The monster could not get to these others; too many priests had broken into the room and barred his way. Their crosses and holy water were too damaging to his fragile skin.

It was time for him to leave; in his weakened state he could be easily overpowered. He had done enough anyway. He picked up six little empty bodies and made a charge for the broken window.

The priests reeled back in horror as he came towards them. They fled from the opening, letting him out into the midnight air. There were nine of them gathered around, all with crosses around their necks. Tonight they had not expected a visit from the devil.

"What are you creature?" A brave one asked. He saw his chance and took it.

"Merely a servant."

He said nothing else as he sped from the church yard, the soil still hot under his feet. There was still the problem of the wall and how to get himself and his baggage over it. Without any compassion, he began throwing the tiny bodies over the wall and to the ground on the other side. That done, he re-climbed the tree and dropped himself to safety with his last bit of strength. The pain of the jagged branches and his bloody hand prints reminded him of sunrise. Only a few more hours to wait and he would have to endure the sunlight again. He hoped that this would be the last. As quickly as he could with his damaged hands, he collected the dead corpses from the slop on the ground and raced to the witches den to dump them.

~~~

The snow that gently began to fall found him in a gutter on a street. He sat in thought, after delivery of his cargo, exhausted after leaving the dead children on the witches' doorstep. He feared the coming of the morning and it depressed and frightened him. Nothing had ever frightened him so much and once again he prayed that this was the last. *"What if it's a lie? What if it doesn't work and the spell is not broken with the witches' death?"* He mused. *"Then death is the only way out."*

The white snowflakes that landed on his sore hands felt good. They melted quickly and sank into his skin, soothing the pain.

"Only blood can heal my pain," he told the sympathetic snow. "And I may need more than this town can supply."

The vampire waited to hear the screaming of the population, but heard nothing. The priests were maybe waiting for morning when the sun strips away the black and things that cannot be seen at night are revealed. He waited and listened, but there was nothing. With hours left to sunrise, he would need to replenish his strength to survive the day. The children's blood was good but he had miscalculated his needs. Six children were dead and his skin had only slightly healed itself.

There was no movement from the coven either. They would not leave until the curse had taken effect; he knew that. So he left them and went to search for the things he needed.

The vampire raided three more houses. This time, the neighbors were alert and came to the rescue. With no pity, they were driven back and slaughtered. The courage of the people was rising, but he smashed it down into silence.

The blood made him drunk; too much made him sick. He had learned that the hard way over the years. One person was enough a night, but tonight he didn't care.

He dragged a woman, still alive, through the streets. Her family he had murdered and thrown their bodies into the street. They had all screamed so loud; they were fearful of letting go of this mortal coil. Surely the priests should have acted in force? But all was still.

The house was still. Only a soft light of a candle burned through the cracks in the window. The woman cried and begged to be let go. He did not listen; he was too drunk on merry wine to care. He dropped her to the ground and picked up one of the children's bodies still scattered around the witch's door.

With no effort, the little girl was thrown through the nearest window on the second floor. It shattered the glass but was held by the wood barricade and so lay in a grotesque position on the window ledge.

The captive woman shivered in the cold. As the vampire was distracted, she took her chance to escape and began to crawl away. But he saw her, picked her up and brought her back to the door. He could feel heartbeats behind the walls and sensed snooping ears.

"It is finished!" he cried out to the hidden witches. There was no reply. Looking down at the woman, he saw her tears freeze on her cheeks. Her eyes and lips shook as much from the fear as from the cold. He bit down and drank, even though he wouldn't be able to hold it down. His body was full of blood and couldn't take more.

Nevertheless, he kept on drinking, until she was empty. The tightness in his stomach began immediately and retarded his efforts to stand up straight. Without help from his mind, his body fought the excess fluid. There was only a slight discomfort as he vomited the blood. It sprayed all over the front wall of the witches' home. The laughing he couldn't contain as the blood. Even while his stomach pumped out the last pints, he laughed and the blood dripped off his lips, which he wiped off with his hand.

Now satisfied, he walked back into the streets to await his transformation and the witches' end. For morning, surely the people with priests would raid them and his revenge would be sweet and his life returned to him.

~~~

The morning heard the cry of the vampire as he was pulled back into his cast. The witches, broken and fearful, awoke. Some had risen earlier and repaired the broken window and retrieved the tiny girl's body from its sad fate. Others had carefully exited the front door to collect the frozen bodies and hide them.

"What will we do?" Celestine whispered to Emmarah. "We can't keep hiding the evidence each night. Soon our house will be full of corpses."

"We have a new threat." Emmarah put her arm around her adopted daughter. "He has stirred the town into action. They are still weak and scared, but they are determined to stamp out what creates that fear. And that source is us."

Suddenly, a pretty blonde girl came up to them.

"Yes, Laideon?"

"Mother, the people are outside."

"What?! Did they see you bring in the bodies?"

"Yes. We only recovered three before we were spotted from the gate."

For the first time, Celestine saw Emmarah afraid. She ran to the window and began to pull off the planks. All of them could hear the men folk screaming from the pathway. Thumps banged against the outside of the house. The occasional window broke and shattered.

With a board off, she could see the mob outside. Her worst fears were now realised. Spread out along the hedgerow was, as it seemed to be, the whole population of Aideon. All of the faces had a mask of anger and hatred. Many threw stones and rotten fruit at the house. In the center rose a giant cross, borrowed from the church. Around it a circle of black clad priests read from their Bibles.

Gradually, those at the gate broke it down. The fear let them advance no further. They waited for the priests, protected by their crosses, to lead the charge. Slowly, the small party edged their way forward, followed by the people. Many had crosses around their necks and strips of cloth sewn to their shirts in a pattern of a cross. As they advanced, they continued to pelt the house with stones and food with gradual accuracy.

The faces of the people, the witches could see clearly. Their anger was now more prevalent and with it a curse more painful and real.

"Burn the witches!" they cried in unison.

A barrage of stones, rocks, and bricks, clearly aimed at Emmarah, ricocheted off the wooden barricade protecting her. She retreated from the window as the barrage continued.

Her flock's faces showed their fear. They were paralyzed with it. In their minds there seemed nothing they could do.

"What do we do now?" sneered Doleen. Emmarah kept quiet.

Only the mob's anger echoed through the warm room. Outside, a cool breeze swept in, but did nothing to chill the resentment inside the people. Still they persisted, following the titanic cross with its sleeping Jesus nailed to its surface. Gradually, they came closer to the front of the house and as they neared, the wind blew harder. It lifted up the snow and threw it at the townsfolk, who quivered and stopped in their tracks, their arms up to protect their eyes.

The priests kept on coming, until they stood at the house. Gently, the cross was put down at the door and rested on the house itself. Like a vacuum in heaven, the snow lifted up from the ground in a wild wind. In a perfect circle, a loose wall rose around the witch's coven, blocking it out from view.

Startled, the priests fell and tumbled. The people pulled back from the frozen curtain with open mouths. They watched the reverse snowfall rage in intensity until it finally burned itself out and the flakes gently fell back to the soil.

It was quiet as the mob recovered, ready to protect themselves against any further witch's tricks. They lay in the snow, waiting for something to happen. To attack or retreat? One priest stood up, then another, then another, until they were all up and at the door. With a mighty cry, the people rose up and charged forward. They brought their axes to bear against the wooden door. Finding the dead bodies of the children aggravated and boiled their blood further.

Quickly, the door was smashed and men soon flooded the lower floor. Here they found nothing but a trapdoor in the floor.

Accompanied by a priest, another gaggle of revenge seekers bolted up the stairs. Here, they found the entire coven sitting in a circle on the floor. With fanatical fury, they pounced on the women. Clawed hands ripped their clothes and beat them mercilessly. If it were not for the priest's presence, the witches would have been killed on the spot.

"No! They are to be tried. Take them outside," ordered the old priest. He turned to a man next to him. "Burn this room."

"No," another priest appeared at the doorway. "Father Letinburg has ordered it to remain."

"So be it," again the old priest looked at the men. "Rip it to pieces then."

With glee, they went about their business. The body of Lucian was stripped and thrown into a corner, her head impaled on a candlestick. Everything was broken, everything was ripped and tossed about. Their frustration had been vented.

The witches were dragged out into the cold morning. They said nothing as the people assembled in the snow and began throwing rubbish. They threw anything that would release the pent-up emotion and repulsion that had brewed for months.

Under the barrage, the witches tripped and fell in the now muddy ground. This got no sympathy, only a jolt in the back and another barrage of projectiles.

Laideon cracked. She broke her silence and appealed to the crowd to listen.

"We did not do it! Only the Nosferatu who lurks in your streets and woods is capable of such barbarism!"

Her voice was a beacon for those waiting for a target and she was pelted to the ground. Only the rough handling of a guard kept her dragging along. She caught Emmarah's eyes as she lifted her head.

"It won't do any good." Her voice was a comfort for the poor girl. Laideon waited for more words but Emmarah said nothing else and looked away.

~~~

Father Dunkat made his way from the upstairs level, where he had gone to investigate the mob destroying its contents. At the bottom level, another priest, Father Letinburg, met him.

"Father Dunkat come with me, I've something to show you."

He led him down to an open trap door in the floor at the rear of the house. A horrible odor drifted out of its dark bowels.

He followed Letinburg down the stairs until he came to a room. Here were a number of men with candles sifting through the lines of dead bodies lined up in rows along the far wall. In places, they were three high and ran the width of the small chamber. Dunkat forced himself away and threw up. Letinburg came over to comfort him and his candlelight revealed another dead body lying at Dunkat's feet, his vomit all over it. Letinburg ignored the dead child, obviously a little one stolen from the orphanage.

"I recognise her."

"Yes, Greta. Except for two females all the others are male in various stages of decomposition."

"What type of evil lurks here?" Dunkat spat.

"Whatever it was they will hang for it."

"Are they all from Aideon?" asked Dunkat, now recovered enough to look at the piles of dead.

"Yes. I recognise those that still have a face still lookable. William Burnster and his family are here. Their bodies frozen stiff and the children from the orphanage are here too."

"Can we find the cause of death?"

Letinburg turned away from Dunkat and called over to a man hunched over the pile of dead men.

"Doctor Grunber. Do we have a cause of death?"

"All the males I have examined have a knife wound running from their chest down to their pubic bone. I am no expert on ritual matters and don't want to offer my opinion--that's up to your good office--but there is a pattern, men pinned down and a knife plunged into their hearts and dragged down passed their waist."

"Good God," Dunkat whispered.

"And the others?"

"The Burnster family are very different." The Doctor got up and went to a pile against a different wall.

"There are no knife wounds. Except Helda, all are clothed in their night attire; their only wounds are two marks on their necks."

Grunber passed a candle close to the wounds so the priests could see.

"My God, it's the mark of the vampire." Dunkat knew what it was instantly.

The Doctor continued. "The bodies are dead one day. Some only hours but they are all drained of blood. That does not happen naturally."

"Witches and vampires joined together in the bowels of our town! This surely is the Devil's work," hissed Letinburg. Dunkat dumbly nodded his agreement unable to take his eyes off the bodies at his feet.

"This is your domain Father Dunkat. I feel your expertise will come in handy," said Letinburg grudgingly.

Dunkat felt the heat of annoyance in his blood. He had been telling them for months that there was something unnatural about this town and no one had believed him. The attack on the church had finally made many of them listen to him.

Now the years of constant cynicism and outright hostility about his work on Lucifer and his followers was going to come to the fore. He had always justified it saying that believers in Christ had to know the evils of the world so as to avoid or defeat them.

"Let us go, Father. We are late for the Council meeting," Letinburg ordered.

The two priests left the pit, followed by the Doctor. They passed the rooms torn apart by the vengeful people, past the snow and mud covered ground the people had left following the witches as they were led to their trial.

In the town square, the hangmen assembled the wooden platform of the old gallows. The people expressed their approval of its use and no more nights of fear.

Cemented in his metal cast was the vampire. His mind was waiting for tomorrow, when he would watch those bitches die and the curse lifted. Tomorrow was freedom. He smiled through his bitter pain, as he watched the rope dangle from the wooden beam.

~~~

Mayor Ade continuously banged his hand upon the bench. His rage terrified the six members present.

"We must hang them now! No trial! The whores must be exterminated to end this!"

"No," Dunkat patiently spoke.

"Why?"

"It must be done in the morning, to safeguard ourselves from whatever lurks at night. If they hang at night, then their spirits will have the full power of darkness in which to spread this disease. It must be finished at morning, so we wait."

The Mayor slumped back in his chair, his head down, defeated. "I just want them off this Earth as quickly as possible." He pleaded his emotions.

"Yes, we all do."

"They still plead their innocence," interjected Letinburg.

"I've heard. They say the Nosferatu was the destroyer." The Mayor mocked the witch's alibi.

"Perhaps they are right your Lordship," Dunkat's bomb stumped the audience. They all looked at him in repulsion and terror. The Mayor looked dead straight into the priest's eyes.

"Are you insane Father Dunkat? What sympathy for darkness inhabits your soul?"

Dunkat turned away and approached the Doctor, sitting motionless in a corner.

"Doctor, was it not two marks upon the necks of the children and Burnster family?"

"It was."

"And what of the other children, dead in the orphanage and the adults on the street?"

"It was also."

He faced back to the Mayor.

"Your Lordship. My fellow Brothers can testify that it was no witch that ravaged those tiny bodies. It was a man. He scooped them up and drank their blood. One by one. Our Brother, Father Heilden, was found dead drained of blood upon the altar. He had been thrown through the church window. I myself saw the beast. A six foot monster with fangs like a wolf."

The dignitaries present remained quiet and listened to the Father.

"It is not one enemy we fight; alas, it's two, two evils working separately. Their paths crossed. How? We do not know, but we do know what for: the extermination of our population.

"Sweet Jesus," whispered Ade.

"Those bodies in the pit were all were killed by a dagger in some bizarre ceremony that I cannot imagine. That was the witches' work and they will hang for it. But what of the bodies over the years that have been found amongst the streets and above all, in the woods? All drained of blood. Two marks, no ritual, no clean dagger cut and no pattern. All murdered by a savage."

"Your conclusion, Father?" asked the Mayor.

"You must understand that the witches have been caught and will hang tomorrow, but the killings will go on, because there is a vampire who we must also hunt down and destroy."

The priests and officials present sat quietly, lost in their thoughts of the swirling evil that spun around their community.

"Where do we begin?" Ade inquired.

"There can be so many places," offered Letingburg.

"We find his house of evil by day and I know where that is"

~ ~ ~

"Such a relief to have the sun disappear," the vampire thought. The burning rays had gone and replaced with a freezing night and light snow that soothed his red skin.

He had to be careful now. The gallows had been erected and with them, a light guard. He must be quiet when he killed, mustn't raise the people into action and attack him. Through the streets, he sought out the weak and those who couldn't run.

He walked on until he came to the town pub. It bustled with noise and celebration; never had it seen such life and joy. Now with the witches caught, the people celebrated their renewed freedom. The vampire smiled; he could celebrate too, for the morning would bring his own liberty. But now there were wounds to heal and he waited in the shadows across the street, waiting patiently despite his immense pain.

It was not long before a dizzy bloated man wandered from the building. He was rugged up against the cold and stumbled on occasion.

The vampire made his move and trailed him far from the liquor joint, its noise slowly fading in the distance.

The man was quite drunk and his reflexes suffered because of it. Quickly, the monster hit him hard about the head and dragged his limp body from the still street. Bewildered and slobbering over himself, the man barely retaliated as the vampire rolled up the man's sleeve and bit down.

It took a little longer to almost drain him. He decided not to kill him, only a tiny drink. He was not sure of the effects that the alcohol would have on him.

"*No, take it all.*" His aching blisters demanded and he obeyed until the point of savagery.

When finished, he wiped his mouth, rolled the man's sleeve back down and left him dead in the alley. Now he could pay the witches a visit.

~~~

"I can hear him coming," Celestine whispered from her chains. As they sat about in the dark of the prison, they were jolted back into reality with her words. Each braced themselves for what was to come.

The jail was bitterly cold; the barred window let in every inch of the freezing night. They had been given no blankets or food to help them through the night. Instead, they huddled themselves in pairs to keep warm.

With trepidation, the witches' eyes were centered on the window. Slowly, a scarred face rose up between the bars. The witches shook and curled themselves up tighter together, as the face smiled.

"Good evening. I hope you're enjoying yourselves?" The vampire began laughing at his mockery.

Emmarah picked up a discarded pottery cup and threw it at him. It smashed aloud, disturbing the guard. At the rattle of keys at the bulky door, the face disappeared. The door creaked open and in rolled a fat old man.

"What are you bitches doing? Stay quiet, I say, or I'll beat you so hard we'll have to drag you out to hang you!"

"It was him," the blonde, Laideon, answered him. He hit her hard with his baton across the back. She whimpered under the pain, but did not cry out.

"Perhaps it is not your usual habit to sleep at night. Maybe you would rather be out killing, eh?"

All the witches' eyes bore up at him. They were weak, but the combined power could still rip apart his soul.

The old man put his hand to his heart, as it began to ache. He struggled to leave the cell. The witches continued to watch and to whisper their words, over and over. The guard closed and locked the door and sat down, exhausted and in pain. Back in the cell, the witches waited.

The guard's mind filled with words and images not his own. Now his head ached and throbbed with every rush of blood, as his heart pumped faster and faster. He groaned aloud at the stress as the witches' words send his heart into overdrive. It pumped until it exhausted itself and blew to pieces. His soul was torn to shreds, as the blood ran out of his mouth and his body slumped dead.

The coven sensed his death and let go of their hold.

"Perhaps you shouldn't have done that?" Emmarah half-joked. She knew it might cause them more grief by heightening the population's paranoia and fear.

"What does it matter anyway, if we take lives? We will all die tomorrow, so we can take as many as we like with us," a brunette snarled.

Emmarah looked over at her in the corner. "I feel it as much, Tainia, but that would bring even more scorn on us."

The girl said nothing and looked away.

"So it has ended?" Celestine whispered to herself. "Will we go to hell?" she continued.

"I do not know." Emmarah answered her. "Perhaps we will all meet again in some place. Have no fear."

"So much for our worship of the Devil! Look what he has let happen to us. He betrayed us. I believed that vampire was our brother. You, Emmarah, said it was so." Laideon attacked her mother viciously. Emmarah, like the other women, was dumbstruck at this attack.

Laideon continued, with even more fury. "This has happened to you before! I saw it in your mind when you slept. Your old coven was destroyed in the same way!"

"Laideon!" Celestine tried to interject.

Ignoring her, Laideon drove on. "How is it you got away? Perhaps he will come and save you and let us hang?!" The tears sprung from her eyes and her voice became choked. "You know more than us and you will be saved."

Celestine again tried to silence her. "That's enough Laideon!"

"Well?" Laideon, hawk eyed, stared directly at Emmarah who was still in a stupor.

"If these chains did not bind me I would turn your face red with my hand!" Celestine once more tried to block her. "Silence."

It was now Emmarah's turn to defend herself. "I do not know how it all works. If I was lucky or was helped that is. I will die with all of you tomorrow. That is certain." There was another long silence before Emmarah directed her words at the blonde Laideon. "Why did you join us Laideon?"

The girl was startled for a moment by the question and searched herself before answering. "I liked the different life. I did not want to be some little housewife, I wanted a life of my own. To do as I pleased and when I pleased. No bonds. No male to treat me as a bed ornament, to do as he pleased. I wanted freedom and to have power. To have drunken males plead for mercy."

All the women smiled, reminded of their short freedom.

"I still gloat of the memory of their happiness at being invited into a room full of women for a special night," Laideon continued gleefully.

"And look what it has done to us," Celestine interrupted. She waited then went on. "What, if the women of the town knew of what it was all about, they would join us?"

"No," Emmarah stated.

"Look where it got us, our freedom gone," an invisible voice spoke out of the darkness.

"One day they will know." Another statement came from somewhere in the cell.

Emmarah ignored them all. Her body language showed her disinterest in the arguments around her. She closed her eyes and tried to sleep. Her dreams of the lost power were clear as day to Celestine.

For the girls, there was no sleep. They were all too excited at the memories and too scared of wasting any more time sleeping. And so they talked on for the rest of the night, until the scream of the vampire reminded them of their fate.

~~~

Soon the dawn of their last day arrived. With their arms bound in front of them, the witches were led in single file from the black dungeon and out into the white morning.

There was some talk still of a trial, but the death of the prison guard only nailed the coffin shut on any fair chance the women had. Some of the coven had tears swell in their eyes as the violent crowd hurled snow, garbage, and abuse their way.

As they neared the gallows, they were already wet from the snow and stained with rotten fruit. They said nothing, most with their heads down and lost in their own thoughts.

All except Emmarah. She faced the gallows, but looked beyond the crowd, which would soon see her death. Behind it, she could see the gold statue sneering back.

"Oh thy fate is sealed. Alas, could it not be in the cauldron of secrecy? Not here in the face of my enemy."

Roughly and without compassion, they were pushed up to the wooden platform. Some of the wooden planks creaked as a foot landed upon it, a testimony to the speed in which it had been put together and the age of the contraption. It had been decades since it had seen the light. The creaking wood only made it worse for the women, as with each step it sang their funeral song.

The seven nooses hung like sweet apples, begging to be picked. Delicate they seemed, as they swayed slightly with the weak wind. Each witch was led to her assigned noose. There was no hood to cover their faces and hide the agony of death. The crowd wanted it that way. They had lived their lives in fear for so long; now it was time for revenge.

The rough rope was placed over each head as the crowd waited in silence. The hangman let them linger on the gallows a little while longer. Let them feel the fear.

It was too much for Doleen. She shrieked in fear.

"We did not kill the children. The monster stands behind us!" Her words were barely distinguished amongst her crying.

As it was with Celestine the morning past, her voice was a beacon and she was pelted with anything that was at hand.

In rage and disappointment, she turned around on her stool and faced the statue. Its shadow slowly made its way across the faces assembled. The sun dented her vision, but she could still make out its shape. She spat, threw curses, threw anything she knew and could at the vampire, until, in agitation, the hangman kicked out the box from under her feet.

A cheer rose from the packed crowd. One down, six to go. The witches closed their eyes and hoped it would end soon.

"Silence!" Father Dunkat ordered the crowd. They obeyed. He paced the platform with his bible until stepping back where he started.

"Do you, whores of Satan, confess to the murders of over thirty inhabitants of God's glory?"

Silence. Only in the witches' ears was there sound. The vampire teased them. He whispered filthy words and threatened crimes against their dead bodies. For once, he let them know of his pain. He screamed a muted scream that only they could hear. Long and slow, loud and torturous.

The witches flinched at its sound. Laideon's will was breaking. She stood next to the dead hanging body of Doleen. She heard the neck snap as the rope did its work and she heard the soul scream as it was dragged to hell.

"We are innocent of the murders of the children and families!" Laideon cried out.

The crowd, repulsed at such blatant lies, again threw a salvo of debris at Laideon. Most of it was way off mark. Pieces impacted with all the witches and priests upon the platform. The rest of garbage overshot and landed among fellow citizens on the other side of the platform.

Then silence came over the crowd once again as they waited for an answer. The silence was broken this time by Emmarah.

"This is true. We are innocent of the slaying of the children, but not of the men. This is our only crime."

The mob swept itself into a fury. "At last the truth be told!" they echoed. This time the crowd did not finish its bombardment. This time it became fiercer. Cries and chants became a chorus.

"Hang them, hang them!"

Even the Mayor, caught up in his rage, pounded his tonsils, "Kill them now!"

His order caught Dunkat off guard. It was out of control now all order lost.

"The monster still lurks amongst you!" Emmarah cried out. She tried hard to ignore the torments of the vampire and the laughter of the devil himself. "He stands as a curse ..." The noose ended her sentence, as the hangman began kicking out the stools before the final blessings and prayers.

The women, now without their mother, cried as one by one, the steady wood beneath their feet was booted from under them.

Celestine braced herself as Laideon was hanged. She was next. She heard all their cries as they fell to hell. She didn't hear the hangman approach; she kept her eyes on the priest who ducked for cover as rotten fruit continued to be thrown. With all her power, she herded a message to him.

"You're right about the vampire. The statue is cursed beyond your imagination. Smash it down."

The priest looked up at her as the stool was thrust out and the light of the day became black for Celestine.

~~~

Dunkat made his way back through the town square, where only an hour ago the witches had been hanged. Their burial was more subdued than their deaths; only two dozen people bothered to follow the procession and cart to a clearing in the woods. There, a large grave had been dug through the night, for the express purpose of burying the bodies.

The square was virtually empty, except a few drunken merry men and women chasing each other through the mess of the ground.

"Such a sight," he muttered to himself.

"We fight so many evils. Evil is all around us and within us. Nothing has or will change," a voice came from behind him. He turned around to face the voice.

"Father Thun," Dunkat waited for the old man to catch up and began walking again in pace with the head of the church in Aideon. Father Thun was the eldest member of the church in Aideon, having lived there for fifty years.

Dunkat's eyes passed over the gallows as they went by. The memory of the women hanging lifeless there only hours before was still very fresh. Now, he saw the statue of Prince Raden nearby. Its gold gleam shone in the sun's rays. Suddenly he remembered the pretty witch's words.

"Smash it down."

"Why?" he asked himself.

The past few days had seen such an upheaval in the ranks of the church and town. The existence of evil had been proven, therefore the existence of God. Many strange things had been witnessed. The power of evil, it was all overwhelming.

"Can we overcome this?" he finally asked Thun.

"Haven't we already?"

Dunkat continued to look at the golden statue.

"I don't think so."

~~~

Dinner in the Rectory was quiet, too quiet. All the men had escaped into their own private thoughts and were contemplating the day's events. They had found nothing in the woods, no hiding place.

Dunkat watched over the meals and brothers. The witch's words would not leave him. On many occasions during the afternoon, when they were burying the bodies, he swore he saw her follow him around the woods. His gut ached, always a sign of his conscience urging him on.

It was nightfall already when he left the church. He had pulled out all his research material that he kept under lock and key. His interest in the occult had forced him to take serious security measures over the years. Some in the church had believed that he himself was an agent of evil. He ran a mental scan over all his provisions, cross, stake, garlic and a mirror. He stayed alert, as he went down the empty streets, conscious of being ambushed by whatever was out there.

At the corner, where the street led into the square, he caught his breath. He gripped the silver cross as he waited and gathered his courage. Hopefully, the cold weather had swept away the merry-makers and there would be no witnesses.

Slowly, he pushed his face around the corner. Only snow covered the paved plain. No bodies. The gallows still stood with a light covering of white.

He dragged his eyes towards the statue mount. It was as if his heart had broken when he saw that sight. There was no golden boy gazing out at the people.

Thinking it was a trick, Dunkat ran to the empty mount. As he climbed the stone, he felt the chill run down his spine--an empty statue mount with two bare feet marks in the thin snow.

Fighting fear, he tried to keep his composure. This was not a good place to be. After surveying all directions out of the square, he made four marks of the cross in the thickening snow layer and bolted back into the dark and back to the church. There, he would prepare for morning.

There was little hope of finding the beast tonight. Morning would come and he would smash it down.

~~~

The vampire fed well on the drunken larks that had collapsed in the streets. The cold and the alcohol made it nice and easy to catch them.

Now he wandered in his woods that had been his old home for years. Their memory had not been burned like the sun, as it had done to his body; he still knew all the paths and hiding places. Being back in his hunting ground made the past few days feel far away. Now he could heal. With the witches dead, he could go back to his former self and leave this damned town forever. He followed the path the grave party had taken this very morning, as it lumbered along with its cargo of dead bodies.

The witches grave was clearly visible. A clearing had been cut for the purpose. A cross marked each grave. This he knew without looking, as the bright light forced him not to stare at them.

"So the witches have entered the domain of God," he sneered aloud. "Let them rot!" he bellowed out at the night sky.

The light was too strong for his sunlight damaged eyes. There would be no desecration tonight, no dancing or mauling. Pity, he so wanted to break them apart and to see the face of death upon each one.

To celebrate his renewed freedom, he raced back from the woods to put his emotions into killing.

One house put up a mighty fight. The townsfolk had learned to defend their lives. A new courage had been created.

They fought with fire. Fire he could not stand. The noise awoke others and they converged into a force of faith and defiance. He had never seen such determination in their faces. Soon he would not be able to hunt and heal his wounds before leaving. It was certainly time to escape this miserable place and find a people who were still frightened of what lurked in the shadows at night.

There was no use fighting them; there were too many and he was too weak. His skin was thin and the forks and knives that pricked and sliced emptied his body of the precious blood.

He escaped back into the darkness of the woods, to heal and await the morning so that he could sleep in the safe surrounds of his grave and plan his flight.

In the morning, the sun crept higher. The vampire slept in his original hole in the soil. His eyes flashed open. A familiar sensation ran through his body.

"God no! No!" He screamed and thrashed about. The next instant he felt the burning hot knives turn into his skin, as the light of the sun bore down on him, as once again the morning found him bound and abandoned in the daylight.

~ ~ ~

Dunkat rose early. Breakfast he missed on purpose; the people had awoken them during the night. A monster had attacked a family. Its teeth were sharp, its skin was blistered and sore.

"Like a vampire left far too long in the sun," he surmised to himself.

He had spoken to the frightened people, quietly and calmly. The morning will see him dead. Bring ropes, horses, and a cart to the square at sunrise; bring all the men and light up the blacksmith's furnace.

Like the day before, the people had assembled themselves in the square. Every space was taken. They sat upon the gallows and to Dunkat's horror, they stood and hung from the walking statue itself.

Slowly, he pushed his way up the stairs of the gallows and through the crowd upon it. He was the only priest that he could see, but he knew they watched from the fringes, not believing his story.

All eyes were on him as he began to speak. "I know the reason of last night's battle. I know its name. Nosferatu. He lurks in this very square. I look at him now. The child of Aideon, the giver of gold, Raden!"

The crowd was in muted confusion. A statue brought to life? They turned their heads and faced the metal figure rising above them. Those clinging onto and around the mount stared at the figure. Could this be true? Some jumped and ran from it, as if the burning felt by the vampire inside was somehow transferred to their own skins. The rest soon took the same precautions and the statue was clear.

"For reasons I do not understand, somehow this has happened. By day, I see it before me. By night, I see only space. Believe me! With these ropes, carts, horses and men we will tear down this abomination!"

They had come to believe every word spoken by priest over the past few days. With the current events that had taken place over the past days, they had come to believe that their woods were alive with evil devils, all intent on winning their souls.

Now that they had found the courage buried deep within them, the people were determined to finish what had begun that morning.

From the sides of the square, the owners of the

horses and carts came rushing forward. Dozens of men broke ranks to join them at the foot of the statue mount.

Dunkat climbed down from the gallows and came over to show them what he wanted done, but he was not needed. By the time he had made it there, the ropes were tight around the statue's body. Hammers had already smashed the stone base, loosening the feet. So, in contemplation, he looked at the golden face and its serene expression, its arms outstretched with piles of gold coins and jewelry in its open hands. They would build another from the metal of the old.

"Father Dunkat! What are you doing?" the Mayor had arrived and was shocked at what he saw.

Dunkat merely raised his hand. "You'll see."

"But that's Prince Raden! How could you?" The Mayor was almost in tears at the sight of the desecration.

"Watch," Dunkat said, without taking his eyes off the statue.

"Pull!" the men cried in unison. The horse teams heaved hard on the ropes, as the men continued to shatter the mount. Slowly it bent. The cracking of the stone that held its supports signaled its slow surrender.

A loud crack echoed out over the hushed square. The statue swayed before the pull of the horses. Finally, as it broke from its moorings, blood splattered volcano like into the air. Its crimson water splashed over men and horses and dribbled over the sides of the mount. Frightened and repulsed, the men fled, as the statue came crashing down onto the hard square ground.

Dunkat, in shock over the blood and the cry of the vampire as it was torn from its bed, was stunned for a moment. He had not expected such gore. The Mayor covered his open mouth with a cloth.

The statue had cracked the stone street when it fell and there was blood everywhere, along with cries from the women and children who had to watch the vulgar scene.

"Father?" a frightened man spoke to him from a few metres away.

"Drag it to the furnace."

The horses were led in the direction of the blacksmith's workshop. Men and some brave women followed in a precession behind them. As the metal-encased vampire was dragged through the white streets, blood seeped from its wounds in its feet, leaving a trail of bright red behind it.

Dunkat had his own battle. The vampire had found the door to his mind. He vomited his vile words into the priest's subconscious mind. Blasphemy and obscenities spewed forth of the like Dunkat had ever heard.

"You like the power of the darkness. I know this," the vampire laughed.

"*You'll never walk again*," the priest fought back using all his determination and faith. Evil would not win. Good always conquers over evil.

Gradually, his mental steel wall blocked out the vampire's curses, until they died out altogether. The vampire, exhausted, closed down his attacks in defeat.

To the priest's relief, the horses had finally arrived outside the blacksmith's workshop.

"Is the fire ready Heinz?" he asked the blacksmith, who had come out to greet him.

"Yes Father, but I do not ..."

The priest cut him off. "You do not need to. For this thing is not human and must be destroyed. If you must understand anything, understand that."

The big man merely nodded and led the way into his business.

Dunkat turned back to the crowd. "Drag it in."

They obeyed, but quickly reeled back, complaining that the metal was hot. The priest threw them his silver cross.

"Put it on his face. Cover it with snow, wrap your hands and bring it in quickly."

Gradually the men heaved it into the rear of the room. A wooden board was put up against the furnace. They hurriedly dumped the vampire upon it, as the end of the wood began to catch fire. Here, Heinz took over.

"Pick up the end and push with all your strength."

Inch by inch, six strong men pushed the statue into the blazing furnace.

Heinz had removed the massive door during the night and the statue just fitted inside.

All of them could hear the monster scream as, bit by bit, it caught alight and melted. Dunkat looked around and saw the men flinch at its cries.

Transfixed, they watched as the statue moved and twisted with the heat. The metal drooped and slid, revealing a human face burning up. Its eyes blazed and its stench drifted out. Covering their faces, those assembled refused to leave the sight; the odor was not enough to quell their fascination.

Gently, the fire burned then retreated and only the glow of the hot metal remained. Heinz poked the small red blob of liquefied metal.

"Is it finished?" he asked Dunkat.

"It is," the priest replied.

CHAPTER II

Doctor Hewen was going through drawers of old files in an unused area of the hospital. He looked aimlessly at the names; he didn't know who they were and didn't really care. He had a reason for coming here straight after lunch. A lunch in which he spoke rarely to the other pathologists and nurses in the lunchroom. He was hiding.

He looked at his watch – 1:30pm. How long could he hide away? *"What about tomorrow you fool?"* He kept on flicking through the pages, and then would pick up another when done so he could drown out the questions that pounded away in his head.

Then his pager went off. He knew exactly why someone would be looking for him. A new body had come in.

"Shit."

He ignored it. It went off again a few minutes later. His hands were sweating as his heart burned inside him. There were footsteps coming closer. A part of him wanted to hide but another told him to finally face his demons. *"Maybe today would be different? It has to end but you know how it has to end. Confess or die."* It was too late to hide now anyway.

The door opened and Nurse Baxter looked in and found him straight away. He pretended to look through the pages but felt her come closer.

"Dr Hewen, what'cha doing down here?"

"Ah, yes," he faked surprise.

"We've been paging you."

"Oh sorry. Sorry I was coming but got distracted. What is it?"

"We've got a body come in, female, early twenties, possible OD."

"Where's Rebecca?"

"She's in the middle of those two murder victims from yesterday."

"Alright give me a minute and I'll be up there."

"Okay."

The nurse turned around and went back out of the door.

He took his time making his way to the ward. His hands were still sweating and there were patches on his body of wetness that made his shirt stick to his skin. "*How am I going to get out of this? Shit! What can I say? What can I do? How the hell am I going to get out of this?*"

Finally he got an idea. He made a phone call to another pathologist whose name jumped out from all the dozens he knew. All the while he purposely ignored the body wrapped in the blue plastic bag on the operating table just beyond the glass.

Each dial tone seemed forever as he waited for it to be answered.

"Hey Jerry, it's Brian. What are you doing now? You want to help me with this cut up?"

Jerry's reply was not the one he wanted.

"Okay, I didn't realise you were on the Gold Coast. Alright, no problem I'll see you when you get back. Bye."

He tried to sound upbeat but his whole heart had sunk.

He replaced the phone slowly as it dawned on him he might be alone to do this one. No witnesses to help him fight his demons, to confirm or deny what he was hearing.

~ ~ ~

Slowly he made his way into the operating ward. He saw his reflection in a mirror. His back was stooped and his balding grey hair was unusually wet looking. He had slowly put on his apron, mask and gloves; the last one took awhile as his bloody hands were still wet. That was good – it wasted time.

Baxter had prepared all the equipment and laid it on a table close to the bed but she wasn't in the room with him. *"Where is she? I have to have her here. She could be my witness!"*

She suddenly appeared from a back office. She smiled and he was glad to have her there but then he realised she was not dressed for surgery.

"You're not assisting?"

"No. I got the afternoon off. Got to see my son play footy at three. I told you yesterday, remember?"

"Oh yes I forgot," he did remember her telling him. "I'm disappointed; I'd love you to stay."

"Well cutting up a body sounds like fun but my son will *kill me* if I don't go and the hospital aren't going to pay OT are they?"

"Alright," he smiled but was bitterly disappointed that it was final. There would be no witnesses to confirm his sanity or madness.

"I'll see you tomorrow okay?" she said as she walked out.

"Bye," he didn't look up but fiddled with the instruments, all of them cold despite his latex gloves.

She was gone now and he was all alone with the dead girl still in her blue bag. There was a photo attached to the zipper, *Adrienne Keith*. She was blonde, attractive, in her twenties as far as he could tell by the photo of her dead body. He remembered when he was 22 and at university where there was unending partying, screwing and drinking. Great times back then but not now.

He took in a deep breath. His hands were shaking as he cut the yellow body tag chord the police put on when sealing the bag and unzipped it. Immediately there was the smell of death. In all his 29 years as a doctor he had never come across the same smell in the real world, nothing could compare to the unique stale tang of rotting human flesh. Thankfully she was reasonably fresh, three days according to the P79 form filled out by the police. Some would come in that were weeks old and they made your stomach churn.

Well there she was. He pulled away the bag and saw she only had shorts and a shirt on. Her limbs were red like a rash but he knew that's where the blood had settled when she died lying on her back. Her face had stains of blood coming out of the nose and mouth along with saliva and mucus. When you died all your fluids ran out of your body.

His tape recorder was running and he begun his external examination of her body, stating her name, gender, sex and any visible injuries. Then he cut the clothes from her body, stating again that there appeared to be no signs of any sexual assault or immediate cause of death. Again he fiddled with his instruments. It was quiet but for the hum of the air conditioner and his breathing.

As he picked up a scalpel he froze as he heard the sniffling and whimpering close to him. Determined not to look, not to acknowledge it so it would go away, he brought the scalpel close to him and looked at its shiny little blade.

"What are you doing?" came a frightened girl's voice.

"No. This can't keep happening. Not again."

He looked down at the girl while holding the scalpel high. Her eyes were wide open with fear and confusion as she watched the blade too.

He took another breath and tried to ignore the tricks his mind was playing on him.

"Please don't hurt me," she pleaded.

"You're dead," he said bluntly to himself more to steady his resolve than to comfort her.

She started crying. Swallowing heavily the doctor went about his work. He brought the knife to the top of her chest, her eyes following every movement.

"No, No, No!" she cried out. Her voice pierced the quiet of the theatre but no-one came running to see what was going on. He stopped to take another breath as he tried to control his shaking hand.

"Please don't cut me," she pleaded again.

His fear had overcome him now and he was angry.

"Shut up! You're dead! Dead! Understand that!" he screamed. Then there was silence, her face still, her eyes closed.

"Fuck this shit!"

His body was shaking with fright. Twenty-nine years of doing this and now they were speaking to him.

What had happened to him? Last week was like any other week. It was the weekend when it all went wrong. He went out to celebrate his brother's birthday. Old bugger was fifty, he remembered them racing around the yard on an old bike that broke under their weight. Somehow they got away from a beating by blaming the rusting frame and laughed together about it. Now they were married and out on the town drinking and carrying on like old drunks.

It was on the way home, yeah, he remembered but didn't want to. Alcohol was great to drown bad memories.

Determined he tried again. The scalpel touched her skin and he begun to cut.

She screamed like a wounded animal and he jumped back. "Why didn't anyone come running with all this screaming she was doing?"

Ignoring her, angry and spiteful he tried again. Damn her. He cut again and again she cried out, "Please stop! Please!"

"I have to do this! I'm sorry alright!" he tried pleading with her as she laid moaning and crying on the table. "I need to know how you died."

He was almost in tears as well.

She didn't reply. It took three hours normally to do an autopsy properly and he had never cut corners but now he was tempted. He stepped away from the table to a bench. Hidden in his drawer marked with his name was a bottle of bourbon, which he took a swig off to calm him down. *"Maybe he could tape her mouth, or put a bag over her head? Or cut the whole thing off and put it in the freezer until he was done."*

The clock ticked away. Three hours. He looked at her squirming on the table, her head towards him, her eyes wide and mouthing the words, *please.*

He wouldn't be beaten. The head had to come off. He went back to the table and grabbed a small saw, which he took over to the slab. Immediately she knew what it was for and how she hollowed with terror.

"No! No! Please don't hurt me."

"I have to it's the only way to shut you up," he yelled back. He was so frightened that he masked it with anger. He hated being scared and hated yelling but it was the only way to cope.

"One day it'll be you old man," came a male voice behind him. It was another body lying on a table; his head was out of the bag and watching him. It was the face he saw on that night, his eyes wide with shock and terror in his headlights. His wife had been sleeping, he told her it was a kangaroo; stupid bloody things just jump out in front of cars. He drank to block out the memory but it wouldn't go and now they were talking to him.

Monday was the morning it began, when they brought that man in. He had to do the autopsy himself all the while the man was whispering, "One day it'll be you old man."

"But not today," he replied with resolve before looking back at the shrieking body of the girl on his cold metal table. The metal blade glimmered in the light and reflected in the girl's horrified eyes.

"Josh?"

"Yeah," he whispered, barely awake. He again wiped the dried tears from his eyes, probably for the hundredth time over the past few days.

"I thought you were asleep?"

"Maybe I'm hoping to still wake up and this is just one of those nightmares."

"Me too," she said as she snuggled up beside him where he sat on the bed with his back against the wall and his legs hanging over the side.

It felt good to have her here; he'd go mad quicker otherwise. Her body was warm but her fingers cold where they touched his torso. Natalie was her name: she was pretty, in her late twenties, short blonde hair and brown eyes. He didn't know much about her yet despite the few days they had spent here, maybe it was because she was crying most of that time.

He had cried too at the start. Mainly because of the pain, the confusion and frustration of it all. Now it was just hopelessness because he knew his fate and there was nothing he could do about it to change it.

"So tell me how you got here?" she asked.

"To think about it cuts me up."

"It might help."

He breathed deeply, his eyes on the furniture of the room. A desk, mirror, cupboard; even horrible wallpaper of pink and red flowers. Shit, they even had the three geese made of porcelain on the wall in the other room. Just like his grandmother used to have. They had been paying attention over the years, probably been in lots of houses and worked out what most of us had in them. Though he wasn't sure how many houses had the flight of geese in them anymore. It even made him laugh inside for the first time. They should have been a bit more varied in their choice of deco.

"What are you laughing at?" she seemed annoyed that he could find humour in their situation.

"Just the décor."

"Yeah it's shit hey ... so?"

"Well, shit I can't even remember how long ago it was. I'm sure it wasn't long, like a week or something. I was driving home from work late at night. I had met this girl the week before ..."

"What was her name?" she interrupted, her hands now warm against his flesh and her embrace tight, her head lying on his shoulder.

"Rachael. So I wanted to call her all day but couldn't cause I was busy in the office and I didn't want anyone to know at work ..."

"Where did you work?" she interrupted again.

"The council, as a surveyor. So I stayed back, rang her, we talked for ages, like over an hour or something. It was dark by the time I left and I had a forty-minute drive home. If only I had rung her during the day like I was going to. I always do that, put things off cause I'm a dickhead and then I get in the shit."

"Like this?" she deadpanned.

"Yeah but this is the worse."

"So what happened?"

"I was driving home, through Yarramalong, the roads are narrow through there and it's pitch black, no street lights. As I was going along my car stalled. I had the shits big time. I promised Rachael I'd take her out and now my car had died. As I was about to get out this bright light exploded about me. I thought it was a helicopter but couldn't hear anything it was just silent. I got out. I had to shield my eyes, it was that bright, then there was this boom and I blacked out and woke up in some cell. I was shitting myself cause I had no idea where I was or what happened. All sorts of things went through my mind like I had been abducted by aliens or did you see Pulp Fiction where Bruce Willis and that black guy end up in that store with Zed and the black guy gets done up the arse?"

"Yeah I saw it."

"Yeah I was thinking it was that or some trick. The worse thing was I kept blacking out and waking up with sores over my body, bruises and stuff. I'd never been so afraid; I finally convinced myself that some serial killer had got me. That was until I saw 'em."

"Did your guys have big yellow eyes and wouldn't speak to you when you yelled at them?" she said while reliving her own terrible experience.

He ran his hand over her hair and spoke in a whisper.

"Yeah that's them. Then I woke a few days ago in here. A house with no windows until the day when the walls open up."

He thought of that day when he was sleeping when the walls of his room suddenly disappeared and there was a bright light and many eyes watching him, all yellow. There had been a few of those lately.

Even now he knew they were watching him. Studying their habits and interactions. Food would appear in the fake oven. It was rice and vegetables and never any meat.

"It must have been scary to be here on your own not knowing what was going on?"

"Yeah my mind's a blur. Couldn't tell you what day it is, or the time. I don't even know where we are in the universe. I'm glad you're here but."

She embraced him tighter.

"I'd be lying if I didn't say I wish I wasn't but I'm glad you're here too."

"I haven't asked about you, do you want to tell me?"

"They got me when I was swimming. I had the same cell and sores. Fuck I was scared but I knew right away what had happened to me."

They were silent for a few moments, his chest rising and falling. He was hurting inside. There would be no escape from here.

"The busiest time must be close to midday here," he finally said while looking at the wall waiting for it to suddenly disappear and watch those never-ending lines of yellow eyes that file past for hours until the wall reappears.

"Suppose they want us to breed."

"Can you imagine bringing a child up here?" he was almost able to chuckle.

"What will happen to us then?"

"Don't know; maybe we'll go insane."

~~~

When the wall did vanish they were asleep. He slowly woke and there they were. Dozens of clustered yellow eyes that came and went. For the first time he could see out of the house and saw the bright pink sky and three blue orb moons and he knew he wasn't on Earth anymore.

LIGHT YEARS

There's a moment when you know you're going to die. For many there is only that flash of time to reflect and then it's all over but for the darkness. For Adon Greer that moment of knowledge had come and past but for him there was no flash, he had plenty of time to think about everything.

Acceptance had replaced the panic - which had erupted in him when he first lost his grip on the recon craft.

Greer had been flying all his adult life, since qualifying for the Space Wing. He had a healthy passion for flying military fighters but as the years rolled on and with a wife to support, he needed a better paying job.

It was that pressure that forced him to give up the job he loved and become a shuttle pilot lugging freight from earth to the outer space stations beyond Jupiter.

It was a bit of a shock to go from being a fighter pilot to the slow and steady pace of a freighter. And it bored him. Over time he took those frustrations out on his family.

Rose, his wife, didn't make the situation better. She blamed him for her depression. She was always sending him messages that she was sick and he needed to come home. How was he meant to when he was delivering cargo to the moon? He couldn't just cut work and be home in five minutes. She knew that. When he was home their fights were furious and he was glad to leave her alone and take another mission.

He started ignoring her messages. He shouldn't have done that.

Flying fighters in the outer territories broke his boredom, something Rose never knew. The thrill of speed had come back. It was only for a few days with a Reserve Unit but all his worries faded away when he was in that fighter again. His great love had returned and there was enough room in his heart for two loves ...

~~~

His small reconnaissance craft was orbiting Triton, a moon of Saturn, when a piece of icy rock has crashed into his engine compartment. This has set off a chain reaction, which shut his craft down. There wasn't much life support inside the craft as it wasn't a long-range mission. A few hours of oxygen and food but with no power meant no heat and he would freeze to death very quickly.

From the damage report it seemed the rock had broken the outer shell and had wedged itself amongst the main cables and piping from the batteries and engine. If he could take the rock out he might be able to restore some life support and wait for help.

He had never had to do a space walk and he was panicking, so much so that he forgot to attach the safety line to the door.

His second mistake was not realising that the outside of the ship was covered in slippery ice. He made it to the engine compartment and attempted to take out the chunk of rock, which had lodged deep in the entrails of the engine housing.

With as much force as he could manage he made the rock move from its position but at the same time his footing slipped and he fell away. He could still feel the grind of metal as his fingertips scrapped against the handle as his body floated away. His heart was beating fast as the distance between himself and his craft increased. It was only then he realised there was no safety line.

He had actually cried. Right after he had screamed all the swear words that he knew for a good ten minutes. There was no going back, there was no chance of living. He was now a man waiting to die and that's when a man does his most serious thinking. About regrets, so many regrets. Anyone who says they don't have any is either lying or haven't lived. *"Oh Rosie what have I done?"*

It took a week for the message to reach him that she was dead. It was from her sister Kath and it was the nastiest message anyone had sent him. The video was only a minute long but it was a blast of anger and spite at his apathy. Rose had gone almost mad being alone.

"You should have known she was sick you selfish bastard. She told you! Why did you ignore it? Why did her mother have to find her dead one morning?!" Kath raged between the tears.

He had to watch it a few times to understand what had happened, she talked so fast and there was so much in that one minute.

He should have done things different. Should have got his priorities right and given a damn about her like he used to when they first started going out. But it was too late now.

He had watched the stars before but now they seemed more beautiful, more brilliant and alive. There was stillness and tranquillity here as he floated above Triton. He was no longer bothered about his plight. He had his peace with the universe and now it was just a matter of time before he ran out of oxygen or the gravitational pull of the moon would drag him into orbit and he would burn up like a shooting star.

He had closed his eyes but could not sleep just yet. His head hurt and his body was cramping as much from the cold as the lack of air. There was no impatience in his soul. Death would come soon.

A strange light that seemed to bounce around him. Maybe it was his mind shutting down but he saw light twist before his eyes. As it washed over him his body came alive with the heat. Then it was gone and the cold had returned.

"Soon my love," came the voice in his head.

"Who is it?" he mouthed. Was he dreaming or would he go insane in his last minutes of life?

"Don't be afraid, soon you and I will be together."

He now recognised the voice. "Rose? I ... I didn't mean to be such a bastard. I'm so sorry," he was crying now.

"Is this where we all end up? Out here in space?"

"This is where we all go. We can be together, two souls together as one swimming the oceans of the universe forever."

He smiled. Such was his delirium he could not compute whether it was really his dead wife talking to him. His oxygen-starved body was shutting down and his mind was already scrambling memories and reality.

"So you've forgiven me?"

"Of course. I did love you deeply."

"And I ... loved ... you," the cold now held him and he could no longer think straight or even breathe. The brightness of the light reflected from the moon's atmosphere blinded him.

His body was falling and his soul was in preparation to part with it forever. He managed to open his eyes one last time to see so much brightness. It was time to die and let his soul swim the oceans that filled the universe and all in it. There he would never be alone.

It was a perfect specimen. It had been terribly wounded. That could not be helped. A creature like this does not simply volunteer to become an experiment. No, it took electric shocks, guns and explosions of all sorts to bring this creature down.

It was so weak it could barely talk. Its blood had flowed out of it from so many wounds. Without that it could not heal itself and would stay weak. That would give us the advantage.

After two hours travelling it was almost midnight when we finally arrived at the Morisset mental home. Abandoned years ago, very few people even know it exists. And if they do, they know nothing of the chambers and rooms underneath.

I'm watching it now. It lies on a bed in infra-red light. It does not like sunlight and even our globes are too strong for its eyes. But I need to be sure of where it is at all times because I do not trust it. And I do not trust it because I fear it. It is so powerful, so majestic and cunning. Glory be that such a perfect hunter exists.

Not that I am here to learn about its killer instinct. It has other benefits that I am more interested in.

Even now, with the small amount of human blood we have given him, it rebuilds its broken body. The small cuts are the first to close up right before my eyes. In a day if not hours, if given more blood, it would be completely healed.

"What do you want?" It sneered at me. Its blonde hair was long and messy and hid its cold eyes.

"Just admiring your attributes."

"What this?" It grabbed its groin. I laughed, it didn't.

"No, nothing sexual. I'm more interested in how you came into being."

"I fell from the devil's arsehole, that's where I'm from."

"No. You were born of mother, hard to imagine that your mother is out there somewhere but it's true. But it's your *other* birth that I am interested in."

"We don't reveal our secrets to humans."

"I thought as much. But the sooner you help me get what I want, the sooner you'll be out of here and hunting young girls again. Understand?"

"So I'm a prisoner. What do you want?"

"I want the secret that lies hiding in your cells, in your very genetic make up. Those strands of DNA that rebuild your body over and over. The secret to how you never age. You don't look like you're a day over twenty-five but I know you're older than that. Tell me how old you are."

"Twenty-five."

I could tell the conversation was pointless and I was just making myself look like an idiot. Truth be told I would have preferred it to help me but knew deep down that wouldn't happen. I had its blood, I had the creature itself and if I had to cut it apart I'd do it.

~~~

In the lab the studying of its blood had begun. It was human but for the strange cell breakdown. While human cells continually divide and then die, the creature's did not die, but continued to rejuvenate for a few hours before they too became black and then green. Its blood outside the body died like any other creatures.

We would have to seek our formula for eternal youth in the creature's body.

It was still weak and easy to keep still. Our drugs had an effect on it, slowing its movements and its tongue.

We took flesh, hair and fingernails. All the while it screamed out in pain and vengeance.

Still it would not talk. I knew this as a lost cause, why would he indulge us with its story after the things we had done to it? We had what we needed to begin more serious research, we would find another to be more ... polite to.

~~~

I don't know how it happened but my staff cried out in panic that only lasted seconds. It managed to pull an arm free and in a split second was feeding on the neck of a co-worker. Each gulp gave it further strength. It was what I feared would happen. It was loose.

I have retreated to my quarters. I will seek to escape. What I am sure of is that all our diseases, even the greatest plague of them all – age - can be conquered with the help of the vampires. If we had the secret of their eternal youth then all humans could live forever and without disease or injury. What a world it would be.

With the screams of the staff and the mighty howls of the creature filling our subterranean laboratory I know this will not happen for sometime. We must control these creatures and take care in doing so. They hold the key but until then experiments are continuing.

THE ROOM

Imagine the sound of fingernails running down a chalkboard. What about the grind of a surgical saw as it cuts bone? The snip of scissors as a ribcage is snapped and then the wet crunch - as the ribs are forced open.

Now watch the knife slowly coming down towards your chest. It pierces the skin, you see blood and you feel pain. Your chest is heaving in panic, your lungs want to burst, you want to cry out with the pain. Stop! Stop! *Please!* But the hand does not stop, it goes deeper and longer as the skin on your breast is sliced open to the wails of your agony.

You always avoided their eyes. You did not want to see the moments of fear. You didn't want to see your face reflected in those eyes. What did you feel? Pleasure? Revulsion? No. You felt nothing. Why? It's simple, you're a monster.

How many were there? You kept count but there were so many more ... collateral victims should we say. These are the lives that have been ruined forever after coming in contact with your venom. Every moment was agony to them. They could not sleep, not work and not enjoy the life they deserved all because of you.

Who am I? I am the voice inside your head just when you die. I am the judge. You don't need to know anymore.

I'm watching you squirm. I like it. Now is the time to be afraid. There is no point in being defiant! Oh you are a sick man, a repulsive bitter wreck of a man. Your father was right you are nothing and your mother did hate you. She even said it to you, do you remember? Of course you do. No one ever loved you. So out into the world you went spreading your misery, to make the world pay for treating you so bad. You think you're original? You are a stereotype and weak. Your daddy was right again. Don't ever think you're special. Don't think by purging yourself you have made yourself better; you should've dived off that cliff, should've put that gun to your temple, or jumped in front of that train. The world would have been a better place, your daddy was right again. Imagine that. It's not natural for parents to hate their child especially to wish them dead.

So are you another victim? Should you be pitied? Maybe if you had lived a better life then perhaps. If you had found a way to conquer your failings, conquer that massive mountain in your life. But you failed. And other souls had to become victims.

Yes they're here. Just through that door into the room. All of them. Every single one that you took from the world as you purged yourself. But they were not yours to vent your anger on. Do you think you could put all that evil into the world, to destroy so much all for your own selfish gratification and there be no ... evening of the score shall we say? There is always a price, always consequences.

Remember the chalkboard? Oh please don't cry now! The knife slicing your skin! The burning of the flesh of animals! The mockery! The hatred! The screaming! It's all here, all waiting for you.

Right through this door and into the room. They're waiting for you. Go now. There is no going back. This is the fate of all of your kind. I'll shut the door behind you.

"Oh my son's such a good boy. I used to sing him a song whenever he was upset. People used to say he was a good boy," the old lady smiled up at her nurse who had come to take away her lunch, moving away the three cans of Aerogard that the old lady always had with her to keep the flies away.

All the staff at Sandlewood Lodge had become used to the strange ramblings of the lady since she moved in a year ago. Always on about her son, even though no one had ever seen him at the retirement home. There were plenty of pictures but they only showed a younger version of the lady with a young boy. All of the pictures were worn and yellow as if they had been handled too many times.

The old lady took one of the cans of Aerogard and sprayed it about, a full five-second burst. It made other residents in the TV room cough.

"You keep those flies away Tudy," one of the other residents mumbled. They had grown used to her constant de-fly program too.

It must be coming on sunset too. It was the usual time of day for her to spray wherever she was and above all in her room.

"I used to sing you a sweet song of icecream and chocolate houses, and you would laugh along," she said as the nurse wheeled her back to her room.

It always took the staff some effort to get her ready for bed. She wanted to talk, to show her nurses her photos, for them to sit and watch TV with her.

"Tudy, I've got to get the other patients ready too," the nurses would say before leaving her alone in the dark.

Then the flies came. Only in ones or twos, no great swarm. But they made that noise in her brain and it always meant that he was here.

"My coffin is full of flies and I've got a coffin just your size Mama," he whispered from a dark corner.

"Oh but I was your friend and I used to sing you songs. Don't you remember?"

"But the things I've done Mama, the things I've done with a shotgun would make you cry."

She did cry. "You used to be such a good boy."

"Oh Mama when will you open your eyes. You never sang me songs. You never thought I was a good boy. You're just full of lies."

She did not look at him but stared at the drawn curtain.

"Even now you look away. Mama! Mama! Oh I'm in pain, the heat Mama and the flies." His body had collapsed and his head was resting on her bed as he cried but she did not look but sprayed her Aerogard until he melted away.

Every night he came to her with his crying. He would tell her his crimes, one by one. With explicit details, such was his good memory. And what would she say?

"Oh he's such a good boy, everyone says so."

Resolve would see her through, ignore him and he would go away. But she had fears, deep inside her she knew where he was and she didn't want to go there too.

The fly buzzing around her head woke her. Even though she could hear his breathing she would not look. There was someone else in the room by her bed playing with her medication.

"They're all here Mama."

She looked up and there was a young girl, about fourteen in a school uniform but it was bloody and torn. The girl was dead. The flies buzzed around her head and worms crawled over her skin. She stared down at Tudy.

"Oh Mama you can't ignore me, this is what drove me to the understanding of the power of my shotgun," came his voice from somewhere in the darkness of the room.

"Each shot that blew away some poor bastard was a scream of rage at you. Each was a count of the suffering living with you. You put me here in this coffin full of flies and worms. I have to endure the heat of hell. It hurts Mama, don't you care?"

She could see him now at the foot of her bed. He wore the same clothes that he had worn the last time she saw him alive. They had argued over him getting a job. He was in his early thirties, lived at home and with no prospects for getting a life. She told him so and regularly. He had no woman, no social life but stayed inside his room playing computer games. One night she threw them all out and locked his door.

When he found out he was in a rage and punched his fist clean through a wall. That brought more screaming and accusations from his mother. It was the feather that collapsed a tonne of bricks onto his fragile frame.

He shot his mother. The young girl was walking past Tudy's house at the time. She was next. Then he went to the Centrelink employment office and shot every single person he could find. Just so he had the excuse that he couldn't look for a job if there was no Centrelink.

She lived but was never the same; she believed he had meant her to live. But he did not; he blew his head off with his own shotgun. Now he was in hell.

The old lady knew it and she cried, as she looked him over.

"You were such a good boy."

She held out her hand as she cried openly. But he did not take it. He was moving away from her on a small boat on a lake of fire. His chest heaved heavily and his eyes burnt into her like hot coals. There was nothing but contempt from him; her tears were all too late. He rode the lake of fire with his flies and he watched her as she cried loudly. It was all too late now Mama.

GUESS WHO WE'RE
HAVING FOR DINNER?

"Is it far? I thought you lived in Yattalunga?"

"Nah, I said Saratoga didn't I?"

Eric didn't answer the question but looked up at the darkening sky and rubbed his arms to keep warm.

"Should have brought a jumper. Don't you hate that? It was hot today and now it looks like it's going to rain."

His companion, Sebastian, only raised his eyebrows in acknowledgement but he didn't really care.

They'd only been friends for a week, meeting in a church gathering last Saturday. Eric thought him a strange creature, he was very young, dressed in black, dyed his hair black and was bejewelled in silver. He was more like those Goths who dreamed of dying and slept in coffins. At the time he was hesitant, quiet, which he at first put down to nerves, but as the hours went on Eric couldn't help but think he was holding in some joke that made him smirk when he mingled with the others of the group. He also couldn't hide that feeling that this kid thought his religion a joke, but over the next few days they met up for lunch and stuff and talked about religion itself, philosophy and life in general. Eric then found him to be quite intelligent though still a little morbid for his liking. There was still that occasional smirk and he had meant to bring it up eventually but maybe tonight wasn't the night.

Sebastian had surprised him by asking him over for dinner at his family's house, who he claimed were all damned and needed God's Light.

He did have plans to go to the Reverend's house to plan the weekend activities while eating takeaway pizza. It was a routine he held for months now but was glad to break, to do the church's work of bringing in new members.

They finally arrived at a two-story house that was at the end of a dead-end street that ran off the main road. There was nothing suspicious about it or strange thought Eric. No cemeteries or cross in the yard or the howling of wolves from the bush that surrounded the street and house. It was in the middle of suburbia anyway.

As he followed Sebastian towards the house Eric could hear a man laughing loudly from inside. Sebastian opened the front door and went straight in. Eric hesitated for a moment as he waited for permission to enter or if it was okay to just follow. No reassurance, so he just followed.

It was as chilly inside in the foyer as it was outside despite the fire that burnt slowly in an adjacent room. He followed Sebastian to the right where there was a door.

"Come on through," Sebastian finally acknowledged his guest with a throw of his head in the direction of the door.

So again he followed his new friend into the other room. It was a dining room set for dinner. Unlit candles, plates and cutlery were set out all ready for a great feast.

A bell chimed deep in the house and there were hurried footsteps then suddenly a little girl rushed in from the door they had just gone through. She was pretty with blonde hair in a ponytail.

"That's my sister Evelyn."

"Hello," Eric said towards Evelyn, who only giggled at him as she walked to the other side of the large table and took a seat.

"I like kids but they don't seem to like me," he joked to Sebastian, who only nodded with his smirk.

There were two doors at the end of the room, one of which opened, and a man and woman entered. They were in the middle of a conversation that ended at the sight of Eric.

"This must be Sebastian's new friend. Welcome!" he said as he walked towards him. He was a well-groomed and dressed man in his late thirties, much too young to have a teenage son like Sebastian. The female was also very well groomed with long dark hair and she also seemed in her late thirties.

"I'm John. This is my wife Indiran."

"Hello I'm Eric."

He shook both their hands, which were cold, but he thought nothing of it.

John showed him to his chair and Sebastian sat next to him. John and his wife then moved to the head of the table.

"I hope you enjoy dinner and can stay after?" John asked.

"Oh thank you, thank you for inviting me."

"It's our pleasure believe me," John smiled as his wife picked up Evelyn and put her on her lap. Sebastian's smirk had not vanished, as he seemed to enjoy some private joke. Eric thought him immature; there was nothing wrong with adults exchanging greetings and manners.

"Where are Eldrid and George?" John asked the room.

Sebastian just shrugged his shoulders.

"Eldrid is probably still deciding on what to wear and you know they're inseparable," Indiran offered.

"True," Replied John with a smile. "You know what I discovered today?" he asked the room, "I never knew this but all retailers double their prices! Extraordinary! And what cheek. Ha! So when you see ten percent or even forty percent you have to think are you really getting a bargain?"

"That's true," Eric added.

"Where are they? I'm hungry," Evelyn moaned.

"Patience," Indiran soothed her child.

Hard footsteps thundered in the house as before and the same door John and Indiran came through burst open and two figures entered the room.

"Finally," John teased.

"Oh poo to your whinging," the first man said. His hair looked like it had been permed like the old ladies Eric would see in church. He also had a large wide tie on with a frilly sleeved white shirt and tight trousers. He seemed very pleased with himself as he walked to his seat at the opposite end to John and close to where Eric sat.

"Fixing your makeup were you?" John joked.

"Do you like it?" the man stopped and put his hands on his hips and stared back before he took his seat.

"You'll always stink," Sebastian this time added to the jibes.

"Yeah you stink," Evelyn cried out then burst into laughter.

"Eric, this is Eldrid."

John put out his hand to indicate their new guest.

"Oh hello, welcome."

"And this is George," John went on.

"Brains," said George.

Eric looked at the man as he slowly made his way to his seat right opposite. He seemed a wretch of a fellow. His eyes seemed vacant holes, his mouth hung open and his skin was grey and patchy. Then there was the incredible disgusting smell that now wavered in the room.

"There's your smell, people," Eldrid said with a hint of satisfaction that he wasn't the one who stank. Eric then noticed that the man next to him had grey skin too and his eyes were black beads which made his own skin crawl.

"Indeed," John laughed then clapped. The candles burst into bright flames. "Now we can feast!"

Eric only then wondered what they would be eating. Lucky he wasn't allergic or had certain tastes as Sebastian had completely neglected to ask him anything about his eating habits. He wasn't sure if he had the stomach for it anymore really; George's hot disgusting breath blew right into his face and made him feel sick.

Suddenly the door right behind John opened up and a huge man entered carrying a long wooden table that he held up in his hands by a chain. John stood up to allow the man to put it at the end of the table and slide it forward.

Eric was horrified to see that on the table was a girl who was tied up. He wasn't sure if she was dead as she had her eyes closed and none of her limbs moved. He watched open-mouthed and wide-eyed at the scene but was waiting for them to all start laughing and the girl to come to life with a wink in her eye. But none moved to end the joke.

They all stared at the girl with hungry eyes and mouths; only Eldrid seemed disinterested while he drank from a wine goblet.

"She's pretty," Evelyn said to her mother.

"She certainly is," she replied.

Eric was still waiting for the joke to end and for John to start laughing. "You should see the look on your face! Ha! Bring out the lamb chops and vegies!"

John was watching him with a slight smile.

"I love it when they don't know," chuckled Eldrid. John's eyes shifted and he laughed.

"Brains," George mumbled.

"Let's eat then," said John.

It was a command for his family to do horrible things to the girl the likes Eric had only seen in movies.

The slurping mixed with the soft cries of the girl unnerved Eric. He shook with fright and confusion. Who were these people? What was going on?

"What are you doing?" he cried out. "Stop!"

He went to stand but suddenly there were powerful hands on his shoulders that forced him back to his seat.

"Sit," a voice whispered in his ear. Then the voice and hands were gone as suddenly as they had appeared. In the corner of his eye he saw John bite down on the girl's neck again. It was his hands and voice but how ...?

Eric couldn't take watching and covered his face with his hands as his eyes filled with tears, "That poor girl."

John lifted his head, "Enough."

His family stopped sucking on the girl and sat back in their seats, their mouths covered in blood. Indiran wiped Evelyn's mouth with a cloth.

"Berger!" John called out.

The giant man reappeared from the same door this time carrying a silver plate with a cover.

"Brains," George called out.

Berger walked past him and placed the plate in front of Eldrid and removed the lid.

There was immediately the foul odour that was just as bad as the fellow sitting opposite him. On the plate was a human arm that was yellow with decay. Eldrid smiled with delight and turned to Eric.

"Three-week-old flesh. Very mature taste, like your vintage cheese."

Next he picked up the arm and bit down on it, ripping the flesh off the bone with his teeth like it was a piece of corn. On sight of the yellow fat tissue and blacked blood Eric immediately threw up. They laughed at him.

Eric struggled to control the convulsions as his stomach continued to pump up his lunch all over his legs and floor.

"Brains."

While he was distracted head down under the table trying to compose himself he did not see Berger go to the girl's head with an electric saw. But he heard it.

The chilling crunch as the blade cut through the bone made him afraid to raise his head but he did anyway. He had to face these monsters and show no fear.

He was just in time to see the saw stop and the girl's brain be pulled out and put onto a plate much to the excitement of George.

"Brains! Brains! Brains!" he shrieked with delight as the plate was brought his way and put before him. He was that hungry that he ripped it off the plate with his hands and took a deep bite out of it.

Eric's stomach again churned as he took a glimpse of the sight. His stomach heaved again and he cried out in pain, as his gut was empty.

"Let me out you bastards!" he managed to call out.

They only laughed again.

"Who was she?"

"Just a guest," John shrugged his shoulders.

"Is this what you do with your guests?" he cried out in anger. He looked to Sebastian who had his smug smile painted across his face. He really wanted to punch that face right now.

"Why did you bring me here? You wretched bastard."

"Don't you wish you were having pizza right now?" he finally said while choking on his laughter.

None of the others said anything but stared at him. George continued to tear apart the warm brain in his hands like a ravenous starved dog while Eldrid sipped on his goblet.

"I'm going to the police."

He went for the door but it wouldn't open.

"No Eric. You're our guest tonight and guess who we're having for dinner tomorrow night?" he laughed and his family joined him. He rose from the table and was instantly in Eric's face, so close he could smell the fresh blood on his breath.

"Dessert anyone?"

Eric felt his legs go weak and his head light as he swayed back and forth before hitting the floor.

"Brains."

TWO PEAS IN A POD

"Gotta make a killing, gotta make a killing," said the bird of prey.

It was so quiet now in the Centrelink Office that the man behind the counter could hear the slow ticking of the clock mounted on the wall behind him as it counted down to five o'clock. Each second it ticked over was another moment before it was knock-off time and he could get out of the place he called hell. He had been sweating all day, as much from the long hours of being in a hot office as from the stress and frustration caused by mindless morons who had lined up all day for their dole, their petty little excuses why their form was in late and then the screaming when he told them they'd get nothing. It made him laugh how they talked about it being their 'pay' like being a worthless bludger was a full-time job, well for most of them it was.

The women, correction, the teenagers always had kids. I guess when you don't go to school or work or have intelligence or have any plan in your life you've got time to screw.

Then there was the smell. Cigarettes, alcohol, sweat and some strange funk that reminded him of wet garbage that had been dried, then spewed on then dried out again and used as an aerosol. Some days he would choke and have to go into a back room and throw up, it was that bad. It was getting harder and harder to come to work and put up with the dregs of society. But after six long years he had found a way to make it better, to bring some purpose to his life.

He moved in his seat, he felt dirty, his skin greasy and his unwashed hair felt oily and he stank too.

"Come on," he muttered.

"I am the bird of prey."

Finally the clock hit knock-off time and he pounced from his work station. Without saying a word he left the office, went to his car parked in the car park. He drove it out into the dusk that had now settled over the small town.

"*Gotta make a killing*," said the bird of prey.

~~~

"One more, just one more," sang the Count.

Elsewhere on the edge of the little town another man walked along a road. He avoided the main highway that ran through the town, as at this time it was too busy, full of working folk in their rich cars on their way home to their mansions. This road was a bypass and only used by impatient people coming from the large shopping complex a few kilometres away, some rich prick would drive along soon.

It was lined with trees and small groups of letterboxes. A few cows were even eating their cuds by wooden fences near the road.

"I am the Count of Doom."

It was getting cold quickly but he put up with the chill, he was used to it, living in a caravan did that to you, you got used to going without luxuries. Good food, good clothes and some of the finer things in life were alien to him; his tattered clothes and skinny frame were testimony to that. But all those rich fucks would pay.

It was the little things at first, like coining some bitch's BMW, ripping out the lights in a driveway, putting graffiti over rich arseholes houses but that was when he was younger. Now things were different, he was making them all pay for lookin' down on him.

"One more and you've got yourself double figures, good show," said the Count.

A car approached from behind him. Its high beams were switched off as the driver spotted him walking along the road. The rattle of the loose blue metal from the bitumen clanged in the wheel housing as the car's tyres ripped it up. The sound of the engine as it slowed as it neared him.

He smiled and put out his right hand with his thumb extended, the universal sign of the hitchhiker. The car slowed even more as it came up behind him. He smiled even wider as it pulled up beside him.

The public servant saw his target in his lights. Immediately he was reminded of the dregs that come into his office. The blue flannelette long-sleeve shirt, unbuttoned to show off the ACDC t-shirt, the dirty jeans and thongs with even dirtier feet. He had a greasy beard and a wide cheesy over-confident grin put on show to seem friendly so someone would pick him up. So here he was.

"Gotta make a killing. Gotta make a killing," said the bird of prey.

As he pulled up he pressed the button to bring down the passenger door window. Immediately the bum's head appeared where the glass had been. Still with that stupid grin across his ugly face and exposing the fact he only had half his teeth.

"Where you headed?" he asked but did not care.

"Just into Gosford thanks matey," he replied with cheer in his voice but lying all the way.

"Get in."

"Oh please get in fuck face."

The bum opened the door and climbed in. He stank of the funk and he had to put the air conditioning on straight away.

"Oh thanks mister, you're a life-saver, bloody long way to Gossie right?" he said again cheerfully naive but lying all the way.

"Life-saver my arse. I can smell the shit on him already," said the bird of prey.

"This well to do chap should be no trouble," said the Count.

It was quiet in the car as it went along. He didn't look at the bloke but only caught a glance when he got the chance. He had glasses on and was going bald plus he could see his fat gut bulging over his pants and straining his button shirt. From eating too much he guessed, too many pork roasts for this chap. The car was new, bought with an inheritance I bet. Money passed down from family to family, building on the wealth of each generation, built on workers' blood.

He turned his head to watch the prick drive; it would make him hate his kind even more.

"So night's almost here mate," he entreated the man with pathetic small talk.

"One more and you've got yourself double figures chap," said the Count.

"I know."

"Yeah it does that," the public servant said. He didn't give a damn about when the night came.

The bird of prey was getting frustrated and began to rant, "What type of left-over shit on a dog's arse is this? I'm sure no-one will miss this turd in clothes except the office when he doesn't come in with his bloody forged dole form, like he's really been looking for work, so he can get his pay to blow on cigarettes, booze and drugs and leave his dirty kids with nothing. Then he'll beat up his wife when there's nothing left but she'll call the cops and tell them nothing happened because she's stupid and weak. That's the way all of them live and they're a drain on society and a fucking waste of space. Wipe the earth of them! Kill em all!"

The public servant looked over at the leach looking out the window smelling up his car and felt the hatred run through his body. It felt good, not long to go. He'd find a nice spot and do the killing.

The bum knew he was being watched and when the rich prick driving put his eyes back on the road instead of looking at him he looked back at his prey once more. The Count spoke, *"Must have finished earning his million dollars today and going home to his perfect woman with nice breasts and big house with two cars and no worries* or qualms. *They'll talk about all the poor people who get in their way when they're out buying stuff. I will enjoy slitting his throat and getting that Italian suit all bloody. I will put the pieces in the river."*

"So finished work then have you brother? Going home to the horizontal lambada then hey?" he joked, but was making himself laugh, he knew that's exactly where he was going. Defiantly going home to a wife who liked a bit of cock and wouldn't bitch about it.

"Maybe," the public servant mumbled, completely disinterested in conversation, his only thought on the road and where he was going. The bird of prey was complaining now, *"My stomach is twitching with having to breathe the same foul air."*

So he put the window down. *"I'll have to remind myself to wear my rubber gloves when I slash his hide. The grease in his blood will stain."*

"Got plans in town then?" the bum persisted in making conversation.

"No. You?"

"Yeah matey. Not sure where exactly, need a map to go where I'm going, you know?"

At that the bum reached for the glove compartment right in front of him.

"What's in here?"

"No!" the public servant broke his composure as he screamed his panic and shock.

"I don't have a map, maybe you can get one in Gosford."

His heart had almost exploded from his chest as the adrenalin surged through his system, but now he could relax as the danger was over.

"Okay man, it's your car," said the loser, the public servant beside him not seeing his red raw eyes become slits as his suspicion began to grow.

"Well well, what are we hiding in there?" pondered the Count.

"This dego scum deserves to die now. Must remind myself not to leave the gun in the glove compartment," warned the bird of prey.

"I've got karate class at seven you see, keeps me all limber and you know karate like. Ready for when the coppers try to throw me out of the pub, you know what I mean matey! Ha!" the loser laughed at his own rite of passage scenario that all at his level seem to enjoy. The loser didn't see the public servant's eyebrow rise.

"You know karate?" he seemed interested.

"Oh yeah mate. For a while now," he said as he looked out the window at the trees that lined the road creating a tunnel of darkness the car travelled through.

"That could be a problem," the bird of prey worried. "I must counter this threat."

"That's coincidental. My neighbour has his own dojo in his garage and I picked up a few moves myself."

The public servant, for the first time in the night, smiled and seemed pleased with himself. The bum became interested suddenly.

"Is that right?" the Count was wary, "Is this a bluff? He could be a little difficult to bring down when we reach Lilli Pilli where I will do the killing."

A song on the radio the bum knew, Guns n' Roses' *Sweet Child of Mine*, broke the quiet tension. The public servant had never heard of it.

"Good song this," the bum seemed happy and hit his thighs along with the beat as if they were a drum kit, a happy naive smile across his face.

"It's just the radio. Don't take much notice of it really," the public servant returned to his glum persona.

"Lilli Pilli, Lilli Pilli, where I'll cut him good, gut him good," sang the bird of prey.

"*Just one more, just one more,*" the Count whispered in the gloom.

There was no talking as each of the men thought about the deed to be done. It was the silence of the mourners walking behind the coffin on the way to the graveyard. Death was coming.

Up ahead a small store-come-garage came into view and the bum took the opportunity to stock up on his essentials.

"Mind if we getting some smokes, nothing else is open at night," he was that confident of a certain death and his double figures. The public servant became nervous at the unusual request.

"I won't smoke in the car, if that's a bother brother."

"No, it's alright."

He slowed the car down and pulled into the garage as his passenger checked his pockets and ran his hands over his shirt.

"Shit. I haven't got any money. Don't get me pay until Thursday," he faked disappointment, which the driver saw through. The public servant wanted to keep his charge happy but also didn't want to be spotted with him because he didn't want witnesses. Still it was dark and this store was off the beaten track, maybe they'd have nothing for him and he'd get his money back, even if he had to take it out of his dead cold hand. He pulled his wallet out of his back pocket and lifted a fiver; the eyes of the bum lit up.

"You're a legend, I'll pay you back," he was given the money and the driver put his wallet in his pant's pocket where it wouldn't fit in properly.

"He is a worm and a scab. Maybe I'll knife his arse and gut him from hole to hole?" the bird of prey mused.

He watched the bum climb out and shuffle into the store. While he waited he played with the hunting knife he had concealed next to the driver's seat by the bottom of the door. It was cold and hungry. This was a piece of equipment created for a simple purpose, to kill living things. He had been putting it to good use. As he ran his finger along the blade his body went into spasms of joy as electric excitement surged through him over and over again. It was good. He loved these little frenzies, as good as sex to him, in fact, it had replaced sex in his world.

In the store the bum picked out his smokes. He couldn't help but laugh on the inside.

"What a fool, easy money and did you see the other bills in his wallet?! Good show. Double figures and extra pay for the deed."

The Count was happy and would soon be orgasmic.

He came back to the car, which had been left running. As soon as he was in, the public servant drove off with a little speed that tore up the dirt access road to the store.

"*This is it*," clapped the bird of prey.

"*Here we go ladies and gents,*" the Count announced to his guests.

The Lilli Pilli turn off was coming up. The locals knew it as a short-cut back to the freeway. No street lights, bad bitumen and plenty of places you can pull over in the dark and not be seen.

The public servant had a spot off to the left near a small swamp and rest area. His eyes watched the markers and familiar trees go by.

The bum had been here before but not for a while, maybe it was number four on his list? He liked the darkness and felt it was a good spot to take the rich fucks to die. He'd make them lay in the dirt and loved the mud when it had been raining. Ahead was a small swamp if he could remember, his right hand twitched as he readied himself to grab the wheel forcing the car off the road where he would then pull out the knife from his shirt and plunge it down and down, over and over it would go in.

The public servant licked his lips, he was hard with the thought of ridding the system of these leaches, this parasite on the workers of the work. Left hand on the wheel, the other stroking the knife handle like it was a wild pet being kept placid.

"*This is it!*" screamed the bird of prey.

The car was pulled over roughly, the tyres screeching and loose bitumen flying about as it hit the dirt in a cloud of dust.

The bum's right hand had reached up but he was caught by surprise by the movement. Did this prick know? He had his hand in his shirt as the car jolted over the potholes and roughly stopped. The knife came out and he turned to do his work to see the public servant armed with a knife and a crazed look in his eyes that suddenly turned to surprise.

"What the fuck are you doin?" the bum cried.

Both jumped out of the car to hide the fear and gain advantage of space and time as both overcome their shock. It was too late to back away, the bum had no car, the public servant couldn't get his gun or drive away without the loser getting in and cutting him.

They charged at each other like bulls locked in a fight to death.

"He knows karate! Cut him! Let the oily blood bleed in the mud!" the bird of prey cried a warning in his excitement.

"Don't let him slash you! You are on your own here! Kill him and you've got double figures," the Count was almost in rapture of the impending kill.

The two fought each other in the headlights of the still-running car. Both avoided each other's knives, which were soon dropped as it came down to fists and kicking. In the struggle the public servant landed two good hits and the bum dropped to the dirt apparently motionless. He then found his knife and plunged into the leach's flannelette shirt.

"*One less! One less!*" the bird of prey cried out to the night sky.

He climbed into his car and drove away at speed, the dust hiding the bum from his view as he went. In the dust the bum had risen and watched the car lights disappear down the road. He was hurting and he was pissed right off. He groped about in the dirt, as it was now pitch black. He found something small and solid that folded open. The bastard's wallet! He chuckled to himself as he got to his feet and the pain faded away.

"The war is not lost soldier, good show. Now into the night!" the Count showed the way, always on his shoulder.

In the car the public servant was sweating heavily and laughed at what had just happened. He couldn't explain why the parasite had pulled a knife on him. It didn't matter anyway, he was dead now. He brushed the dirt off his pants but something felt amiss ...

"Fuck! Fuck! Fuck!" he screamed and pounded on the wheel.

He was back at the spot in under a minute and got out to have a look around. Nothing. No body and no wallet! In his panic and shock his hands pulled on his hair and he turned around and around looking for something that wasn't there, kicking the stones leaving small clouds of dust wafting in the lights of the car.

"*He'll find me! What do I do? What do I do?*" he asked over and over. The bird of prey said nothing.

Even though I was asleep I could feel the searing pain. There was only seconds of it before I woke, barely able to stifle my scream. I had to hold it in; I didn't want to make any noise.

I bit down on my lips to hold it in and suck it up. I instantly knew what had happened but was still in shock that it was still occurring. My hand on my chest was wet with warm blood and my skin was stinging with pain.

I climbed out of the bed and looked at myself in the mirror with my chest exposed. The three letters were there again, carved into my skin. *Run*.

I was only fifteen and far from home. I had nowhere to run too. I couldn't go home, even if I knew how to get back there. I hated it here at Northwood Farm. The house was old and creaky. There was dust over everything and Frank Morgan, the farmer, was creepy. He was ugly and cruel.

I had been sent here by the agency to be safe while a relative could be found to look after me permanently, not to be a slave. I don't know what the foster agency was thinking, placing me with this weird freak who liked shooting live animals and would watch horror movies all night.

It was almost morning and already hot. The heat I'm used to, but city heat is not the same as living out in the country. It seemed to just hang on the ground, burning everything up and making every movement an impossible effort.

Run

I was breathing heavily as I thought things over. Every night for the past week, since I got here, I had gone through this agony. I couldn't do it anymore.

Dressing in my pathetic worn clothes, I then left my room, trying not to make any noise on the wooden floors and steps.

The heat was just bearable as I entered the backyard. I walked to the well. I hated this well. It had freaked me out from day one. Even now I couldn't look down into the black darkness. But I was thirsty and I had no water to take with me.

Run

There was a voice.

"Who are you?" I whispered.

I saw a small hand on the inner edge of the well. Somehow, despite the heat, I went cold.

The banging of the rear house door broke my stupor. I instantly looked towards the house and saw old Morgan standing behind me. An axe was in his hands.

"Shoulda listened to those voices boy. Now you gunna join all those other kids," he said while he licked his lips as he always did when excited, his eyes looking into the well.

He took hold of my collar and began hauling me towards a shed.

"Now, there's no use crying. It'll be all over soon."

Only now that the thick trees of the forest had blocked the warmth of the sun and a tingling chill reminded that sunset was near did George begin to panic.

He had stormed off from his family's farm a few hours earlier and sought refuge in the woods that bordered the length of the farm. Without much thought as to where he was going (he was still too angry to care), he stomped through the trails that wound endlessly through the scrub.

George had been in here before, but only skirting the edges. He was new to this area of England, having moved to his Uncle Jimmy's farm with the rest of his family when their home burned down two weeks ago. Having nowhere else to go, his father's brother had let them stay.

That's when things became difficult. George was almost eighteen and wanting to do things on his own and his way. It was a shock to his system to have to uproot his life and move faraway. He understood animals needed to be looked after, and he was more than willing to do his share. It was when his Uncle would yell at him for making mistakes or using equipment that wasn't his own that made George really despise his Uncle and his farm. George was getting the feeling his Uncle was tired of his family stepping on his toes.

So, after yet another yelling match after George had forgotten to close some gates and let the sheep get out, George fled to get some space. Now as the trees became thicker and the sun disappeared, he realised he didn't really know where he was.

Having spent his anger in great strides along the paths, he was tired now and ready to return to the farm. Seeing the best way was to simply retrace his steps, he began to do so.

"Stubborn old ox," he mumbled to himself as he thought of his Uncle.

As he walked it became dark very quickly, and he was sure to lose his way. Soon, he believed he had done so. Exhausted, he sat on a rock to gain his bearings and figure out what he was going to do. He looked about, trying to remember if any of the trees and features around him looked familiar, but they all seemed the same shade of green and withering brown.

"You're lost in my woods?" came a soft female voice.

George sprung to his feet, partly surprised and partly afraid he had stumbled onto a Lord's private estate.

He looked about but could see no one.

"I apologise my Lady, I am lost. I did not mean to intrude onto your land."

There was a gentle laugh. George strained his eyes in the dying light to see who was speaking to him.

"What a nice boy to have such manners and expect this forest to have a Lady."

George swallowed hard, not daring to say anymore.

"Step away from that rock so I may see you better."

George took a step forward. Then, suddenly, there was a female form stepping out from a large tree trunk immediately to his right.

"Don't be afraid. I do not get to many brave men wandering in my woods anymore," the voice said sadly.

"I am sorry my Lady."

George could see her now. She was slender with a black dress with a golden necklace. Her hair was brown and long, tied away behind her back. Two great green eyes bored into him, they were the greenest he had ever seen. There was a smile on her delicate face.

"You are George from the Blacksmith farm," she said, not as a question but as a statement of fact.

"I am. May I ask who you are?" George stammered.

"I am Luna and this is my forest. Do you like it?"

"At the moment it has me lost, so saying I did would be a lie."

She smiled. "Of course, in the dark things seem strange." She stepped closer to him and George could see her skin was beautiful and flawless. Her eyes seemed to be scanning him as if checking off items some checklist only known to her.

She ran her hand over his cheek, her touch cold as the night breath that now hung throughout the woods.

George did not know who or what she was. He had heard tales of old witches from the olden times that still lived secretly in deep forests. Old witches trying to hold onto the old ways of the Celtic life that every invader of England seemed to be intent on wiping out.

"I will show you the way out, if you promise to come visit me sometimes. I get lonely, you see."

"I don't have any friends either." George admitted.

"Then we must become friends," she said, and laughed and held his arm tight. George saw her eyes widened in great excitement. It made him feel special and at ease.

"Close your eyes," she whispered.

He did so. Moments later, she whispered again for him to open them. When he did, he found himself outside his Uncle's farm. He was stumped.

His Uncle was waiting for him. Uncle Jim with his crooked nose, thinning hair, and fat face. It was a rude shock and brought him back to reality like the classic bucket of cold water in the morning. He had once been handsome but had inexplicably scarred himself years before in a moment of madness.

"Where have you been? Your mother is worried."

"I got lost."

"Go inside, clean up, we've got a big day tomorrow."

George stepped passed him, not noticing Uncle Jim giving the woods a final scan before following him into the house.

~~~

His family wanted to know where he had gone and George gave them a simple answer. Of course he made no mention of Luna.

Some nights had passed. His Uncle had him working all day and most of the night. Ploughing fields, picking vegetables, and butchering meat. Being covered in blood at the end of the day did not suit George at all. It stank and was sticky. At least his Uncle did the hard business of the actual killing.

As had now become his habit, as soon as he was allowed to go to bed, George fell asleep quickly.

"Georgie my sweet! George ..." a sweet voice echoed in his dreams. In his dreams, the voice became the roar a beast "George!!" and he woke suddenly.

There was a form on the open window frame. It was Luna.

"You haven't been to visit me," she whined.

"I'm sorry, my Uncle keeps me busy all day."

"I can smell blood on you."

George looked about, he always bathed at the end of the day but he saw his dirty blood soaked clothes crumpled on the floor.

Luna stepped into his room. It was only tiny, a simple addition made to his Uncle's house when they moved in. Being the eldest, he was allowed more privacy than his younger sisters.

She sat on the bed. Tonight she wore a red dress and her hair was flowing without any ties. She looked beautiful.

"I thought we could wander in my woods again, if you like."

"Now? How late is it?"

"Oh George you should see my woods at night. There is not a soul about, the birds sleep, the animals that crawled under a log to die days before rot away, and the wind dances with the leaves above our heads."

Her eyes had closed as if seeing what she was saying. For a moment George felt uneasy at her strange antics, it was peculiar to him. That all was swept away when he saw the warm desire in her green eyes that bore straight into his soul. It was the shape of her body and knowing that he and she would be alone together.

George dressed, he was conscious of his messed up hair and bleary eyes but she didn't seem to notice. He followed Luna into the woods. She said nothing until they were deep within the forest. It was cold and he rubbed his arms to keep warm.

"Here we are," she said.

She led George into a small clearing where a fire burned at the centre. "We can warm each other while we talk of our greatest secrets."

George was glad to sit by the fire and immediately began to defrost. Luna danced about the clearing, her head up towards the canopy. As she did a number of laps around the fire, George realised she had suddenly become naked.

He had never seen a grown woman naked before, and certainly never one as beautiful as Luna. She had the most beautiful curves, and he imagined running his hands over them. George watched as she twirled and danced; at times she ran her hands over his hair and kissed his cheeks as she passed.

"Put some clothes on woman!" came a gruff man's voice out of the dark.

George, surprised, turned and saw a large man as big as bear forcing his way through the undergrowth and into the clearing.

"He's just a boy," he went on.

"So?" Luna replied bluntly, "I can do as I wish."

"Not this way," the man replied, all the while looking at George. He had wild long hair and wore a strange suit of purple and a white ruffled collared shirt, which George thought was odd to wear in a forest.

"Leave me be!" Luna warned, "My Luc will never return to me, what else am I to do? Why can't I make new ... friends?"

The man just grunted. His eyes shifted to George, before he turned away and disappeared back into the darkness.

"Who was that?" George asked.

"A nuisance. Do you have an elder always telling you how to live your life?"

"Yes, my Uncle. I really wish I didn't have to live here," he replied.

She came and sat next to him, wrapping herself in her previously discarded clothes.

"Well now you have me, young George, to keep you company." She smiled.

~~~

For many nights, George continued to see Luna in secret. They would wander the woods and talk. He would complain about his life and Luna would always talk of a man called Luc. A Frenchman who had come to her woods long ago, but it seemed would never return.

"He was one of the greatest. So brave and romantic," she smiled at the memory.

George didn't have much to say. He was not wise in history or geography; in-fact, the trip to his Uncle's was the first time he had left his county.

"Don't you want to see it all?" Luna would say, "to walk through Paris or Rome. There is a whole world out there."

"I would," George would say. But it would make Luna sad for some reason. It took some courage for him to ask her why.

"Because you will leave me and never return."

"But you could come with me."

"No, I cannot leave this forest."

George never received an answer on why. Instead, Luna would give him books to read, which he found difficult, as he was not a good reader. Many nights Luna would read them to him, and he was enthralled. There was Shakespeare, tales from old Celtic lands and even heretical books banned by the Catholic Church. Luna said they had been told by the devil himself. Those he didn't like. She made it seem all so fantastical and within arm's reach of achieving it.

"I want to sail around the world and see all these things," he announced one night by the fire in the clearing.

Luna smiled but seemed sad. "Good," she whispered, "come here to me."

George went and sat in her arms. He was drowsy; despite the constant night visits he was still not used to being awake so late at night.

She played with his hair while he looked through another book. It was written in German and he had no idea of what it was saying. He could feel her lips on his neck and her arms tight around his waist. In moments, they were naked, with Luna sitting behind George, her cold hands running all over his body and her lips soft on his neck. The German book was long forgotten.

George had closed his eyes and given in to the pleasure of his flesh being touched so. Such was his enthrallment that he barely felt the sharp pain in his neck. Luna held him tight and she was strong; the pain he felt seemed to evaporate as she rocked him, her hands wandering over parts of his body no woman had ever touched.

He didn't know how long it lasted, but as always in moments of pleasure, it seemed to end too soon. Her lips lifted from his neck and there was the sweet, metallic smell of blood, his own blood. As he fell from her embrace he looked up to see Luna, her mouth covered in red scarlet, her teeth with animal-like incisors and her eyes so green they seemed great swirls of emerald. Her chest heaved and there was the low grunt of an animal as she breathed.

George landed, unconscious, on the grass.

While he was out cold, the same gruff man appeared in the clearing again.

"You should either kill him or leave him be Luna."

"Why should I be alone?"

"That's just the way it is."

"Well, Hadrian, this is my forest and I do as I like."

Hadrian took one more look at the unconscious George and left the clearing.

"We will see," he whispered.

That Luna had carried George home was the only theory he could come up with as he awoke in his own bed.

~ ~ ~

There was no sleeping in at Blacksmith farm.

"Get up," his Uncle roared.

George rose, bleary eyed and with a pounding headache.

"What's this? You're bleeding boy."

"What?" George ran his hand over his face and neck. There was the stain of blood over his hands and neck. His Uncle came in for a closer look and almost jumped to the ceiling when he saw George's wound.

"Get out! Get out!" he bellowed.

"Why? What is it?" George implored, feeling scarred and confused by his Uncle's reaction. At this time, his mother came running in to see what all the yelling was about.

"He has the wounds. I've seen them on me cows and sheep in the mornings," his Uncle said, while pointing at George.

His mother sat down on the bed. George was still in shock, he was now remembering what had happened last night and he was desperate for an excuse or distraction.

"Come on Jimmy, these are just wounds from mosquitos and fleas. He's probably riddled with them, this place is so open to the elements."

"I am itchy," George said, trying to act as if the relief he felt wasn't plastered across his face.

"Fleas?" Jimmy laughed. "Bloody big fleas." He left the room, leaving George with his mother.

"It's alright dear, I'll clean them up so they won't get infected. We have to make our keep here at Uncle Jim's, so we can't lose you."

~~~

George still had to work during the day, despite the bandage around his neck. His Uncle watched him all day, but never spoke to him.

Now it was night, and George became apprehensive. He wasn't sure if he wanted Luna to come to see him. Though he felt like some ravenous beast had been unleashed inside him, there was something about Luna's green eyes he had never fully understood. Now the memory of his blood smeared over her face chilled him to the core. He came to the realisation that he didn't really know what Luna was. Surely, she was some Celtic creature imprisoned in her forest, or worse, some demon sent by the devil himself.

It was some hours after sunset when Hadrian came to Blacksmith farm. George was tending the fire when the main door of the house was kicked in. Uncle Jimmy stood up from his chair, but very quickly backed away when he caught sight of the intruder.

"Wh ... what do you want?" he managed to stammer.

Hadrian pointed at George. "You boy, have to die or leave this place ..."

Before he could finish, there was an almighty howl from the darkness outside the house. Each of the humans inside curled up into balls by the fire. Even the great bulk of Hadrian seemed to shrink at the sound.

Long slender arms caught Hadrian by his head and with a great pull, he was ejected from the house. George recognised those arms: they were Luna's. He went to the door and saw a mighty fight between Hadrian and Luna.

They screamed at each other in a language George did not know. Their faces were not human but beasts', the eyes blazing like blazing stars and the teeth horribly animal like.

While Luna was slender, she was strong, but Hadrian was stronger. Very quickly, he had Luna by her neck with his giant hands holding her out like bag of rags.

"Is this what you love?" Hadrian spoke to George as he came towards the house with Luna still being held tight.

"Look at her."

George could see her teeth and her emerald eyes in the dim moonlight.

"Look at us, we are not human. She wants you to be like her. Do you want this? To live as a demented beast, suckling on the blood of others to survive?"

"What are you?" George whispered fearfully.

Hadrian laughed.

"I am dead and so is she. She died a long time ago my friend, but lives on now in a shadow world. It is something you could never fully understand."

"George," Luna managed to say as her throat was held vice like in Hadrian's mitt.

George could see she was pleading with him for understanding.

He was a young man stepping into adulthood, a God-fearing man who wanted to live. Her tales of tortured men, soulless wandering the world, did not appeal to him.

"God has forsaken us George. We are hunted, feared, loathed. You will never feel the embrace of your Jesus around your body. You will see him turn away from you and the light of heaven will fade, leaving you all alone in the dark, the cold winter wind and the ghosts of your existence your only companions."

George could not take his eyes off Luna. The unnatural features he had seen before had disappeared and there was the Luna he knew, her eyes still bright and pleading. But if Hadrian was right, then he wanted no part of her existence. He knew that God would not forsake him.

"She has already bitten you." Hadrian raised his fingers on his free hand and tapped them on his own neck.

"You are only a step away from becoming one of us. She is mad and you will go mad too."

"George, no," his mother begged him.

He looked at her as she came up behind him and held his arm.

"We can't stay here," she added.

"Yes. Listen to your mother George, mothers know best," Hadrian said, while he looked at the face of Luna. She had gone whiter than before.

"Please George. I need you to love me," she squealed as Hadrian tightened his grip.

Georges's mother had pulled her son into the house and the door was closed.

"Leave tonight!" Hadrian called out.

George and his parents did just that. By morning, they were nearing their old home. The sunrise had never looked so welcoming and safe.

~~~

For all his life, George could not forget Luna. At times, he thought her near, her scent on the night wind that blew in from the river Eyre, a naked dancer running through the trees, her eyes afire like brilliant stars.

He would not know the torment he left behind. Luna had lost all hope. She needed someone to last with her for all immortality. It was only now that she was coming to realise just how hard that was; immortality was too long a time. She would go into the earth and wait. Then decide her fate.

Uncle Jim was glad to see his brother's family go, but he was afraid of what lurked in the forest. He couldn't believe the trouble that boy had brought to his farm. He ran his hand over his scarred face. Harpies love handsome boys, but he had known all about that long before George arrived.

TWO LITTLE HANDS

Gosford Hospital is set upon a rise overlooking the small city it's named after. Easy to see, but not easy to get to if you're on foot and in need of urgent medical attention. Many of the streets around the hospital were inclined at almost a 45-degree angle.

It was well past midnight, but there was still the trickle of cars and ambulances coming and going from the accident and emergency department car park. The quietness of the night belied the massive social problems of Gosford: the constant domestics, the drug use and the alcohol abuse perpetrated by people of all ages and demographics. A police car, its flashing lights and siren filling the night, roared down a main street as if to emphasise the point.

Only about a hundred metres away was the railway station, where a few drunken youths were yelling out at each other as they walked along the footpath.

Ambulance 513 suddenly came roaring up the road, its red and blue lights flashing off the parked car windows. Its driver pulled the large van into the accident and emergency car park and brought it to a stop outside the sliding doors.

The driver went to the rear of the ambulance, opened the door, and assisted his partner with pulling out the stretcher. With few words, they brought their patient into the hospital.

A team of staff waited. It had been a quiet night for once and the waiting room wasn't full.

"Has she been out all this time?" a nurse asked.

"Yeah. Here's her chart," the paramedic handed it to the nurse. The nurse was looking at the female on the stretcher. She was blonde, in her late twenties as far as the nurse could tell. The dried blood across the woman's face made any further identification impossible.

"Who is she?"

"Don't know. The police found her by the side of the road."

"Looks like she's been hit by a truck," the nurse muttered under his breath.

~~~

At 1 AM, Detectives Paul Mullen and Joe Delves were at their office at Gosford Police station, ready to knock off. It had been a quiet shift and they had spent most it finalising a few briefs for court.

Mullen was making himself a final cup of coffee. He was blonde but had just shaved all his hair off; it had been beginning to fall out anyway. He was patting his expanding stomach when the phone rang. The two men exchanged worried looks when it first begun ringing. It was either a duty officer checking whether they had knocked off early, hoping to get a scalp or - just as bad - some new incident where the detectives were needed.

"Yeah? ... Who is she? ... Right," Mullen spoke while Delves held his breath.

"Alright, we'll go and have a look," Mullen then hung up the phone. "Shit!" he cried out, while Delves reluctantly grabbed his jacket. Delves was in is mid-thirties, the same as Mullen, but had a more solid build as a result of his time in the gym. He had a full head of hair with flecks of grey, so he didn't need to shave it like his partner did.

"So what is it?" Delves asked when they got to the car.

"Jane Doe presented at hospital. Found by the side of the road."

"Dead?"

"Nah. Unconscious. Head wounds, fractured ribs no ID," Mullen's answered.

"Been dumped, you reckon?" Delves asked, yawning.

Mullen looked at him and merely nodded his head with a knowing smile.

~~~

When the two Detectives arrived at the hospital, they were surprised by the quietness of the place. They had a quiet chuckle at the only person in the waiting room, a large fat man who was staring directly ahead and breathing heavily in controlled breaths. The front of his shirt was covered with food scraps or vomit, they couldn't really tell.

"All you can eat really has a lot to answer for," Delves whispered to his partner, who was trying to look professional as they waited to be taken to the bed of the Jan Doe.

A nurse led them to a separate room where the woman had been placed into a bed. There had been no change in her condition.

Mullen and Delves weren't medical experts, but being in the job for fifteen years each, they had picked up a lot of the acronyms and medical jargon that hospitals use.

"Life threatening?" Mullen asked the Doctor, a balding Indian man in his mid twenties.

"I can't see why it should be. A few broken ribs, cuts and bruises. Her coma is my only concern. She has suffered a blow to the head and we are running some tests to see if there has been any damage to the brain. Until then, it's a waiting game."

Delves had wandered into the room where the woman was lying with the standard drip in her arm.

"No ventilator?"

"No, she's breathing on her own."

"Any property?" Mullen asked.

"Yeah, on her bedside."

As Delves went to get it, his eyes were distracted by red spots on the side of the blanket that hung over the edge of the bed. He looked closer and was surprised to recognise their shape.

"Where did these hand-prints come from?" he asked.

The Doctor stepped into the room to have a better look.

"I don't know. Maybe it's paint." he shrugged. It had been a long shift and his interest was at a low.

"Looks like some kid's handprints." Mullen had also had a look.

Having no answer, the doctor left the detectives to go through the brown paper bag. Delves pulled out a wet and dirty handbag that contained only wet mud.

"Shit. They pull her out of a river or something?" he looked about for something to wipe his hands with.

"Don't know." Mullen was quiet, "There's nothing we can do here. We'll get dayshift to come back with a fingerprint kit."

~~~

It was hard to change sheets and bathe some patients; some people were too fragile. The only chance was when they would be moved for surgery or temporally taken to another unit for the unending series of tests that hospitals seem to impose on patients.

A nurse came in to ready the woman for another brain scan. The room was cold and she glanced at the window to see if it was open. Seeing it closed, she checked the air-conditioning. The dial read 25-degrees, but the nurse was sure it felt like only ten.

While moving the sheets, she saw the two red coloured handprints on the side of the sheet. She had a better look at it and knew instinctively that it was blood.

~~~

Mullen and Delves started a new shift at 1pm the next day. They had their day planned, but that all ended up being shelved by the new developments of the Jane Doe case.

"Blood? You serious?" Mullen exclaimed, while drinking coffee.

"How?" Delved added.

"No one knows." Sergeant Anderson shrugged his shoulders. "It took all day to get a warrant to get her prints. The boss even went on the news to get some public help."

"Anything?" Mullen added.

"Not yet. You'll have to get the prints yourself and get an update."

Once again, the Detectives drove to Gosford Hospital. There was something about the smell of a hospital that made Mullen's stomach turn over. Probably the amount of disinfectant used on the floors and walls to kill germs and cover the stench of death. He was surprised that in the morgue there was no such smell, there was just nothing ... well, except the smell of chemicals coming from the big fridge.

They made their way through the corridors where nurses and patients walked about, all coming and going from different places. Finding the room, they went straight in.

"Do we need to show the warrant to anyone?" Delves asked his partner.

"Nah. Well, next of kin or the patient, but in this case we just need to send off the completion." Mullen's body suddenly shuddered. "Is it me or is it freezing in here?" Mullen's asked while he began setting up the small fingerprint kit.

"Very," Delves replied, while looking about for the air-conditioner.

"Hey, look at this," Delves had spotted the little red hand prints on the bed sheets.

"Thought they would have changed the sheets."

"They did," came a voice from behind them. It was a nurse.

"She went to x-ray about an hour ago, the sheets were changed. She came back about twenty minutes ago and no one had been in here," the nurse began to leave, "and it's always cold in here, despite the air conditioner saying it's 25-degrees. Freaky, hey?"

"Yeah," Delves replied, while looking down at the two little hands.

"Any luck on finding out who she is?"

"Nah, hopefully this will start something," Mullen replied, while taking the woman's fingerprints.

Having done that, the two Detectives were glad to leave the ward. Mullen didn't want to say he was freaked out, but he was. All the time he was in that room, he felt like he was being watched.

The fingerprint analysis came back with nothing. The blood had been sent for DNA analysis, but there was little point in having these results without something on a government database to match it to. It seemed Jane Doe just didn't exist anywhere on any database.

All they needed was a name, or something to lead them to a name. Then they got two calls. The first was from the staff at the hospital. The two little hands had reappeared in the morning after the sheets had been changed. The staff were beginning to get freaked out and they wouldn't go in there alone, because when they were in the room they felt like they weren't alone at all.

Mullen didn't know what to say to the nurse. "We've got a few more leads. Is there any change in her condition?"

"No. Well, we'll let you know, of course, if that changes and if the sheets need to be changed again. At first it was a bit weird, now it's just creepy," the nurse said.

"Yeah, I can only chase bad guys who are alive, not ghosts," Mullen's laughed.

The second call was what they wanted to hear. A car had been found at the back of Somersby.

"GD crew said it looks like it came off the highway and been under the bush for a few days. No-one in it, but there's a woman's purse, Julie Wisher from Penrith. Car's registered to a Michael Wisher, same address." Delves smiled, he was glad of the break through.

"Penrith cops going to knock on their door?" Mullen asked.

"As we speak."

Penrith was a long way from Gosford, a good 200 kilometres, and a bit of an effort to get to. First you had to travel the Great Western Highway into the city, the M5 if you could afford the tollway. Then it was through the congestion of Sydney's roads and then north up the F3. Mullen didn't think it too extraordinary: plenty of families had left the high crime areas with their lack of employment and general dreariness to move to the cheap land of the central coast, not to mention that the beaches were generally less than twenty minutes away for most residents. No wonder Gosford's crime rate had risen, though no one would admit it in government circles. 'Westies' had moved to the coast in large numbers and brought all their social problems with them. Well, that was another story, Mullen thought.

All they could do for now is sit back and wait.

~~~

A detective crew from Mount Druitt arrived outside 34 Paris Street. There was no car in the driveway. The grass was overgrown wherever wheel ruts hadn't turned the ground into pools of bare earth. Scattered toys were strewn about the front yard. The house was part fibro and part brick. From the wear and tear, it seemed the occupiers didn't spend too much time or money on the place. Detective Tracey O'Malley had been here before, years ago, when she was still in uniform. It was for a domestic, the common currency of the police in Western Sydney. She remembered a woman and a drunken man who was an arrogant fuck; she had found it hard not to hit him around the head with her baton. And there had been a little baby. Computer checks on the house didn't reveal anything new; just a few lost property reports and another domestic incident about a year previously.

O'Malley's partner, Terri Hatchen, knocked on the door. No response. Knocking twice more produced the same result.

"Let's go around the back," O'Malley suggested.

They passed through the open rotting wooden gate to the backyard. It was more overgrown than the front, with the customary toys strewn about, a moss-covered kids swimming pool, and the stereotypical rusting old Holden in a far corner.

There was still no response to their knocking and calling.

"Has someone tried to contact the father?" O'Malley asked.

"Yep, nothin'. They tried his work, here, mobile, and nothing. Goes to message bank."

O'Malley was about to give up, but took one last look by stretching herself across the balcony to look through a rear window. She saw men's boots dangling unnaturally in a doorway.

"Shit!"

"What is it?" Hatchen asked as her partner went to force the wooden back door open.

"Someone is hanging in the lounge room," she replied. She checked the handle and was shocked to find the door wasn't properly locked. With one push she forced it open, and the two Detectives entered the house.

They found the husband, Michael, hanging by a piece of rope from the lounge room light. All the curtains were closed and there was a god-awful smell hanging in the air.

"Looks like he's been dead for a few days," Hatchen stated while pointing a torch at the face of the corpse.

O'Malley quickly checked the other rooms. There was a little girl's room, but it was empty. The whole house was empty but for the human chandelier.

"There should be a little girl here," O'Malley yelled out.

"Come look at this," Hatchen yelled back.

O'Malley came out to see Hatchen hunched over a table, torchlight on a piece of paper, which she was reading.

"Suicide note?"

"Sort of."

O'Malley began to read.

U stupid bitch and ur stupid runt of a kid. I've taken it and dumped it just to piss u off. Maybe now I can hav a life without u fuckers. Go find her slut.

"Nice."

"What an arsehole," O'Malley said while looking up at the remains of Michael.

"Now we've got a missing person. I'll check with the neighbours. We got ourselves a crime scene," Hatchen was already on her feet.

"Hey Tracey, you okay?"

"Yeah. It just shits me that's all. Fuckers like this do this to people."

"I hope there is a hell, I really do," Terri said as the two walked out of the house.

"Should we cut him down?"

"Nah, let him hang, crime scene can do it."

~~~

Mullen and Delves were back at the hospital. Finally having a name made it much easier to try and formally identify Jane Doe. Julie Wisher's drivers licence had been accessed and all her old photos downloaded. Dentist records had also been checked. It was all adding up to confirm that Julie Wisher was lying in a coma in Gosford.

But this didn't explain how or why she ended up here. Or why her husband had hung himself after seemingly making their daughter disappear. Had Julie been driving about looking for her only to become distracted and drive off the road? Why hadn't she called the police? Why would a father do this to a child? It seemed answering the question of who Jane Doe was just opened up the proverbial can of worms. Who was Julie Wisher?

Delves and Mullen's didn't have those answers. Their first priority was finding Julie's daughter, Penelope. Penrith Detectives had told them Penelope was about four and autistic. She never went anywhere without her mother, never.

Mullen was looking at the fresh blood on Julie's sheets. He wasn't going to admit it to anyone, but he felt sure that Penelope had found her mother.

"What the hell happened in that house Greg?" Delves whispered to him.

"Don't know man, it's all beyond me," Mullen whispered in return. His eyes fixed on the two little hand prints.

PENANCE

A telling of an event three years ago ...

It was late at night. Sue looked at the clock at her desk once again. 11:53pm. She couldn't believe they were actually working so late and getting paid to do it. She hadn't worked a night shift since she was in her early twenties packing shelves in Coles on the weekend to get herself through uni. But now it was the big world and rich companies in America would pay for workers in Sydney to stay up late so they could converse with each other, being daylight in the USA.

"Why couldn't it be the other way round?" she'd ask aloud.

"Because they're paying," would come the answer.

She yawned again and stopped typing.

"You want another coffee Sue?" April asked as she walked by, empty coffee cup in hand.

"Love one. Even though my doctor says I shouldn't be drinking all this caffeine during night time, I'll be wired for weeks."

"Only a few more days and we're back to normal time."

Sue yawned again as she stood up. She was going to be lazy and give her cup to April but decided the walk would wake her up.

Inside the small office were a number of cubicles most of them empty but for three. Another one of the night walkers, Brad, was typing away while talking on the phone to a client in LA. Other than that most of the lights were out and it was quiet.

"You still going away on the weekend?"

"Oh yeah, it'll be good to have a break after this. Three days of doing nothing but laying in the sun."

"Two sugars and milk right?"

"That's the one."

April prepared the cups while the water boiled. Suddenly a phone rang in one of the cubicles, by the tone of Wham's *Wake me up before you go-go* it had to be a mobile.

"Tell him I'm working," Brad called out.

"Who'd be calling me at this hour?" Sue said as she hurried back to her bag at her cubicle.

She picked up the phone. The display read – home -

"Hello?" Nothing. "Hello?"

"Mum! Mum! Help me! Help me!" came a frantic female voice before the line went dead.

"Leah? Leah!" she looked down at the phone in confusion and growing panic. That was her daughter's voice, she was sure of it, as all mothers know the voice of their children.

"Who was it?" April asked as she came back with the two cups of hot coffee.

"I think it was my daughter."

Sue's voice was frail and crackling. She dialled her home and waited impatiently for it to be answered.

Seconds seemed like minutes as she waited. Nothing. Agitated she slammed the phone down on the desk.

"No answer?" April queried as Sue began to get her things together in a panic.

"I'm going home, something's wrong."

"Yeah do what you've got to do."

Sue ran out of the office to the elevator dialling again the home number. She had dialled three times while in the elevator; each time there was no answer. She tried her daughter's and her husband's mobiles but both were switched off. Her panic levels were increasing as she got to her car and fumbled madly with the keys.

Even while she drove she continued to ring home.

"Come on! Answer the phone!"

She gave up and concentrated on driving home as quickly as possible. It was an easy half an hour at normal speed but this time she went over it. She was getting frantic, her heart raced and her hands sweated on the wheel as the worse scenarios flashed one after the other in her mind, broken only by the thought that the cops would probably be out and catch her speeding.

The half an hour became twenty minutes as she pulled into the driveway. The double-story house was in darkness and her daughter's old Gemini with only three wheels was still in the driveway.

Somehow she had managed to calm down slightly so that she was able to open the door with a key quickly.

Inside it was darkness and everything looked normal and in its place. She went upstairs to where the bedrooms were.

"Leah? Pete? Hello?" she called as she climbed the staircase.

Upstairs was cold, which was unusual; there must be an open window somewhere. She went to her daughter's room, opened the door and turned on the light.

There was her daughter fast asleep in bed. Her art supplies and paintings all around the room plus her clothes in piles near the bed. Leah stirred as the light came on and her mother's quick footsteps came towards her.

"Mum? What are you doing?" she whispered, still half asleep.

Sue sat down on the bed. "Did you ring me at work tonight? About half an hour ago?"

Leah looked at the clock on the table next to her bed, 12:55am, then back to her mum, "No. Why?"

"Didn't you hear the bloody phone ringing? Where's your father? Jesus the house could be on fire and it wouldn't wake you two up."

Leah laughed.

"It's not funny Leah. I was absolutely beside myself and had to race home because I thought you were in trouble, I mean the phone call, you sounded frightened. Are you sure it wasn't you?"

"Mum. Why would I call you in the middle of the night to play a prank? I'm not a kid."

"Alright. As long as you're okay?" Sue seemed satisfied but still wary as a mother can be. She looked her daughter over; her hair was still blonde with the black stripe she had coloured in last week, against her mother's wishes. Her eyes were still green and barely open.

"I'm okay but I'll be cranky in the morning."

Sue stood up off the bed and went for the door.

"I hope you're not practising for this weekend when you've got the place to yourself?"

"No," Leah was already wrapped back in the blankets and near the point of sleep.

Sue turned off the light and closed the door behind her.

"Now I'll wake the other deaf caveman called your father."

She went into their bedroom and turned on the light and closed the door.

Leah had already fallen back to sleep.

~~~

Ourimbah University's car park was crammed with students who had all walked the short distance from the railway station to the uni itself. Leah yawned for the fourth time since getting off the train. It was the end of a long week and she had been working on her major piece for her half-yearly exam. She had a bin of mistakes, not likes and maybes, but had finally settled on painting a group of photos of her grandparents when they were young. She had found similar photos of her parents and thought it was odd and arty to do a collage of time repeating itself. Hell it would do, she loved art but sometimes she had to be in the mood.

Near the gate her friend Jo Armitage, wearing her trademark black jeans, red flannelette shirt and pink hair, was waiting with a large case containing her own painting of wild horses. She had a thing for them but she always painted them in black or in war-like poses. Being a half Goth/punk and cynical as a piece of lemon gave her a dark outlook on the world.

"Ray called me this morning. He got dumped by Claire again," she jumped straight in.

"They're always breaking up and getting back together. What is this, the third time in four months?"

"I think it's the final time, she hooked up with this other guy last weekend and I guess she spent the next few days making up her mind."

"Poor Ray he tries so hard."

"He'll get over it," Jo said bluntly.

"So what are we painting today?" Leah changed the subject.

"Fruit."

"Ohh," Leah moaned, "I'm sick of painting that, when are we painting nude men?"

They both laughed at the thought.

Inside the classroom the students were still coming in. Scattered around the art room were paintings, sculptures and art supplies. Leah and Jo sat together at the large table that held the whole group. Next to them was their friend Ray Sajer, who sat head down drawing in a scrapbook.

"I like your new hair cut," Jo smiled and rubbed her hand over Ray's short crew cut.

"You okay doll?" Leah asked as she put a hand on his shoulder.

Ray didn't move from his sketching. "Yeah I'll live." *Little bitch.*

"You still want to come over tonight? We can talk about it then."

"We've got the whole weekend for you to cry your eyes out," Jo added.

"That won't happen. But I'm still up for it, cause Brett's bringing along a little game to lighten the mood."

"It's not European porn? You know Michelle's religious and it'll freak her out," Leah was suddenly suspicious.

"Well you can tell your friend that she might enjoy a little porn. Jo does."

"Don't all perverts?" Jo smiled.

"But no it isn't porn nor anything sexual, so don't fret my little pets."

Jo was going through her bag, which she had on the desk. "That Brett's been a bad influence on you. You used to be the nice one."

Ray smiled, "I'm still nice just getting a bit rough around the edges now that I'm a man."

"Whatever you think Ray," Jo said with a wink.

Once uni was over Leah and Jo headed towards the local shops to stock up on supplies for the night. It had been years since Leah had any form of sleepover, only in high school, and now this was more adult.

"What about Mexican?" Leah posed the question as they walked down the aisle.

"You don't want boys eating spicy food and then having to be in the same room for the rest of the night, if you get my drift?"

"Yuck. What about movies? Action, scary or girlie?"

"Is Michelle allowed to watch them, being a Mormon?"

"She's a Jehovah's Witness and I'll have to ask her. That would suck, you know she *has* to go out and door knock, it's part of the religion. Can you believe that? I'd be so embarrassed."

"You'll have to call her soon so we know."

Leah's eyes widened in excitement as she remembered a tale she had completely forgotten about all day.

"My mum woke me up this morning asking me if I called her at work at like midnight or something, she rushed home to check, she was freaking out."

"That's weird, was it a wrong number?" Jo asked as she lifted some noodles in a cup complete with vegetables.

"She said my mobile number came up on her screen. I was thinking it was some computer geek who hacked into our personal records and is now enjoying playing pranks. That's why you don't buy stuff off the net."

"I've bought books off e-bay and never had any trouble."

"Not yet."

Jo had settled on some chocolate and a big bag of assorted lollies, her usual weekend diet.

"Only pay in cash and cards are for emergencies."

"Your kids are never going to have any fun are they? You'll be one of those paranoid mothers who won't let them buy i-pods or computers or TVs cause the government might be watching."

"Like Michelle?" Leah joked.

"Poor girl, she needs a night out," Jo said while containing a laugh.

The day was near its end now. The sun was melting into the horizon throwing up a bright orange haze across the sky as it sank away.

Two parents had hurriedly packed their little hatchback both eager to escape the doldrums of the working week. Sue gave her husband Pete the final bag as her daughter watched and counted the seconds until they were gone.

"You'll be alright?"

"Yes," Leah said sweetly.

"Call the police if any gate-crashers turn up, just keep the doors locked."

"Alright Mum," she was getting annoyed now.

Sue moved to the car and opened the passenger door. "And keep your mobile on all night; keep it on the charger to be sure."

"I will," she kissed her mother on the cheek.

"Bye now."

Her father came up to her and kissed her forehead.

"Please don't let me find anything rubber in our bed, okay?"

Leah was both embarrassed and disgusted, she wasn't sure which, at the thought that her parents thought she was doing it or doing it in their bed.

"Yuck Dad. It's probably yours."

He chuckled as he walked back to the driver's side and got in. Sue waved goodbye as the car rolled down the driveway and onto the road. It would be the last time they would see their daughter again.

As the car drove away another car, a white Charade with music pumping loudly was coming the other way. Its horn beeped as it passed her parents. It had to be Jo. The Charade pulled into the driveway and out got Jo and Michelle.

"That's timing," Leah said as she walked to meet them. The two girls were busy now pulling out bags full of food and drink both fizzy and alcoholic.

"How much stuff did you bring?" she exclaimed at seeing all the bags.

"Hopefully it's enough."

Leah took hold of one of Michelle's bags. Michelle was a slip of a girl with straight shoulder-length blonde hair with rosy cheeks. The guys thought she was hot if she dropped the old virginal Britney Spears look.

"Mum packed me a few religious books for inspiration."

"Really?" Leah seemed incredulous. "Van Gogh?" she added excitedly.

"Vincent is a sinner in my house so I have to hide his stuff."

"Did you look through his book? Don't you love starry night?"

"We're not talking art all night are we?" Jo pipped in as the three moved towards the front door.

"Well this is a study weekend," Leah smiled. A phone rang forcing Michelle to dig into her pocket.

"Hello? Yes I just pulled up ... No they just left ... I don't know how late we'll be, it's Friday ... That was Jo ... she's harmless," Michelle was rolling her eyes now as her two friends started laughing.

"Did you bring the batteries for the vibrator Leah?" Jo said loudly, intending for Michelle's parents to hear.

"Turn that porn down!" Leah added.

Michelle flung them a death stare that quickly became a smile.

"No it was the TV. I have to go. I'll call you tomorrow," she turned the mobile off. "She heard you two."

"Oh well," Jo shrugged. "Where are the boys?"

"They'll be here soon."

"They're not the type to get me drunk and try and have sex with me are they?"

"No. Well Brett might have a go until he realises he's getting nowhere. But Ray's too shy," Leah assured her friend.

By now the sun had set and darkness hung over the small suburb by the water. It was chilly outside and a fire was lit in the fireplace in the large study at the back of the house on the ground floor.

The boys had arrived hours before and had set up home in front of the TV with the playstation and most of the food; so intent on the game that most of the crumbs were spread over their shirts. Finally Ray, still eyes on the screen, wiped them off with one hand.

The girls had been talking amongst themselves but Leah was getting tired of that so she decided to annoy Ray.

"Ray, did you get any of your project done today? I'm putting this night on for that reason you know."

Ray's eyes didn't leave the screen and only a small portion of his concentration was spent on Leah.

"I was trying; I brought it with me but just can't get into it. I was drawing Claire as Queen of the Harpies and that made me feel better."

"There's plenty of pussy out there man," added Brett. He was a solid young male with a three-week beard and messy brown hair.

"There's my cousin Jenny."

"Nah. If I stood behind her you wouldn't see me she's that ... biggish."

Jo, who had said little, now pricked up. "Fat! What is it with you guys who want the skinny bimbo?"

"I didn't say that."

"But that's what you meant."

"I was trying to think of a better word. There's fat and then there's voluptuous, Brett's favourite."

"Don't try and deflect to me man!"

"Is that your type? The curvy girl?" Leah teased.

Brett was trying to ignore them and continue with his game.

"Yes I like girls with a little meat and big breasts. Ray's the one who likes the pale skinny model type."

"It's true. The more addicted to crack and heroin the better."

"That reminds me Brett. I've heard this rumour going around that you're into drugs big time. I'm shocked," said Jo.

"It's all bullshit. I've smoked a bit of weed but who hasn't? Plus a quarter of an ekki which fucked me over good time but that's it."

"We're art students and musicians, isn't that part of the script?" a sarcastic Ray added in mock defence of his friend.

Jo then turned her attention on Ray. "So you have too then?"

"You may be surprised by the fact I haven't. I want to keep my 140 IQ and go on to greater things."

"What you're saying is I'm a deadshit?" Brett protested with his mouth full of chips.

"Nah. But I went to school with this kid who was brainy and got good marks until he discovered the weed and it was down hill from there. By the end of school he was a brain-dead zombie."

"So what about you two then?" Brett turned the tables on his accusers.

"Pot," Leah bluntly replied.

"Same. But hopefully crack and heroin so Ray will love me," Jo smiled. Ray winked at her playfully.

"God is there anyone who hasn't tried pot?" Leah mused then seemed to remember Michelle was there. Then everyone else remembered as well and it went a little quiet until Leah bit the bullet and asked.

"What about you doll?"

Michelle rolled her eyes. "Come on, you know I've never smoked anything except smoked ham … all I've had is a few threesomes."

There were a few seconds of quiet as each of them made sure she was joking. All of them suddenly broke into laughter.

"For a second there I'm thinking oh shit really!" Brett laughed.

"I'm surprised I can eat hash browns," Michelle went on, giving an insight into her life in a religious house.

"So are we going to study or paint or what?" Leah once again tried to bring the party back to business.

"Nope," a disinterested Brett replied.

"We need more food."

"I'll get the pizzas then," said Leah as she got up off the couch and went to the kitchen.

Ray stood up to stretch, pieces of food falling off him like a waterfall.

"Are you going to let me play pro wrestling or what?"

"What just like you two do together in bed?" Jo jumped in before Brett could answer.

Brett and Ray looked at each other with a disgusted look.

"I just wanna play wrestling on playstation with you man, that's as far as it goes," Ray warned.

Brett looked to Jo. "You're fucked up Jo."

"I don't get how men love the idea of women having sex with other women while man on man action is repulsive, even to women."

Ray decided to offer an answer. "Because men think visually, women react differently with emotions and touch and stuff. Men just wanna see tits and arse, the more the better."

Defeated, Jo turned to Michelle. "Can't win can I?"

"Nope."

Leah returned with a few plates with pizzas. "Come and get it."

Brett pulled himself off the floor. "I've earned a little break."

"You haven't done anything," Leah pointed out.

"That takes a lot out of you," Brett indicated towards the playstation now idle on the floor. "It's very exhausting."

They all gathered around a table and began grabbing bits of pizza.

"That looks so good," Ray eyed the plates of steaming dough, paste, meat and cheese. They each took a piece and went back to the couch. Leah sat next to Brett.

"So where's this thing you were going to bring over?"

Brett got up and went to his bag, picked it up and dropped himself back on the couch. He opened it and pulled out a square board.

"What is it?" Jo asked.

"An Ouija board," Brett replied with a twinkle in his eye.

"A what?" Leah's face contorted in confusion.

"Mystics in the nineteenth century used them to contact dead spirits," Ray offered an answer.

"Like the one Regan used in The Exorcist to bring out the devil," Brett went on.

"You're joking. Let me look!" exclaimed Leah.

"You two are kidding right? Where did you get it?" Jo seemed stern with her words, mixed with anger and fear.

"I bought it last week at some hippie, tree-hugging, new-age shop in Newtown," Brett dismissed her.

"Actually they were Goth witch types," Ray corrected.

"Whatever."

Leah looked over the board with great interest. "How does it work?"

"You've never seen one of these?"

"No," Leah came from a straight family, no witches in her bloodline.

Michelle had been watching them fawn over the device with revulsion and fear.

"They're dangerous. The bible says you shouldn't deal with witchcraft and sorcery."

"This isn't witchcraft, it's just some fun," Brett said as he put it on the floor.

"We're not going to bring on the end of the world by speaking to Ray's dead Pop. We might even be able to speak to Jesus, how bout that eh?"

Michelle was able to take most people's jokes about her religious family and its values but her patience had worn out now and she gave Brett the biggest death stare she had ever flicked someone. She was fired up now.

"I'm just saying we should be careful, you never know what's going to happen that's all."

"Michelle babe. I could get hit by a car or a falling tree if I stepped outside but that's not going to make me stay inside forever is it?" Brett condescendingly replied.

Michelle still wasn't convinced but could tell stubborn Brett wasn't going to change. Jo finally came to her defence.

"Maybe she just wants to sit it out and watch?"

"It's okay if you don't want to," Leah added.

"Yeah, I'll just watch you all turn into rats," a defiant Michelle was then silent. Her and the popcorn sat back to watch.

Brett looked at each of his friends. "Leah? Jo? Ray? Are we all in?"

"Of course you idiot."

Leah and Jo looked at each other before answering in the affirmative.

"I think it's a load of crap but I want to see you turn into rats too," Jo added. Leah's face of concern creased even more in worry as she turned to Brett.

"Could that happen?"

"No. Do you want to see how it works?"

"Yeah."

"Let me look at it first."

Jo reached out and picked up the board and the glass sitting on it. It looked normal but for the edges surrounded by letters. She looked under it and into the glass and found nothing that made her suspicious.

"No batteries, no strings," said Brett as she gave it back to him. He replaced it on the small table.

"Ray, the lights."

Ray got up and turned off the lights leaving them in the glow of the fire. Leah turned off the TV and stereo.

"Okay. We all put our fingers on the triangle and concentrate."

They all did as Brett asked while Michelle watched from the couch.

Brett closed his eyes and began to speak. "Spirits of the underworld, hear me."

The others cracked up with laughter.

"Luke I am your father," Ray mimicked his favourite Dark Lord, Vader. There was more nervous laughter. Brett wasn't laughing.

"Stop it!"

He closed his eyes again. "Spirits of the underworld, hear my call."

The girls suddenly jumped.

"Did you do that?" Leah sharply turned on Brett who was wide-eyed in excitement.

"Did you feel something?"

"Sorry that was me, nervous twitch," Jo half-heartedly apologised, then broke into giggles with Leah.

"Girls, stop pissing around, it won't work otherwise," Brett was getting annoyed.

"Where are all the ghosts Brett?" Leah asked innocently, but he knew she was taking the piss. Ray took his hand off the glass and sat back.

"This isn't working."

"You're meant to be the brains of the group, you and your 140 IQ," Brett turned on his friend. Ray just shrugged.

Brett's mind was racing as it looked for an idea. It didn't take him long to get it.

"Where's there a cemetery round here?"

~~~

By now the moon had risen and was a great silver disk in the dark sky. The few clouds had been moved away by a gentle wind.

The opening of a door and the running of footsteps and laughter broke the quiet of the night. Brett and Ray ran towards Brett's car parked at the end of the driveway. Jo and Michelle walked behind them seemingly bored and carrying the loot while Leah locked up the house behind them.

Brett opened the doors on his car.

"Do we have provisions?"

Jo held up the bags of lollies, chips and alcohol. She threw them into the back seat. Ray jumped in after them. Jo followed. Michelle stood by the door a little unsure of what to do.

"You coming?" Leah asked her.

"I don't know," she was a little hesitant.

By now Brett was in the driver's seat with his head out of the window. "Come on. We're not smoking dope, robbing banks or rooting. We're young and we should be up to no good and damn it I want some mischief and I'm gunna conjure up a ghost."

Ray put his head out of the rear passenger window. "Yeah cause we're uni students."

"Yeah, we're letting the cliché slip here; we have to do something crazy. Jo's in."

Jo gave a half-hearted wave while eating a bar of chocolate. "Let's get into some shit, we're art students," added Ray.

Leah got into the back while Michelle gave in and got into the front. Brett had the car out of the driveway in reverse quickly and away down the road.

As the car drove along the only road through the sleepy suburbs to the only cemetery in the small suburb it swerved to the right then back to the left as the roars of laughter came from within it. It slowed as the cemetery approached. It started to jump and jolt as Brett played dumb with the gears and brakes forcing more laughter from their overstimulated laughing gear.

Finally it stopped and the five piled out. Brett looked around satisfied.

"This is it."

"Did we even bring the board?" Ray asked while choking back tears.

"The board! Where is the board?!" Brett roared.

Jo handed it to him. "I have it here my master."

Brett took it and kissed it. "Very good my son. Let's go in shall we?"

Jo was already walking towards the small gate, which was connected to a low sandstone wall. It didn't seem to need a gate because you could just jump over it. It was only a small cemetery; about a dozen headstones were in neat rows with overgrown grass. It was the final resting place for many of the early settlers in Saratoga.

"Can you feel the spirits at your bosom my master?" Ray mockingly asked.

"Yes my apprentice they suckle to me and I feel their anger."

"If you're lucky Marilyn Monroe might come and suck your dick," Jo added.

"Cool," said Brett and Ray in unison without even looking at each other as they walked.

The group approached the cemetery and for a strange reason they had gone quiet. The laughter and pissing around had stopped.

Leah approached Michelle. "Are you alright with this?"

Ray overheard the question and before she could answer had asked his own. "Yeah, are you even allowed in here?"

"I'm alright; I'm not that much of a dork. Now Mormons, they're your bible-bashing weirdos."

Brett had now joined in the questions of Michelle's religious beliefs. "What is it with knocking on people's doors anyway? Don't you know how much we hate it?"

"I know but I have to or I'll go to hell."

"I realise it's part of your dogma but don't they realise that the bible has been interpreted in so many different ways by so many different groups," Ray went on. "Why do you expect you'd go to heaven while say a Catholic won't when in reality that started the concept of modern Christianity which is based on Judaism anyway?"

"So you're saying why is my way the way, and yours isn't?" Michelle gently asked. She didn't mind answering these types of intelligent questions; in fact she enjoyed it.

"Yeah like it's all about earning your way into heaven but if you go out and do good things isn't that enough? Why do the details of like what food you eat or giving or not giving blood count?" Ray continued with his probing.

"We're all hell-bound anyway. All the best people are in hell," Brett interrupted the conversation with his own thoughts as he usually did.

"You know who else is a Jehovah's Witness?" Michelle smiled as she put the question out there.

"Umm, Jesus?" Leah innocently answered. Ray gave her an 'are you stupid?' look.

"No. Michael Jackson."

"No way!" Leah exclaimed.

Brett was laughing at his own thoughts. "Imagine him coming to your door." He changed his deep voice to mimic the self-proclaimed King of Pop. "Hi, I'm Michael Jackson. Look what God has done to me, so go to church."

They all had a good laugh over that as they reached the gate.

Ray leant in close to Michelle. "You didn't answer my question."

Michelle innocently shrugged and smiled. "Why do people like different flowers or different types of music?"

"Variety is the spice of life huh? I suppose so."

The group entered the graveyard, except Brett, who stood at the gates, eyes closed and breathing heavily.

"What is he doing?" asked Jo.

"I'm about to cross into the netherworld woman," Brett replied as he shook his body.

"Okay I'm ready."

"Where's a good spot?" asked Ray as he looked around.

"This one," Brett pointed to a grave with the only above-ground slab. They all gathered about it while Brett placed the board and glass on the stone slab.

Jo sat next to Leah. "When I was little I was petrified to walk on graves. I was waiting for the hand to come out of the dirt and get me."

"Me too, they're freaky."

Michelle took a seat next on another grave an arm's length away. No-one noticed her.

"It's expensive to be buried these days. Plus there is the chance in two hundred years of being dug up for some building development," said Ray.

"Really? Don't they let the dead lay?" asked Leah.

"Nah. Town Hall in Sydney and Central Station used to be graveyards til they were dug up and the coffins moved to Rookwood, or so they say. The headstones are there," Ray smiled.

"The price of progress," Jo lamented.

"So are we going to do this or what?" Leah asked Brett.

"Yeah is it charged up?" added Jo.

"Eager to talk to the dead are we ladies?" Brett gave his best smile.

"No my arse is freezing on this grass," Leah smiled back.

Brett took a deep breath. "Okay, let's begin. Like before, fingers on the triangle thingy."

The others did as asked while still giggling with each other. Michelle watched. Brett closed his eyes again. "Spirits of the underworld. We are here at your death's door, awake and speak to us."

"Are you making this up?" Jo contained a laugh.

"It's very cryptic," Leah added.

"Guys!" Brett was getting annoyed again. "Concentrate."

"Yeah Jo."

"Piss off Ray."

Brett closed his eyes. "Come on spirits. Hello, we're here, talk to us." He knocked on the stone of the slab. "Hello? Wake up."

Everyone broke into laughter.

"This place has no power or energy," a disappointed Brett announced.

"Does anyone have any batteries?" Ray called out. Michelle was having a laugh at them too.

Leah stood up to brush off the grass from her pants. "What are we going to do?"

"Go home?" offered Michelle.

"No," said Brett. "I've got a better place, if you dare."

Jo breathed out a breath of frustration. "You're not going to drag us around all night with your ghostbuster bullshit are you?"

"This will be the last place and if doesn't work I give up," he started packing up the board, "Come on."

Once again the car travelled down a lonely road. Here the road divided a marshland of wet earth and salt-poisoned trees. There was no light as the clouds gathered to veil the stars and moon.

The car jolted and shook like before as Brett continued with his trick of faulty gears. The laughter was just as loud coming from the car as it echoed through the quiet night. It stopped off the road on the grass and the doors flung open.

"This is it," stated Brett as he spotted the small posts that indicated the path that ran into the marsh.

"Come on Scooby gang," Ray encouraged the others while eating a bag of Smiths chicken chips. One by one the girls got out of the car. It was chilly now and the cold made them rub their arms. Michelle looked forebodingly at the dark ugly marsh. "This place is freaky," her eyes taking in every shadow behind every twisted tree, looking for monsters she was sure would live here.

"Some people find the woods more of a frightening place than a cemetery," Ray said into her ear.

"Yeah I see that."

Brett led the group down the path. A few mozzies buzzed them immediately. All of them brushed and slapped them away but they kept coming in ones and twos.

There was no laughter as they busied themselves trying to keep the bloodsuckers off their skin.

"Are you sure this is a path Brett?" Leah called out as she swept her arms for about the sixth time.

"There's a clearing up ahead," Brett replied, his voice clipped with concentration.

"Just remember the way we came in," warned Michelle.

"I've been dropping bread crumbs," Jo smiled as she dropped a gummi bear onto the ground.

"It's alright, we're not too far from the road and the woods aren't that dense, just lots of trees, weeds and no undergrowth. Like a pine forest, so you can't get lost," Brett reassured the group, but they didn't seem too convinced except for Ray who was still eating.

Finally the group reached the clearing and followed Brett's lead as he sat down with the board. They sat in a circle with him at its apex, all except Michelle, who sat behind them looking uncomfortable at her surroundings.

"One more time eh?" Ray winked at his friend.

Brett didn't reply and turned to Michelle.

"You joining in this time? The more we have the more energy we can put out."

"You've been reading up on this shit haven't you?" quizzed Jo in surprise.

"I've done the research," replied Brett.

"Well nothing has happened so far girl," Jo said to Michelle.

"It'll be okay," added Leah.

"Alright I'm in," she moved over to the group, who made a space for her.

"Okay. Same as before, fingers on the glass this time," Brett once again was the mouth piece for the group.

"Is there anyone out there who wants to talk to us?" Silence, and the board did not move. Brett repeated the offer, but still nothing.

Then the glass with all their fingers on it began to move across the board.

"Are you doing this?" a stunned Jo asked.

"No," whispered Brett. "It's working."

"What's it doing?" asked a frightened Leah.

"Spelling a word," answered Ray, who watched the glass as it moved about the board stopping at each letter.

H-E-L-P.

"Help? Are you doing this bozzo?" again Jo quizzed Brett.

"No. Just go with the flow would you."

"What should we ask it?" asked Ray.

"Who are you?" Brett asked the night.

C-A-N-D-L-E. The board spelt out.

"Candle? Why does it want a candle?" Leah asked.

Brett was already in his bag looking for one.

"Supposed to channel the energy better," Ray answered. Brett has a green candle out and put it on the board and lit it. Its warm light reflecting in each of the innocent eyes that watched its flame dance.

"Okay," he put his finger back on the glass.

"Can you feel anything?" Jo asked him.

"The only thing you'll feel is my cock up your arse!" Brett's face had mangled for a second into an old man's and his voice had changed into a gruff bitter man's.

The others jumped in fright, Jo's mouth was open and the gummi bears she was eating fell out.

"Oh shit! Did you see that?" Ray exclaimed as Brett shook himself.

"What happened?" he asked.

"What was that?" Leah was frightened.

"Your face man," Ray went on.

"You turned into an old man and you were fucking rude!" Jo yelled at him, the quiver of fear in her voice.

"We're serious man."

"Maybe we should stop?" Michelle offered but no-one took her advice.

"It must be working. Let's try again," Brett smiled.

"I don't want to do this," Michelle said bluntly.

Brett turned on her in frustration. "Come on girl, don't be such a bible-bashing pussy."

"Brett!" Leah yelled back.

"I'm sorry, just getting excited. But isn't this cool?"

"Alright. But only so you turn into a madman and die in a basement killed by another madman you resurrect."

"Cool by me."

"Peer Pressure," laughed Ray.

They all put their fingertips back on the glass and it immediately began to move.

R-E-V-E-N-G-E

"Revenge. Nice," said Jo.

"Who are you?" asked Brett.

S-A-T-A-N

"Satan. Oh come on," Ray dismissed the idea. "Spirits usually play games and riddles."

"But the Dark Prince himself, what an honour," a sarcastic Jo added.

"What's your real name?" Brett pressed the spirit world again.

G-O-O-D-B-Y-E-D-A-V-E

Brett screwed up his face in confusion. "What does that mean?"

The glass moved again.

A-N-G-R-Y

"Who's angry?" he asked.

"I wanna ask it something," Leah gathered up some courage. "When will I die?"

T-O-N-I-G-H-T

"Tonight? It's telling me I'll die tonight," she immediately regretted opening her mouth and vowed not to say anymore as she was officially scared.

Y-E-S

"It's just playing with you," Ray tried to comfort her.

"Yeah, just words," Michelle whispered to her with a tight worried face.

"Is this Dave?" Brett was confused and trying to work out who he was communicating with.

N-O-T-D-A-V-E came the reply from the glass.

"Then who the fuck is it?" a frustrated Brett spat.

I-K-I-L-L-E-D-M-Y-S-E-L-F

When the group finished reading the glass' reply the mouths opened and each gave the other a worried look, as this little lark was somehow now turning serious.

All except Brett who breathed heavily, his wide eyes pinned to the glass as it moved about quickly. Its reply coming so soon as the question was asked.

"I killed myself," Jo whispered.

H-E-L-P-M-E

"Are you reading this?" she asked Ray who was also silent with fear.

"Yeah."

Jo had taken her finger off the glass, quickly followed by the others, leaving Brett's finger the only one.

"Who are you?" Brett's voice breaking with the terror he was hiding deep inside him.

I-T-S-M-E

"Who?" he screamed so loud and suddenly that the others jumped. The candle flickered in the darkness and danced brighter as it seemed to burn on the atmosphere of fear that hung now over the group.

"We should stop," a frightened Michelle said, her eyes misty with tears.

C-A-N-D-L-E

Brett went into his bag looking for another candle.

"Brett no!" Leah protested while the others groaned.

"It'll be alright I wanna see what happens," he replied as he pulled out another candle and lit it. Immediately its flame burned just as intently as the other one.

"Enough Brett, I'm shitting myself," Leah protested again but her calls fell on deaf ears.

"Who are you?"

The glass spelt a name that the others didn't recognise, except Brett, who went white as a ghost. His hand on the glass started shaking.

"Where are you?"

H-E-R-E

The others began to protest loudly then stopped suddenly as the candle burned white, making all their hearts pump even harder than they were.

"He's here," Brett whispered and took his finger off the glass, but it was too late.

A branch snapped in the darkness and all their heads swung as one in that direction. Their breath was heavy and their eyes twitching with fear as they scanned the darkness looking for something to reveal itself.

Another snap of a branch and Michelle began screaming in panic and raced from the group. The others act as one and did the same, running panic-stricken from the clearing and back down the path they had walked in on.

"Run! Run!" Brett called out, terrorised at the back of the group.

Michelle was the first out of that marsh with the others close behind. They ran to the car still parked on the grass by the road.

"Come on man! Open the fucking door!" Ray demanded, while looking back to the marsh, his body twitching with fear.

Brett fumbled with the keys, the same fear running through him too. "I'm trying alright!"

Finally he got the door open, which unlocked all the doors and they were able to scramble in. Brett got the engine going and they were away with a burn out in the wet grass as the car sped down the road.

The girls were crying and trying to calm down.

"What the fuck was that!" Leah cried out as Jo held her. Ray sat beside them and looked out the rear window.

He saw a figure of a boy standing on the road where the car had been.

Brett saw it too and floored it even more.

"Go man, just get us out of here!" Ray warned his friend. They all turned their heads to look but they had turned a corner and whatever was back there was left behind.

"That was bullshit," Ray was regaining his normal breathing pattern as the danger had distance and time now.

"Is everyone ok?" Jo asked.

"Michelle?"

Michelle was wiping her eyes. "Yeah, I'm okay."

"Who was that?" Leah asked.

Brett was slowly shaking his head as some thought rolled around in there that he didn't want to believe was true. His knuckles were hard on the wheel and his mouth clenched.

"Brett?"

"I had a friend from school kill himself in there. Hung himself," he whispered.

They were all shocked, which quickly turned to anger.

"You took us into that place knowing that! You arsehole!" Leah screamed at him while Michelle made the sign of the cross even though she wasn't Catholic and pulled out her crucifix that was around her neck.

"What were you thinking!?" Jo attacked him too.

"Alright! Stop yelling at me!"

Michelle kissed her crucifix and closed her eyes while whispering a little prayer.

"Can I kiss that?" Ray asked her.

"I'll just whisper a prayer for all of us."

"How the hell was I supposed to know it'd work? Fuck! You all thought it was bullshit before."

"Can you take me home?" Michelle asked him.

"Yeah."

"I don't blame you girl," said Jo.

"I feel safer there."

They said nothing while it took the five minutes to drive to Michelle's house. There she got out and went to the back door.

"Um, thanks for the night. See you in church on Sunday?"

They all had a little laugh but didn't reply.

"We might go shopping on Sunday, I'll call you," Leah replied.

"I don't think I'll be able to sleep tonight."

"We won't either, call me later tonight. Is your mum home?"

Michelle turned to look at her house. There was a car parked in the driveway.

"Yeah she's home. I'll see yas later."

"Okay bye."

"Bye."

Brett moved the car off. There was still little conversation until Ray began talking.

"We really scared the shit out of her didn't we?"

Brett made a gruff. Jo looked at Ray.

"What about you? You've got the highest girly scream I've ever heard from a male."

"Yeah Ray, what are ya? I think you were trying to hold my hand the whole time," Brett chimed in.

"Wasn't my hand."

"Well it was someone's."

Back in Leah's house the group had now regained their composure with a few stiff drinks and hot food. It was getting late, well after midnight, and the yawns were coming in every few minutes.

Ray came out of a room with just a towel. Jo, who was getting a bed ready in the lounge, wolf whistled.

"Mum didn't pack your jammies?"

"I sleep in the nude, see," and he dropped the towel to show his bare backside. Jo threw a pillow in his direction as he wrapped the towel about himself.

Brett had remained silent since they got back; he was in the kitchen having a beer, his fourth. Leah came out of a back room loaded with blankets, which she dumped in the lounge.

"So what did you think about tonight Jo?" Ray asked.

"It was probably some guy walking his dog and came across us at just the right moment."

"I think Brett's freaked out," Leah teased.

Brett emptied the bottle and put it with the rest and came out of the kitchen to join his friends.

"Yeah a little. Maybe it was just some guy walking his dog, who knows."

"Total blood rush but."

There were no lights and the house was in darkness and quiet as the four friends slept. Ray and Jo slept soundly but Leah and Brett lay there in the dark not knowing that each other were awake.

Brett's mind was turning over with worry and confusion. He wasn't sure of what had happened tonight,

305

whether some spirit out there was trying to play with him or if it really was Mark. Why would it be anyway, he hardly knew him at school, they went to primary school together as they lived in the same street but had little to do with each other in high school.

As he lay there musing over recent history he had barely noticed the distant howl of dogs wildly barking. They had been going on for almost half an hour but the barking was getting louder as dogs closer to Leah's began barking.

"Can you hear that?" he asked aloud hoping someone else was awake.

"The dogs?" Leah whispered.

"Probably some pissed idiot walking along the road."

Suddenly a few houses down a dog began a wild hell howl that woke them all up in fright.

"What the fuck is that?" Jo spat.

The dog kept barking madly and they began to relax at the recognition of the sound. Ray lay back down and tried to go back to sleep.

There were a few seconds of stillness that was suddenly broken by a loud thump on the front door. Again the group jumped at the sound and all eyes immediately jumped straight to the front door. Leah covered her mouth to hold in a scream.

"Okay now what was that?" Jo demanded.

They sat transfixed as they heard the door knob being jiggled as something on the other side tried to open it.

"Someone's trying to get in," Leah whispered what they all knew.

"Oh shit," swore Ray.

"Fuck off!" Brett yelled out towards the door. At getting no response he got up and started to run down the hall to the door, Leah franticly trying to call him back.

Brett reached the door, quickly unlocked it, opened it and stepped out ready for action. But there wasn't anyone there but the chilly night. He had worked himself up with anger to mask his fear and now he felt naked standing outside.

He stepped back in and locked the door then returned to his friends who were wide-eyed in terror.

"Well?" Ray asked.

"Nothing."

"What are we going to do?" said Leah.

"About what?" Brett replied nastily.

"Whatever the hell you woke up!"

"Bullshit."

"We don't know what it is."

"It's probably some guy trying to scare the shit out of us," Jo tried to bring some reason and calm to the tense atmosphere.

"Exactly. Some dipshit saw the whole thing and is fucking with us."

"Maybe he's gone away now?" Ray offered hopefully.

Suddenly there was a flash of a human figure as it ran past the large sliding glass door that led from the lounge room to the backyard.

All of them seemed to jump out of their skins, Ray had scrambled an arm's length from his bed while Leah held in another scream and closed her teary eyes hoping it would go away. Jo breathed heavily, her eyes pinned to the glass. Brett was breathing in heavily too, his chest heaving up and down in rhythmic beats. He was shitting himself and getting to the point of completely freaking out the longer he denied what he believed was going on. There was no doubt now to any of them that there was someone in the backyard, they had all seen the figure dash past.

"Fuck this prick! I'm gunna smash him."

"What are you nuts!?" Jo protested.

"Go away!" a crying Leah called out, while Brett looked around the room and found a golf bag full of clubs in a corner.

"Come on Ray grab a club."

"You're not really going out there?" again Jo voiced her protest.

"You saw what went past," Leah countered her.

"Yeah some prick is going to get this around his neck," Brett predicted the prowler's fate and a chance to vent his fear.

"Let's just call the cops," Jo again tried to plead a different way of solving their problem.

"They could be hours ..." Brett broke off as he heard the banging of tins falling over coming from the backyard. He went over to the window and watched the small aluminium shed in the far corner of the yard.

"What if it's a ghost?" Ray asked, fear in every syllable.

"It's not a bloody ghost, I'm telling you now. Come on."

He slid back the door and stepped out, club at the ready and Ray right behind him. They both headed to the shed.

It was cold in the backyard and mist blew from their mouths as they took quick panic breaths.

"What are we doing out here man?" Ray protested to his friend in hushed tones. Brett didn't answer but kept going towards the shed. He didn't notice that Ray had dropped back and stopped.

Brett moved close to the shed and could hear shuffling, which became pacing that ended with a smack on the tin wall every few seconds as whatever was in there went from one side to the other hitting the wall. Each crash on the metal made his heart jump and he began wondering if Ray was right.

"Hey," came a cold whisper, which for a second he thought was Ray, but it came from the shed. The pacing and banging had stopped. For some reason Brett kept stepping forward.

"Why didn't you stop me man. Why?"

The voice sent a shiver down his spine at every word.

"Wanna see what you look like dead?" came the same voice again.

He reached the shed and with a shivering hand slowly opened the shed door, which groaned as metal scraped against metal.

He immediately regretted it. There was a boy in the darkness, his eyes bulging and his tongue blue and swollen as it hung partially out of his mouth. The rope around his neck contoured the head as it hung from some invisible beam in the dark. Suddenly the eyes flickered and an arm reached out for him as the dead always do when pleading with the living.

The small courage that he had somehow gathered was blown away as a wild panic tore into him. He couldn't even scream as his body convulsed with terror; he was so scared he wasn't cold anymore but flooded with adrenalin.

He ran back to the house, past Ray, who was standing on the grass looking at him with wide eyes. In seconds he was at the sliding door.

"What was it?" Ray yelled as he looked about the yard and shed with its gaping black hole where the door was left open. He followed his friend back inside.

Brett felt safer inside with the others, who all gathered about him with worried and frightened faces. He sat in a corner with his hands over his head, trying to stay calm, trying to get the image of that kid's face out of his head.

"Brett. Brett are you okay?" Leah soothed her hands on his.

"What did you see?" Jo asked Ray.

"I didn't see anything. He opened the shed and then just freaked out."

"Oh shit, oh shit," Brett moaned through tears. "We're in fucking trouble man. It reached out to me, oh fuck, I did it, I did it. I fucked up big time."

"We should call the cops," Leah again tried to get outside help.

"What are they gunna do? Call fucking ghostbusters for fuck sake!" Brett yelled at her.

Jo went over to the liquor cabinet and grabbed a bottle of whiskey and came back with it. Brett snatched it from her hand and gulped it down. He cried out in a mixture of pleasure and pain.

"What are we going to do then?" Leah questioned.

"I can't think," Brett stated.

"We let it out, maybe we can put it back where it came from?" offered Jo, who usually didn't believe in such bullshit and was compelled to believe that it wasn't a real person in the backyard.

"It's not a bottle of milk you can put back in the fridge," Brett spat after taking another gulp of whiskey.

"Well you got us into this!"

"We should talk to it," Ray calmly said, his mind overcoming his fear so he could think straight.

"How?" Brett demanded.

Ray turned to Leah, "You got some candles, pen, paper?" Leah nodded.

Ray turned back to Brett, who was still slumped in the corner. "You remember those books about automatic writing? You get a pen, paper and concentrate. Then it's possible to communicate with spirits and they write through you, like they channel you."

At the thought of talking more to dead people Leah's face turned sour. "I don't want to do anymore talking to ghosts. I'm shitting myself."

"Well we didn't get off to a good start with this thing," added Jo.

"I don't know either man. I'm thinking Michelle was the smart one in going home."

"If it's a ghost then it might want something, maybe we can help it."

"You're crazy!" mocked Brett as he got to his feet, the panic finally subsiding.

"I think Ray's right. We should talk to it."

Brett looked straight at Jo.

"You didn't see what was in that shed. You're all nuts, we should just leave!"

"No way!" Leah protested. "And leave me with it! I don't want a bloody ghost hanging around, my dad would kill me."

"Maybe this is the only way to get rid of it."

Brett ran his hands over his face, resigned to defeat.

"Okay. Let's do it."

~~~

The required items were found and put on a table, which the four gathered around. A candle burned in the centre of the table next to a writing pad and pen, it was the only light and cast creepy shadows onto the walls, which danced as it swooned with every breath from the nervous group.

They had chosen Brett to pick up the pen and see if the kid would write through him. He seemed to be the one it mainly concentrated on, he knew him, and they secretly were suspicious about his involvement in the kid's death.

"Ready?" asked Ray.

"Yeah," replied Brett, who picked up the pen and put it to paper while closing his eyes.

They only had to wait a few seconds before Brett's hand quickly began racing over the paper. Finally it stopped and Brett opened his eyes.

"Did you feel anything?" Jo asked. Brett shook his head and Ray took the piece of paper and read it out loud.

"Sad, so lonely. I killed myself, I was angry. You should have stopped me. Now I'm angry, it hurt, I didn't die straight away, I was stupid. I cried out, you saw me and ran. Help me, help me, but no-one came and I died."

Before he even finished the others were looking at Brett who had guilty tears in his eyes.

"What did you do man?" Ray was aghast at the realisation of what he believed his friend had done.

"You left him there hanging. You saw him," Leah was crying too.

"I'm sorry," Brett mumbled through the tears. "I was shitting myself and took off. I didn't know what to do, fuck I was just a kid."

A silence came over the room as they didn't know what to say or do now they understood the kid and his anger.

"We should keep going," said Ray.

Brett nodded and put pen to paper.

"What do you want from us?" Ray asked the invisible presence. Again Brett's hand began scribbling, they watched the writing fill the page before it stopped, leaving Brett to wipe his nose and his tears. Ray read the page.

"So I killed myself. Let me be your friend, has Leah forgotten she'll die tonight?"

He wasn't able to finish it as Leah had grabbed the paper and ripped it up in a crying frenzy.

"Go away! Go away!" she screamed out.

Then there was a cry as an invisible voice somewhere was wrecked with pain. It sobbed loudly and yelled between sobs. The group gave each other quick glances to check that it wasn't any one of them. When they realised it wasn't their bodies froze.

Just as suddenly as the crying started it stopped. Immediately the lights in the lounge room flickered on and off, doors opened and closed with such force that they almost broke. The fridge door swung open like an invisible muscleman had the handle and then closed it so hard it shook on its mount. Even the fruit on the bench seemed to decompose right before their eyes.

Then the terror stopped and the group were left in the darkness as the candle had gone out through their heavy breathing. There was only the sound of beating hearts and twitching eyes as each tried to steady their broken nerves. They were so scared they were actually petrified, such was the scene.

There were then footsteps and creaking boards. At each step a board creaked. All eyes looked above them at the roof. It was coming from upstairs.

"There's someone in the house," whispered Jo.

"Yesterday there wasn't," Leah answered dumbstruck, her head skywards as she followed the steps along the hallway and the boards that she knew creaked.

"What are we going to do now?" Brett wondered aloud.

Leah got up and raced for the phone on the wall near the kitchen. When she put it to her ear all she got was loud interference that hurt her ear so much she had to put it down.

"No good."

"Let's just leave," Brett offered again his solution and made for the front door of the house. The others followed. They went past the kitchen and through the small hallway and passed the front lounge room to the door. Brett tried to open it but it was locked and couldn't be opened.

"This is bullshit! Try a window."

Jo pulled aside the curtains and went to try and open the window but jumped back in terror. The others also jumped and Leah put her head in her hands her resolve totally shot. Even Brett had jumped so far back he was back into the small hallway.

Jo pointed to the window and could only stutter. "He, he's out there."

They ran back to the rear lounge room all jumpy, frightened and confused.

"This is fucked up, we can't keep doing this, try one of these," Brett ordered as he tried the rear door. He didn't really want to go out into the backyard again and when he couldn't open it he was secretly glad these doors wouldn't open either. His eyes trying not to look at the black gap on the shed where the door was open.

Jo padded her pants.

"Where's my mobile?"

At the same time the others also started looking for theirs, they were always on them but none could find them.

"Where the fuck did they go?" Brett demanded.

Ray pulled his mobile out of his bag near his bed and they all smiled at being possibly saved. He tried it but his smile turned to a frown.

"It's dead."

"Why won't the doors open?" Jo cried out as she kept looking down the hallway waiting for something to come out of the dark.

Brett was angry he was that scared; he hated weakness and being afraid was taboo in his house. "I can't believe this shit! Is this really happening? What are we gunna do? We can't get out of here and we can't call anyone. Fuck this I'm smashing a window Leah."

He picked up a chair and raised it above his head but some invisible force ripped it from his grip before he could use it as a battering ram and threw it across the room.

They all stood there, petrified mouths opened and teary eyes. Their bodies were shaking and their systems on overdrive.

"I've got my phone upstairs!" Leah cried out with joy.

"It's probably dead too," said Brett.

"It's on a charger."

"Do you think you can get it?" asked Ray.

"I can't go up there by myself," Leah's courage had disappeared as quickly as it came as the thought of being left alone in her house now sent her cold.

"I'll go with you," offered Ray.

"Me too," added Jo.

"You can't leave me alone down here!" protested Brett.

"Alright, I'll stay here with you but you two better be quick. Get it and come back."

Jo, against her better judgement, volunteered to stay with Brett.

Leah turned to Ray and they both took a deep breath, she held out her hand, which he took.

"Let's make it quick."

"It should only be a minute."

They then ran for the steps leading them upstairs.

"Let's hide under a blanket," offered Jo.

"Good idea."

It took only moments before Leah and Ray had reached the second floor. It was dark, which made the fear factor rise in their bodies. A window somewhere in one of the rooms was open and there was a slight breeze coming in from the night air.

Leah fumbled around for the light switch and turned it on. The hallway was then bathed in light.

"Maybe he's gone?" Leah said hopefully, but Ray didn't believe it; it couldn't be this easy.

They reached Leah's room and went in; she turned the light on and went to her bedside table. Ray stayed by the door impatiently, his eyes looking out for danger.

"Is it there?" he nervously asked.

Leah was franticly looking around the table. "It was here! That prick's got it! What have you done with it!?" she screamed out as the tears of frustration and fear flowed down her cheeks.

"Where else would it ...?" Ray said before being abruptly silenced.

Leah was in such a state she didn't hear Ray. She ripped back the blanket of her bed and found a bra of hers tangled up with her mobile phone. Quickly she grabbed it and pulled out the mobile dialling madly. It still worked and she got a dial tone to her mother. "Mum! Mum! Help me! Help me!" she cried out frantically before the phone went dead and was ripped from her hand. She screamed out as her nervous system convulsed with the sheer terror of it all.

She was unable to move her body as the room had suddenly grown ice cold. She could move her head and immediately noticed a pair of sneakers sticking out from under the curtain near the window only an arm's length away from her.

"Ray," she managed to gasp. "Ray."

But there was no response. She managed to back away to the door but her friend wasn't there.

"Ray!" she called out in the hallway.

Suddenly there was a massive thump against the wall opposite her, coming from inside her parent's room. A few seconds later it came again and was so strong it jolted some of the photos hanging from the wall.

She went forward despite her fear, the door was open and she could see inside in the night light Ray being picked up and thrown against the wall by something invisible.

"Ray!" was all she could scream before she was knocked back out of the doorway and into the wall near her room.

~~~

Downstairs Brett and Jo waited impatiently under the blanket shivering with fright.

"Why are they taking so long?" complained Jo.

"This is all my fault, I'm sorry about it."

"Well you'll know next time not to wake the dead. What time is it?"

Brett looked at his watch but it wasn't working.

"Bloody hell it's dead too. It's dragging on but, hope the sun comes up soon."

Suddenly there was a thump from upstairs and then another one and Brett stopped what he was going to say next to listen.

"Fucking hell!" Jo said worriedly.

"Come on you two, fucking hurry up!" Brett yelled out. Then there was a footstep and the sound of a bottle being knocked over and hitting the wooden table.

The two were frozen and their breath fast and sharp as they followed the footsteps as they came closer.

"It's in the room," Jo managed to gasp. There was a tugging on the blanket and they tried to hold onto it. They were frantic with fear as they tried to keep hold of the blanket but they lost and it was flung away from them to the accompaniment of Jo and Brett's scream.

~~~

Upstairs Leah was sitting on the floor of the hallway silently sobbing to herself. She wasn't sure if she had been asleep or what had happened to her. For a few moments she had forgotten the past few hours and wondered why she was on the floor. Then she remembered.

There was a piercing scream which she immediately knew was Jo. She got up and ran for the stairs but found the door was locked at the bottom. She couldn't open it and had to endure listening to her friend's screams.

"Jo! Open the door! Brett!" she called out.

"Oh fuck! Ray! Ray!" she heard Brett's cries and knew he was petrified.

"Open the door!" she called out again and pounded hard on the wood.

"Leah! Oh shit Leah. Don't! Don't!" Jo's frightened cries cut her deep and as the cries went on and she couldn't get to them to help she crawled up in a ball crying uncontrollably. She knew they were hurting but there was nothing she could do.

Eventually the screams stopped and it went quiet. It took Leah some minutes to regain her composure and try the door again. It opened and she slowly opened it, absolutely petrified of what she would see in the lounge room.

"Jo? Brett?" she whispered. She then remembered that Ray was gone too and she had forgotten to check her parent's room, but she couldn't go back up there.

With unsteady legs she stepped out into the main area of the lower level of her house. It was dark still. The kitchen was neat but the lounge room where they had only hours before being talking was a mess. Bottles were strewn about, tables turned over but no sign of her friends.

As she paced about biting her nails and trying to comprehend what had happened and what to do there was a horrible groan from a male's voice. Leah began to cry again as she knew whoever owned the voice was in pain.

She looked about her but there was no-one. She had lived in this house for fifteen years and knew the sound was coming from the garage. Her father had made a staircase from the garage to the lower level so he didn't have to walk all the way back to the front door or back door when he parked in the garage.

The groan came again. She knew she shouldn't go down there and should make a run for it. But the last time they checked all the doors were all locked. There was nowhere to go and her friends needed her. God knows what she could do but something made her step towards the open staircase.

She began to step down the turning staircase, each step in her heavy legs took her some moments as her body and muscles were tired and so worn from the night's experience.

As she got closer she saw there was a light that was swinging.

"So what if I wanted to die! So what!" came a chilling male voice that was full of anger and rage.

She stepped down and could see into the garage. There was no car but she saw her friends Ray and Jo hanging by their necks from a metal beam. Their eyes were wide and their tongues hanging from their blue lips as their bodies swung in the light.

Brett was kneeling on the ground, a rope around his neck and standing over him was just a boy with white raged eyes and dirty torn jumper and jeans. Brett saw her and reached out his hand. But Leah broke. She was so frightened she couldn't move and it was only when the fast approaching kid came for her that she moved and began to run as fast as her tired legs could carry her back up the stairs.

She got one hand to the top of the stairs before she felt the cold clammy hands of the kid on her neck, pick her up and drag her down into the darkness. There was one final scream that was drowned out by gargles that finally went silent.

~~~

A man stepped out of his house. It was cold and he rubbed his hands together as he went to his car in the driveway. He put his briefcase down as he fumbled for his keys.

He looked up at the quiet street as he heard footsteps on the road. There was a boy in the distance walking away from him, the street's lights flickered as he walked by each one and the dogs howled as one choir.

Michelle was the first to come over in the morning. Leah's parents were furious about the mess they found when they got home as it looked like they simply left to go somewhere and left everything as it was. As the days wore on and they heard nothing from their daughter or her friends a sudden wave of worry came over them. Putting Michelle's story and the ransacked house together their fury turned to worry and fear.

No sign of the friends was ever seen again. Leah's mum, after moving six times, changing phones and phone numbers still receives the same terrified message from her daughter every year on the same day. It is always traced back to Leah's mobile phone at the family home even though the house at 112 Hampden Road no longer exists.

Eyes wide, eyes bright.
I see her shape, a shadow in the night.
Smile fierce, smile tight.
I sit in the cold, on a bench, in the snow.
"I had a little girl once, torn from my womb she was.
I never got to hold her tight."
Eyes wide, eyes bright.
She smells my scent. I recoil.
Face white, face fierce.
"I've been everywhere to find her. The thief, as we
speak, she draws near."
Snarl black, snarl fierce.
"Who are you?"
"Torn from my womb, by my very blood. There is a
thief, as we speak, she draws near."
Smell blood, fresh blood.
An open wound in her belly chills me.
Her eyes so black, her face so white.
"So many years, so many tears."
Whispers cold. Her touch like ice.
"Here she is, as we speak, my baby thief."
Eyes wide, eyes bright.
My mother cries.
"Sister, sister. I have returned."
Eyes of tears. Heartbeat fast with fear.
Three of us in the snow.
Now I know.

ABOUT THE AUTHOR

Kristian is originally from the Central Coast of NSW but is currently stuck in Darwin, Northern Territory, waiting for a train that will never come.

More nightmares are coming. Sweet Dreams.

www.ingramcontent.com/pod-product-compliance
Lightning Source LLC
Chambersburg PA
CBHW020401260626
47156CB00007B/2194